D1557443

Albina Lesi Detrow

A SPARED FATE

Acknowledgements

This book would have been impossible
without the help of my husband.
A big thank you to the early readers of my first drafts
and my editor, Kathie Weaver.

Based on data from the Institute for the Studies of
Communist Crimes and Consequences in Albania,
34,135 Albanians were imprisoned during communist rule
and 59,009 were deported and persecuted. (ISCC, 2020)

Dedicated to my mother,
who lived under the communist regime for thirty years.

CHAPTER 1

I was a worker in the 1970s in a land owned by a psychopath. Supreme Comrade Enver Hoxha, First Secretary of the Party of Labour of Albania. It was a battle to keep alive under his control. Our days began like this: the moment we woke up, we left our house and went straight to work. Then, at work in the fields, we kept our mouths shut and worked from seven a.m. to seven p.m., six days a week. Each day, after viciously cleaning our hands and taking the dirt out from under our nails, we had one hour to get home. Eight o'clock p.m. was our curfew. No one was allowed outside after eight except the military. But that was a joke rubbed in our faces because who the hell had the legs to stand around outside after working twelve hours a day for six days straight?

Once we finished middle school, labor began unless you were one of the few chosen for high school. For most of us, that graduation was the first and last one we would ever experience. For the celebration, we would gather at our local party office to be nominated for a job, and the selection was usually mining, farming, or the military. The few who were sent to high school had to have exceptional grades, and the even fewer who went to the university had to also possess a clean ancestral biography with a dash of Communist adoration. I was an excellent student, but since the second criteria was not sufficiently evident, I was sent to the fields.

In the fields, women were treated the same as men. Our leader had declared that women are equal to men, and therefore, women must produce as much as men. Of course, motherhood and housekeeping were not taken into account because production was the only thing our leader cared about. It was just another joke that left every woman cruelly tormented, but each of us had no choice but to swallow it.

It was even harder to remain alive on military training days, which were every Saturday morning. First, one of us, chosen at random, would have to recite the oath of the combatant:

Kujtese! Çdo shtetasi te Republikes Popullore Socialiste të Shqipërisë ka për detyrë të jetë kurdoherë një luftëtar i denjë, besnik dhe i papërkulur deri në fund, i gatshëm në çdo çast për të luftuar kundër kujtdo që do të guxojë të prekë vendin tonë, dhë të mos kursejë as jetën për mbrojtjen e interesave të larta të popullit, atdheut, revolucionit, dhe Socializmit.

(Attention! Every citizen of the People's Socialist Republic of Albania has a duty to always be a worthy fighter, loyal and inexorable to the end, ready at any moment to fight against anyone who will dare to touch our country, and to offer his life for the protection of the high interests of the citizens: homeland, revolution, and Socialism.)

After the oath, our officer would approach us, and we'd line up. Then, his soldiers quickly handed out their old, green uniforms to us, and while we changed into the uniforms, the soldiers put up a paper target. Forced to practice shooting an unseen enemy, one by one we lifted the rifles and began firing. If you were dying from starvation and you could not pull the trigger? There, in front of your peers, you were killed instantly. Needless to say, that would be a good day for the officer because he had demonstrated what would happen if you did not take orders.

Pregnant women had to practice with all the other workers. Once they shot at the unseen enemy, just after the bullet left the gun's mouth, vomit would shoot from their lips. Pregnancy was a weakness because pregnant bellies could prevent women from escaping the real enemy. But in the fields, pregnant women escaped punishment, not because the leader was tender and understood women's struggles, but because their babies would be needed for labor later on. Nonetheless, there were no exceptions to the military training because, as our officer often told us: "The enemy doesn't care for the weak."

As a country, we were not overpopulated, but we surely were overmilitarized. I saw more men in the army than men living on the land. A slew of soldiers in secondhand green uniforms often marched tirelessly along our rugged roads like ants coming out of the earth. I say secondhand because we were isolated from the entire world except for our two foreign allies, Russia and China, and they sold us their old uniforms, old weapons, and old books. Even our Communist ideology did not come from our country's men. It came from our foreign allies.

Following our allies' tactics, our militant leader conducted surveillance in every town through the party's offices. These offices knew and ran everything about the people who lived in their territory. Every person's age, work record, family, health history, school record, ancestry, ancestors' conduct, and so on were amassed until they had documented every hair on us. If a person from outside of a town came in, as sometimes newspapermen or doctors did, for example, they were first required to report to the party office of that town and get approval to do the job they come there to do. That was how they weeded out the nonconformists. As for the conformists, we had to get permission from a party office for every act.

There were a few mountain peaks in our country that were not controlled. The land was too remote to be regulated and cultivated, and therefore, the party offices did not extend to the people there. The mountain people were left alone, while the country people were forced to survive in an open jail.

Isolation and surveillance became so ordinary that the next generation—my generation—was fully accustomed to it. The mind of a worker was crippled, blank, dull as a rock, and even if we sensed the unfairness and the wrongdoing, we were too scared to challenge our regime. We knew that our government was cruel, but we denied it. Psychologically, it was hard to acknowledge what they were doing to us.

However, despite the suffocating severity of the restraints on our lives and our ignorance about the outside world, our people held on and remained proud and resilient. When we were in the fields, wearing our rustic clothes, our feet touching the dirt, we humbly bent and drank water from the same bucket while enduring our undesirable fate.

Albania's absolute ruler, our mentally ill leader, made us serve every day except for the Lord's Day. When Saturday's sun went down, the sky became free, and then, we were permitted to live in the light of day. Those mornings, when we did not have to run through our doors to the fields but could sleep a bit longer, were ours. Yes, Sundays were ours to catch up on housework, gather with family, and possibly—to dream. But, needless to say, we could not have it all.

A day free from labor was always a threat for our leader. The threat was even greater when it was combined with a religious celebration. Therefore, once a year, on Pascha Sunday—Easter Sunday—it was obligatory for every adult to work. Pascha Sunday, the holiest and most important Christian celebration, was not a day to let the people loosen up. From its mightiness, their souls might begin praying, and from prayer, hope might come, and from hope, their spirits might be liberated, and then, they might offer themselves to a greater good and seek righteousness. That was the ultimate fear of our leader—mass uprising, and Pascha Sundays could be the match to that fire. So, he kept the people tired and declared, "It is for the people's good."

Every year, Pascha Sunday was sunny and overflowing with blue skies. Young buds, butterflies, ladybugs, and frogs would come out from the earth and their hibernation, cheering and proclaiming the arrival of spring. On that day, we ached to be at our homes, resting our bodies, of course, rather than laboring for the seventh day that week, but our ruler was paranoid about the possibility of any other figure being worshipped more than his party. For that reason, he demolished all of the faith objects that had been put on our land prior to his regime, and he banished all objects of faith—from churches to temples to crosses, and even hand carvings that had a special significance. Pascha Sundays were the epitome of his paranoia about religion and faith, and thus, he made us work for fourteen days straight. That Sunday, we were reminded that there would be no *Zot* (God) coming for us. It would have been nice to have a savior, and we prayed for it. Yet, the truth was that no one tried to relieve us from our dictator. From our prayers, we knew there would be no heaven without a fight, and he knew we were too tired to fight.

Perhaps our people were too tired to start a revolution, however, our leader led an unwinnable battle because, even if people put a lid on their faith on the surface, in their hearts, they couldn't forget their dogmas. After the priests gradually disappeared or were jailed and murdered, people began mourning and craving their own lives and rights. Deprived, they would hike up to the peaks of the mountains, where it was harder to get caught for showing signs of faith, and create their own churches. Others remembered the old sacred soil in the high hills, and they would press their knees on its shattered bedrock, praying to find their supreme selves. In the long run, it became one battle in the war to keep their own pride and values. Hence, even after those knockdowns and maniacal attempts at censorship, people still found a tonic for their inner needs. This left our leader aghast and in disbelief that his people would rather devote themselves to something unseen rather than devote themselves to him.

"It is a disgrace," he said and threatened to torture the brave ones who were hiking high up on their free days.

In fact, he ordered us to believe that the only *Zot* (God) to worship was the Zot who had skin, bones, and his likeness. He claimed he was not only the leader of the Communist Party—he was our Zot and he was saving us.

He suffocated us by indoctrinating us with false beliefs and terror. From the day we were born, his voice rattled through the radio, telling us that our country was our temple and invasion was what we should fear. We couldn't understand who we should fear the most— him or an enemy we had never met. Everything was unclear, from the enemy to faith to fear. By design, it left us spiritually exhausted, confused, and lethargic. We swallowed our questions and conformed because who in their right mind would dare to speak up to a sick man with so much power? To do so would mean certain death.

When a sunny day would come by, it would kick out our worries along with the trash our leader tried to feed us. He was a mad genius for predicting that these sunny days were like Zot—hope and cheer would come from them. To keep us quiet and paranoid, even about trivial matters like expressing enjoyment at the lovely weather, he spread rats to watch us. His spies surrounded us like the air, and every word could be turned into a negative mark if they so desired. His rats kept us subdued because they had the authority to distort the truth. If you just said a favorable word that did not refer to his regime, it was suspicious enough to make a case against you. Cheerful expressions were questionable because they indicated a change in the authoritarian way of living, and that was wrong too. We cheered only if our leader ordered us to cheer. Unwarranted joviality was forbidden—along with laughter and hope. Laughing in public was like committing suicide. Anyone could see and hear your laughter, from your neighbor to the field worker, the teacher, the brigadier, the doctor, the office worker, and the random man on the road. Each and every person could be a spy.

To avoid paranoia, we understood that the trick was simply to keep everything to ourselves. Starting when we were very young, Mother preached the lesson of how to be invisible and how not to be invisible. "Don't be too happy, too loud, or sad. Just don't be," Mother always said. As for the rats, I am not sure what our leader promised them or what they got in return, but undoubtedly, it was something precious because they were ubiquitous. Perhaps the rats were promised some extra food for their children's mouths or had somehow been totally radicalized. For the rest of us, the cost of going to jail and sealing our entire family's fate was too big a risk to take, so we kept mute.

We lived alongside the spies in the hell we had built together. Our paranoid leader had forced his people to construct tunnels, bunkers, stock rooms, escape passages, shelters, precise weapons, traps, and great jails. On the coast, there were entire naval facilities, including naval ships, hidden underground. Beneath the land, there were secret underground paths that led to facilities with rooms big enough to fit an entire village. Across the nation, the land was studded with cement bunkers like whitecaps on the sea. Out of all the projects, the bunkers were by far the most prevalent, with an average of six bunkers every fourteen square miles. Along the road—a bunker. In your yard—a bunker the size of your grown son. High up on a mountain—a bunker that was impossible to hike to. At a canal, at a stream, at a school, at a hospital, you name it—there was a bunker. Without so much as a single battle, we had more bunkers than bodies to use them. We felt constantly watched, so once we built the bunkers, we watched.

When I was a child, the cement bunkers had an air of nobility when they stood next to the pothole-strewn roads that connected the old stone *kullat* (houses) with untouched nature. The only contemporary art in our country was the mass cement project of bunkers. Some of them were covered by weeds or thorns, and a few of them had flowers displaying some hidden hope. As kids playing hide and seek around them, we smelled the cement as a fine, modern thing, but when we grew up, we smelled war and realized that their purpose was to seek, hide, and kill. Upon arriving at that conclusion, our stomachs turned, and we never saw the bunkers in the same light again.

Secret doors in the fields led to dark passages with train tracks running through them. As a child, it was bizarre to watch a single cart filled with lumps of coal driving itself down the tracks when you didn't know its destination. When we would see empty bunkers while an army was marching on our deserted road, we would guess that our country was under invasion, even though we saw no battles. He forced us to believe that the gray zone—the rest of the world—wanted to fight us. "The enemy can hit any day, any time!" the officers would bark during military training while we stayed on high alert, boastfully carrying our guns. In the end, we never identified one enemy, but we were prepared to fire.

The sweat and pain we went through to build that hell—and then to live in it—is more than one can fathom. Hard labor was what really ambushed us, and the truth was that we only used our weapons and jails for our own people, those who took action about what our country had become. Carrying out our leader's sick plans and projects like fools, both young and old built the "necessary" defenses to fight the enemy.

Ironically, we were ready for the attack, but no one ever came to make war with us. We waited and waited for decades to get the hit, but none struck us. It was understandable—why get involved with a sick country owned by a psychopathic leader? The gray zone was wise and gave neither a care nor a dime, forever ignoring us while we lived permanently in a land covered by an oppressive sky.

CHAPTER 2

I started working in the fields when I was almost sixteen years old. I had just finished eighth grade. I had been denied high school because my grandfather, a prominent writer and member of the country's art league, had been arrested for "favoring the enemy with his pen." I never met my grandfather because he died in jail.

When my *nëna* (grandmother) tried to bring him clothes and food in jail, the officer told her, "He is dead. He was a traitor and got what he deserved."

Nëna left the jail that day with only his clothes to bury. After that, she dressed only in black. Grandfather was thirty-seven years old when he was taken, and after that, his family never saw him again.

"We have no place to mourn him properly," Mother would say.

Our bloodline was said to run with a traitor's blood because my grandfather had been taken, so we were scrutinized by the state. Because of his "treachery," the state denied higher education to our family and sometimes even food—for two generations.

Back when I was a student, I didn't have time to do my homework. My notebooks remained closed after school because I had to do the housekeeping. Still, I understood the subjects very well, and I was an exceptional student. Sometimes, I felt that Mother didn't want me to be a good student. Perhaps she was afraid that I would put a word in an essay that would cost me my life, or perhaps solidarity with her father's loss made her want me to remain illiterate. However, my good grades and my grandfather's treason were irrelevant to our day-to-day life. Dogged labor was what mattered, and once I finished middle school, I was sent to work with the others. It was that simple.

Somehow, all of us were blended in the same pot like human cattle, with no room for independence or initiatives of our own. Clearly, we were domesticated for free labor in support of Communism. In the pasture, our only job was to serve our leader's vision and to do what we were told. Sadly, the oppressive sky swallowed our cries, and our most important task was to try to remain alive in a land ruled by someone else's principles. As a member of the herd of cattle, you were simply sent to wherever the state wished you to work. You were not asked. All that for a piece of bread.

"In the fields," was all the party officer had said to tell me what my first official job would be.

And so, after the weekend of my last day of school, on Monday morning, I began working in the fields. Although I was fresh at the task and had a scarred arm from an accident, I tried very hard because what I witnessed there was beyond comprehension. I saw thin arms fighting with shovels, old bodies quarreling with the dirt, skirts battling in the trenches, and shoulders saddling sacks of grain that ripped young flesh while spines grew twisted. Young bodies shrank and broke until they quit. I thought I had witnessed austerity and hardships in our home and at school, but when work came along, this notion plainly broke down. As a mark of respect at seeing their elders, the youth knelt, bowed their heads, dug holes, and lifted sacks without question or resistance. Nearly my entire family worked for the state's farms, and while I was expecting it to be hard, the truth was that it was unbearable.

CHAPTER 3

Our *kulla* (house) stood on the crest of a hill like a sturdy tree atop its roots and had been built to withstand the blasts of the Adriatic winds. The *kullat* (houses) were old houses that had been made by our grandfathers and passed on to us. Built of stones from the mountains, they were strong and had deep foundations to withstand tremors, and their thick walls sheltered us from the blasts and whine of the winds and the rain of the storms. There were kullat in our village that were two hundred years old, and ten generations had passed through their doors. If a member of a household made it to sixty years old, they were considered lucky to have enjoyed its shelter for that long.

Our kulla's thick walls kept us warm in the winter, but they were very, very, very ugly looking. Their asymmetric stones were a dark gravestone-gray and unevenly put together. The windows were made of rough, hand-molded glass that did not let you see any distance, and the rooms were dark because the translucent patch of glass let only a faint light pass through. Every kulla had a big triangular roof, and inside, there was no ceiling between the floor and the roof. Instead, beams made of pine logs spanned from wall to wall to support the house.

"Having a ceiling is a lavish thing," Mother would say.

We used the pine beams in the kitchen and basement to hang braided garlic bulbs, onions, and, sometimes, meat—if we were fortunate to have it. Behind the kitchen, a hallway led to the basement, which had no windows and never saw the light of day. That was a good place to hide food or people, depending on the need. I did not like going into the basement because a cool, damp air hung in the room, as the mismatched stone walls had sunk into the earth and never saw the daylight, and the darkness stretched off into uncharted corners. It terrified me to be in a space that was so damp and dark.

"If the devil exists," I told my mother once, "he lives in the basement."

Mother laughed and said, "One day, you will be brave enough to not care about dreqi."

Dreqi was our word for the devil. Mother was reminding me that she was not afraid of him. Perhaps she even loved him a bit because of how often the word dreqi came out of her mouth.

The sea winds were a living wonder in Lezhë, the province where we lived. Out of all the winds, the gales in winter were the hardest to put up with because they battered our kulla without respite and whined angrily in our eardrums. Out of the whole country, our city was the windiest, and we were called "the windy people" because our hair was always messy from the wind. It rained a lot in our city, but the city to the north of us was closer to the mountains and had enormous valleys, so it had a greater amount of rainfall and tremendous flooding. We called its residents "the rainy people" because their hair was regularly wet.

The best way to predict storms was by examining the gusts that preceded the rains. As the windy people, our ears could register the different whining notes that would reveal the next day's weather to us. By my eighteenth birthday, I had learned to flawlessly predict the weather. One night, I saw a clear sky above our kulla and heard an unusual whining of the wind, and I reported to Mother that bad weather would come the next day. But she did not hear me.

"Bora, take the clothes and bring them outside," she said.

Late every evening, I was the one who washed the family garments for the next day. That night, I gathered the clothes together and walked around the back of the kulla. Mother was already there, down on her knees, trying to make a fire while the wind played with her headscarf. On winter nights, we made fires around the back of the house because we could strike a flame there behind the thick stone walls of our kulla.

"Here, take the big pan and fill it with water from the spring," she said, her voice distorted by the whines of the wind cutting through her words.

I dragged the pan around the house and down the shallow hill. Then I placed the pan beneath the spring to fill it. The spring pulled icy water all the way from the white peaks of the mountains, and the pressure at the mouth of the spring made the water spatter against the pan. Once it filled up, I lifted the heavy pan to just above my belly button, hugged it tight, and walked it back up. I set it over the fire that Mother had made behind the house, and when the water was heated, I dropped my pants and the other clothes into the pan and began the wash. The boiling water quickly warmed my hands, but as soon as I took them out, the cold blasts of wind brought back the chill.

I quickly drained the clothes and threw them into a bucket. Then I began placing the clothes over a rope that stretched from the bars of the kitchen window to the branches of our pear tree, but the wind kept blowing the clothes down as soon as I would put them up. I always enjoyed the breeze on a summer day when the wet clothes would swing in the hot wind and chill my skin, but I did not enjoy it when the blast was icy. Cursing at the wind, I overlapped the clothes with one another to keep them from blowing off the rope.

Each day, six days a week, Mother and I would walk down to work carrying our heavy tools and a light lunch. The administrator would be standing at the entrance to the field. His job was to take our names and bring the daily summary of our work back to the party office. We called him the foreman for short. Every morning when we arrived at the entrance, Mother and I would split up, as we worked in different brigades on different crops. Both our bags did not have lunch that day because we knew that we were not able to work after such a heavy storm. Nevertheless, we were required to get to the entry of the fields and claim our presence if we wanted to get points.

The party officers translated the points into wages, and based on our pay and the number of members in our family, our earnings were rationed into paper stamps for buying food. After that, all that would be left were a few coins for the head of the family to collect. Of course, by the end of a normal day, it was obvious who had been absent based on the work that had been done. But even when rain had turned the fields to lakes, it was obligatory to go down and give our names, just as if it were a regular day. It was like a ritual. In both bad and good weather, we went there and gave our names, but to what effect we did not know.

"Bora Zefi," I shouted to the foreman, who was sheltered under his black umbrella.

The rain was flowing from my forehead into my lips, sending droplets of water flying with my words. Once we had shouted our names, we were permitted to go back home, so I turned my wet shoulders and left the field. My shoulders were not itchy anymore because the wool sweater was completely saturated with rainwater, making it smooth. I did not wait for Mother and ran fast toward our warm kulla.

As I was passing the water-filled potholes on the road, I saw other field workers coming out from under their roofs to line up and yell their names. There were no exceptions to the ritual, and perhaps it acted as a morning reminder of who we belonged to, in case we had dreamed and forgotten the night before.

Among the people emerging from their homes was my neighbor Kol.

"Good morning Bora!" he said.

"Hey, morning," I replied, pleased to see him.

"I'll talk to you later on, perhaps on a good day," he said sarcastically as the rain ran in streams around his lips.

"Sure," I said.

But he had already taken off, running along the wild thorn bushes toward the field, so he did not hear me. While I was trudging back up in the rain, I assured myself that it wouldn't be long before the storm was over, and Kol and I would meet up again later.

If it had been a nice day, I'd have come out of my kulla ready to sweat. Then, once I gave my name to the foreman, I'd go straight to my task in the field. There, instead of Kol greeting me with charm, cold shovels would blister my hands. Good mornings and smiles were forbidden, not by the brigadier, but by the racing clock. The brigadier was the person who delegated our tasks and wrote down our production points. He usually delegated an impossible amount of work to us so he could look good to the higher-ups by making us run like maniacs. And since we needed the points, it was a mutual, unspoken rule to not talk while we worked.

Every evening before we left work, our brigadier would gather us and tell us what to do the next morning. That was how we did not lose time because the next day we would know exactly what to do. If we did not, it was our negligence, and it came out of our points. Most of the time, the brigadiers were men, and they appeared to be formal and proper, but they used their manipulative ways to favor their people and themselves. Their favors led to our amount of work becoming increasingly harder and, at times, impossible to finish. However, regardless of what the brigadier did or did not do, it was unheard of for a worker to speak out. We understood the rules and that the brigadier was our authority, and we knew that authorities exercised their rights in their own ways.

The storm ceased without me seeing Kol again, and the next day, the sky was washed and shining a pure blue. It was a good day in the fields, and once I had sweated out half of my work, I dropped my equipment and lined up to wash my nails. After a good cleaning, I sat down to take my break with the other workers. A white sheet had been thrown on the soft, plowed soil, and each of us put our food on the sheet so we could share it. Women and men sat in separate groups but were close enough to hear each other.

As we were enjoying our food on the white sheet, a woman with her infant sucking milk from her breast said, "It was only poverty that made us generous."

I began breathing serenely and staring at the washed sky, trying to make sense of the woman's wise words. We share a lot because none of us has much to share, I thought.

Shortly, more workers came to sit on the white sheet. The mothers picked up their babies and began to nourish them, having already cleaned their hands with water from the buckets. The babies looked dead until they touched their mother's breasts, and they all had the same iron-flat heads. Perhaps it was because for five hours straight, six days a week, the babies were tied stiff to a baby bed, waiting for their mothers. By the fifth hour every day, the babies looked paralyzed. Some mothers kept their children in the beds until they were four years old because there was no one to look after them. If the baby's grandparents weren't alive, some mothers left their babies with elderly neighbors.

I took a piece of cornbread and a few crumbs of cheese that another worker had brought and looked up at the sky again. I wondered how long Mother had kept me on that bed and if my flat head was a result of waiting those five hours for her every day.

As I was chewing a piece of cornbread, I watched an elderly woman take off her corset and breathe a sigh of relief. Nearly everyone wore those corsets to handle the heavy lifting in the fields. Without the corset, the elderly woman's stomach spread out across her skirt, and from the looks of her belly, I speculated that she had twelve to fourteen children—at least. I watched her as she started to viciously pull the dirt out from under her nails. Every worker was obsessed with eradicating this dirt. It was the fieldman's syndrome, and it could not be cured.

On one side of the blanket, the men were talking about jails, weapons, and the same old stories. Near me, the women were talking about their daily problems in small groups of two or three. As they shared stories of their children, miscarriages, and illnesses, some of the women looked mischievous, while others looked bored with each other. One group was quieter than the others, and of course, that was the one group complaining about their husbands.

As a young worker, I didn't care about the grown-ups, but I longed to have their status. After two years of working in the fields, I was still considered a schoolgirl because of my pants. A skirt was required to change my status. The skirt, a mere strip of fabric around my belt, would mean I was married, or at least ready to be looked at, and that I worked, earned money, and was equal to the other women. My pants betrayed that I was not a woman because women wore skirts over their pants. Even if I worked as hard as the other workers, I was still treated like a schoolgirl because of my pants. Up until the end of eighth grade, young girls wore pants. Once school was finished but before work began, most young girls wore their first skirt—if their mothers could afford it. Immediately upon betrothal, the mother would have to buy a skirt for her daughter whether she could afford it or not. It was one of the several unspoken rules we performed without discussion. I was not engaged, and Mother had no stamps to buy the fabric, so despite my age, I was left in between being a woman and a girl. I was stuck with having a title I disliked, but until I wore a skirt, I had to swallow it down.

I knew I wasn't a woman, but what bothered me the most was that our state called me to serve and perform duties and meet expectations without exceptions regarding my age or gender. A high-pitched voice of a state representative would crackle through the many tin loudspeakers at the fields, saying: "Women and men are equal and therefore they share the same work roles and duties." I could not call foul because that was a twisted truth. They granted us the privilege of being equal with men in hard labor, but nowhere else. Young girls and women with or without skirts had to work equal to the men, when actually they were as equal as a lizard and a lion. And as far as my brigadier was concerned, I had to obtain the strength to produce as much work as the other workers in order for his sheets to be satisfied and my points to be filled out. Yet, in his eyes, he did not have to invest any time in showing any acknowledgement of my work or the work of any other girl or woman because we were just someone's daughter or wife. While holding shovels, we were equal at best, but once those were gone and we were on the rugged roads and inside our kullat, the message was sharply painted, putting us in our place. And that place was at the bottom.

CHAPTER 4

It was an ordinary day in the fields the day the old man recited his story. He was sitting on the white blanket on our lunch break as we were eating our lunch. It was spring by then, and there was still a chill in the air, but the old man seemed to be enjoying the warmth of the sunlight. He had a long nose girdled by two empty cheekbones with rips of wrinkles going down his jaw. His face seemed tired but gratified. His hair was gray with hints of white. He was skinny, and his shoulders were flat but crooked. He was seated with his legs crossed, and his spine pressed through his shirt, looking like a thin chain against his back. He had just gotten out of jail after twenty-five years.

As we sat together on the blanket having lunch, a young man asked the old man the question we all had in mind.

"How did you survive?" the young man said.

All the workers sitting nearby stared at the old man, waiting for his answer. Even the young man's friends paused their soccer talk and opened their ears to hear.

"Talk old man!" one of them shouted.

The old man stuffed his mouth with a big piece of cornbread, staring at the vast horizon.

"Did they torture you?" the young man asked.

The rest of us felt embarrassed by his audacity, yet we were sinfully burning with curiosity too. Choked by the question, the old man stopped chewing and swallowed a mouth full at once. We hung on to every movement of his compressed lips, waiting for him to speak. He cleared his throat.

"It was the small things that kept me alive," the old man said.

Not satisfied with this answer, the young man asked impatiently, "Did they torture you?"

Silence.

"Did you try to escape?" he pressed, not letting go.

The old man bowed his head, and his lips uttered a pitying tsk tsk while the wrinkles moved around his face.

"I will tell you," he said, taking in a deep breath and letting it out slowly, bracing himself. He shifted his body and settled it again. Then he opened his ancient mouth and let his story out.

"On bad days, they put me in a room that had a long, clear tube. The tube was only wide enough to fit one or two men at the most and was made of hard plastic. Once I got in, they filled the tube with cold water up to my chest. My whole upper body was left sticking out of the water—half my chest, my shoulders, my neck, my head. We were always cold in jail. Every inmate, the same. No matter whether we were tortured or not, cold was the long-lasting *dreqi* (devil) that ate into our lives with every sigh. So, I was used to the cold, but not like this. When the freezing cold water touched my feet and started to rise up, I felt spikes driving into my brain. As the cold water rose higher and higher, the spikes hit faster and faster and sharper, blasting my head. After that, my ears pounded from the pressure, and my body sank down in the tube. At that second, I would lose my breath."

For a brief moment, the old man closed his lips and got lost gazing at the sky. His audience stared at him shamelessly, hoping he would go on with his story. Then, he inhaled deeply, forcing himself to continue.

"I do not wish for any man, even the worst, to go through those tortures," he warned us and then flipped the page with his white eyelashes and began again.

"When the cold water stopped right here"—he put his hand on his chest—"my entire body started throbbing." My chest raced so fast that it did not let the air reach my lungs, and soon my mouth spoke only in mute tongues. The cold air in the tube was suffocating me, and my face succumbed to the temperature of the rest of my body and went numb. My eyelashes trembled, fluttering like birds with clipped wings. In a short time, my lower body changed color from bright white to blue, the same color as the slate in our mountains. After a few minutes of the cold seeping into me, I could not see anything else besides my feet swelling. Next, my sight was blurry and my hearing slow. The guards' voices came into my ear only when they talked about the length of my time inside the tube. Three hours was the usual amount they kept me there.

"Every time I was taken into that room, three guards escorted me in. But every time, one of the guards left because he couldn't bear to watch it. That forced the other two guards to stay and watch the torture because they couldn't risk the chance that my frozen, paralyzed body might escape."

He turned his head and spat.

"Idiots," he said.

Then he turned back and faced us again.

"They called these sessions 'contacts' for reasons I never discovered, but boy, in the tube I knew that each of us contacted our mothers, our children, the mountains, the fields. But the thoughtful part of the contacts did not last long because we dropped fast from the pain, and there, only death touched us by cruelly licking our pain. And believe me, in that second, even the most well-built man gives in without a fight.

"The first time in the tube, I moved a lot because I was trying to ward off the chills from stealing my warmth. Later, I learned that I could retain more energy by keeping my body still. I held so still that I became a stone column. I used to look over at the guards with loathing, but soon I understood that even that was only exhausting me further. In the first hour, my body moved no matter what I did, but I stiffened my muscles as much as I could, fighting the movement that was coming from the throbbing. The pain came and went in waves, but the shivers never stopped. I'd tighten my whole body against them, trying to grip them and hold on from sliding into a deep sea. And there I'd stand, confined inside the tube.

"Sometimes, my face would drop into the water and jolt my senses. Then, I would steal myself once again to see out the remaining moments. By the end, the sorrowful sounds of my lungs aborting me and my heart mourning came from deep within my ear tunnels. Beyond keeping count of my breaths and trying to soothe my heartbeats, I could not do much else. Deadened and helpless, I stayed inside until my time was done, just flirting with my own demise. I underwent the cold waters of the tube for three hours on each contact. Each time, the guards pulled out my bones one step before they dissolved."

The old man paused and took off his shirt, and we saw that his flesh had been weathered by the cold of the water tube. Deep furrows snaked and zig-zagged across the skin of his arms and torso. He grabbed his own arm and pressed it hard with his hand. Then, he paraded the swollen veins under his frail skin in front of us.

"See," he said, "See? It was impossible to not allow the pain to occupy you, yet, Zot, it is mighty to witness your flesh and your blood doing unnamed things to keep itself alive."

He pulled his shirt back on, and then he continued, quiet and intense, looking into the eyes of those who were listening.

"When that moment of pulling me out would come, my body felt like a heavy marble statue. My limbs had lost all feeling, and I couldn't move them. Once the air touched my wet skin, my body flapped like a fish out of water. It was brutal. They wanted us to die without dignity. Seeing me shivering like crazy, every time they'd throw a blanket at me. Oh, that thin blanket felt as warm as the ray of sunshine that is hitting my skin today. Each time, the two guards would slide me back into my room like a dog. Right? Because in the cell, we were worthless Kullaks."

He turned his head to the side and spat on the ground.

"Dogs," he said.

He stopped for a moment and inhaled deeply, steadying himself, but his fury only grew.

"That's what they wanted us to believe because that was what they needed to believe too. Otherwise, how could they convince themselves to complete these cruel orders? I had two pieces of clothing to wear. Two! And after they threw that blanket at me, I'd be lying on the floor in a grey corner of my cell. Like a rag doll. My whole body was shivering under that blanket, and my arms and legs were locked up so I couldn't move them. And pain was shooting through every one of my cells, every single inch of me."

He stopped for a few moments, and his voice quieted again.

"After a long time, I was finally able to reach my hand up to the bed and pull off the sheet and dry my body. It always soothed me for a moment—until I'd see my skin peeling off. I could not bear the sight of my own body so weakened, so I'd force my legs to unlock, get up, and put on my two pieces of clothing. Then I'd lay down on the bed. I longed to find warmth in the harsh mattress, but there was none. I laid there for hours, inhaling and exhaling, but I could not control my arms and my legs, and my fingers and toes twitched from the pain.

"After a lengthy lethargy, my body would dive into a deep sleep. In that state, I did not know if I was alive or dead. The sleep was good, it repaired my frame and made me feel better, but still, waking up was a slap in the face. It was not the cell or the jail that wrecked me when rising, but the memory of contacts and tortures and what I had gone through. What I remembered, I could not bear, and in spite of the trouble that those memories brought, the wait for the time they would take me again was what I could not withstand."

He grabbed a piece of cornbread and began chewing it slowly, giving himself a break from his tortures.

"My days were bitter. I went crazy speculating about what they were going to do to me next, and needless to say, I would have killed myself if I had the chance. Because their tortures conquered any desire for living, even though my heart held. But that opportunity did not present itself, and I had to carve out a way to exist. My bed and the walls retained me until I found a new companion.

"The tortures stopped after two years, and they let me live in my cell. I could plug the leaky pipe of my loneliness for a week by remembering my wife's face. Then she would visit, bringing me food and stories from the outer world, and with her stories, I would last for another week. It was in those days, on a break, that I found my closest companion. It wasn't a spiritual figure or a friend, but an object that helped me live through the next twenty-three years.

"The break room was a square, muddy place with no roof. One day, I was sitting on my haunches after getting out of a long, lethargic sleep. The sun was shining on my body, which had lost any fat and muscle that I had ever had. I was too weak to gaze at the light, so I held my face down, looking over the mud. I pulled some buried rocks out of the damp dirt and rolled them around in my shriveled hands. Then I threw them out at the four walls like the wind throws petals away from the hills on a June day."

The old man's voice became more excited as he remembered that day.

"In the next handful, I gathered many rocks, a round one, a spiky one, a glittery one, and a muddy one. I rubbed the dirt from them, wanting to set them free, washed and cleaned. But when I rubbed the dirt off the muddy rock, it turned out to be too white, too soft, and too comforting for me to let it go. I dragged it across the gray wall to see what it would do, and lo and behold, it left a white line on the wall. It was a piece of chalk. I brought it into the cell with me, and after that, I never stopped writing on the walls.

"But I did not write words because words are worse than weapons and could be used against you at all times. When the guards saw me writing, they lowered their heads, understanding that twenty-three more years was a lifetime and that I deserved a piece of chalk to help me to live them. And when a new guard began working, he came and inspected my walls, peering at them with confusion. But shortly after, his colleague said to him: 'Forget about him, he is one of our olds here,' even though I was only thirty-five years old."

"Olds" the old man muttered to himself, a sardonic chuckle slipping out of his mouth as he wrapped up his bread and put it in his lunch bag.

"Soon after, their orders for contacts ended, and we developed a victim and perpetrator relationship, each party deciding that it was best for both sides to forget and, perhaps, forgive."

The old man's ancient mouth closed once more, as if to let us soak up the rain of wisdom that he had just dropped. The faces in the crowd looked dazzled by his oratory, and everyone was silent, waiting for his creased lips to open. The old man looked from face to face, making sure he had each person's full attention. Then, he spoke again.

"Every day on my walls, I wrote four math equations, and each day, my mind raced to solve them. I left the morning equation unsolved so I would have something to occupy my mind while I was taken from my cell. It was that small exercise that gave me a reason to live long enough to tell you of my hardships. When I wrote the first problem of the day, it did not matter if later they made me dig tunnels through solid rock, or build bunkers, or mine coal, or lift stones. I had an equation to come back to and solve. Every day for more than twenty-two years, I wrote on that wall and then erased it, in order to feed my mind and keep it sailing out of the walls of my cell."

The old man turned to face the young man, who was digesting the story, his mouth wide open. Then the old man's eyes went for a walk through the crowd, but he soon turned back to his target, the young man and his friends.

"Young men, your drive and impatience will not serve you on bad days. Keep those for the good ones. And for the bad ones, be quiet and patient because no matter how much you flap, your fate has its own script," he said.

Then, the old man gave the young man a look that seemed to make the young man ashamed and regretful for the lack of respect he had shown. The old man ate his last piece of cornbread and looked upwards, once again cherishing the warmth of the sun. We began to realize that his story had ended and that he would speak no more.

I traced the long wrinkle that cracked his skin from his cheek to his jaw and grasped that it had been made by the freezing cold in the tube. The mystery of his worn face was solved like the equations in his cell. By the time he had finished his tale, our break was over, and we had to return to work in the cornfields.

When I lifted myself from the ground, each one of my garments, from my pants to my shirt, felt heavier than when I had sat down for his story. Yet, the beauty of working in the fields was that everything was erased by the end of the day. From my experience, I had seen that fields gave a type of exhaustion like no other, a lassitude that deleted stories, troubles, loves, opinions, and names—even your own. From the hard labor, sweat, and dirt, all our legends were forgotten, leaving us to rush home for some comfort. And there, aching under the layers of the covers, we hid the day's stories and slept innocently and deeply.

CHAPTER 5

It was a usual gray day taken by the mists, only a few weeks after the old man had let his story out. After visiting a neighbor's house for her son's engagement on a Sunday, Mother and I were walking along our ragged road toward our kulla. The wild thorn bushes kept pricking my scarred arm as we made our way up into the fog. March was even more intolerable than the winter months. We truly needed the sun to dry our bones, but the sun was stingy with its warmth. Mother was up front, stepping up onto the rocks of the unpaved road and carrying an empty bag. The villagers had made the road with their own shovels to make a path to their kulla. The rocks were one of the ways we kept the winter mud away. Our road was ragged, but despite its roughness, leaves and stems from wild weeds had cracked the soil, rooted, and birthed a boisterous natural *gardh* (fence). In some parts, the gardh had bushes even taller than me, and some of its nettles were poisonous, but I liked the brambles, and the curly, wet leaves that unfolded on the ground.

That day, the flowers and green berries on the prickly shoots were tipping downward, announcing that the time for blossoming had come. I saw a blackcap bird standing on the moistened bushes, sipping drops of water from its glossy, green leaves, and a whitethroat hopped over onto the arms of a neighboring tree, singing of the birth of spring. There were a few walnut trees along our path, and their gnarled roots buckled our ragged road. Although Mother was a tall woman, she looked tiny next to their big trunks. She looked good next to the wild pomegranates with their red fruits and in front of the rustic, green olive trees.

Beyond the bushes, Kol's kulla appeared through the gardh, and I peeked in to see if he was home. Kol and I went back a long way, as far as we could remember ourselves, but our relationship had changed as our adult lives began. He was older and had begun working two years earlier than me. His shoulders had become wider and muscular, and his face looked more mature. After a long day at work, I often saw him walking, his body held straight and his golden hair glimmering, bright and clean. He had a long neck and a square jawline, and he said good morning and good night with a kind, genuine voice.

Even though Kol had grown, his smile remained kind, and his cheeks still blushed shyly. His light skin blushed even more when we would hike up steep hills to find wild fruits. He had forever melted my heart when he had pointed out the sunset to me on top of our hill, two summers earlier. Now, when we would run into each other, he blushed humbly without a true reason. It was impossible not to fall for him. At the party office, I had wished to be placed on his farm, but Kol and I had been placed on different fields and rarely saw each other anymore. Although when we did, we both enjoyed it very much.

In the summer, the thorn bushes on the road offered wild berries. The wild plants and trees were important for us, as they bore the few kinds of fruit that we could eat freely from the *tokë* (land). It was not feasible for the state to ask us to collect berries from thornbushes, pomegranates from ravines, quinces from cliffs and hills, or persimmons from a soggy, muddy lawn. The ripe berries ranged in color from light red, to dark red, to purple, to blue. Before the ripening season, the color of the berries was green. Through my childhood years, I awaited the green color turning into a deep, dark shade so I could eat them. For many of us, a handful of red, blue, or purple berries was a day's meal. There were days that I boiled them with a dash of sugar and then drank the liquid hot. It tasted like a fermented juice with a bittersweet flavor that gave my stomach occasional aches, but better a filled stomach with an ache than an empty one.

Some nights, Mother would boil a dry, spicy pepper, throw in a handful of berries she had picked on her way home from work, and then add the crumbs of bread left on the table from our meal. It was her soup, and sometimes she put some salt in it to give it some taste. I tried her recipe once when I was very young, but when the spicy, hot liquid lit my mouth on fire, I threw away the cup, breaking it. Mother had yelled, unhappy that I had broken the cup because we did not have many to begin with. But I was not used to spices, and perhaps it needed another dash of salt to mellow the taste of the juice.

I knew that salt and sugar were expensive, and we were careful about using them unless it was a birthday. Birthdays were special days, and we honored them accordingly, using our stamps to buy sugar. For the birthday boy or girl, we soaked a piece of bread in olive oil and put it on the stove to let it dry. Once dry, we covered one side with sugar and gave it to the birthday girl or boy to eat. Children waited eagerly for twelve months for that meal and, just as eagerly, for summer to come when they could eat the wild berries.

As my mother and I walked along the road that gray day after celebrating a neighbor's engagement, I could see the old stone kullat through the bald spots of the gardh, and I peeked in at their residents. The homeowners looked like ants next to their kulla, which in turn appeared like rabbits tucked in between the elephantine mountains.

"Bora, *move*! Dreq," Mother yelled when she saw me standing and looking into one of the yards.

But I kept peeking while her long figure headed up the road. In the yard, there was a woman in a white headscarf sweeping her rugged *trojë* (land). Close by, her baby was wrapped tightly in a wooden bed. The wooden bed was a miniature crib that was made to precisely fit a baby's frame. It was the same bed used by the women in the fields. It looked almost like a brown coffin for babies. I never liked those beds, but I knew that no babies had died from them, and in fact, they were very useful for mothers. Every time I saw the crown of one of those cribs, my skin got goosebumps. It looked like a three-foot section of a wooden water trough balanced on two perpendicular rocking-horse feet that allowed it to swing from side to side. On each side of the crib, there were cleats where you could tie a rope to prevent the child from falling out. That method was safe and saved the mothers a lot of time.

Mother had taught me how to use it when my younger brother was first born. I started by putting my baby brother over the sheet while holding his hands down. Then, I took the upper corner of the sheet and folded it in the form of a triangle to free his face and his neck. Then, I tightly covered his body with the triangle-shaped sheet and slid it under his little hairy back on both sides. Next, I took a long, thin cotton string and fastened his body from his shoulders down to his legs. Then, I pulled the string up to his chest again and made a knot. My baby brother moved a lot, and once, he almost fell on the fire when he unfolded himself.

"You cannot miss the feet and hands, Bora," Mother said as she grabbed him and showed me again how to wrap him.

After that, I knew how crucial it was to tie the baby well. He was a lucky baby because he did not have a flat head. He had a beautiful round-shaped head. That's because I was always around to get him out of the bed. Mother was pleased with my bed skills too. She told me that I would make a great mother when the time came. I felt delighted to make her proud, even if that meant making my little brother wail when I secured the knot tightly.

To say that the wooden baby beds were adored by mothers like a piece of gold jewelry would not be enough. Feeding, washing, and tying the baby up was all the time mothers had to spare. All mothers brought the beds to the fields and left them in a shaded spot while they worked. Many times, the babies woke each other up from their crying, but because of the noise of the tractors grinding the tokë up and down the field, often the mothers did not hear the screams. If they did hear them, it took only one mother giving the babies a moment of care for the babies to soften up. That was how desperate the babies were in their stiff wooden beds. By noon, on the lunch break, the mothers would go and unbind them, wash them with some cloudy water, the only water available, and then hold them in their arms. The mothers relished these moments, cuddling their babies with love, just as the woman in the yard was doing now that her sweeping was done.

I left the mother and baby to themselves and ran fast to catch up with Mother. I kept running after I caught up with her, passing her by, but I stopped after a sharp curve where the road went along the edge of a cliff and the gardh was short. There, I could see our town beneath my feet. Mother rounded the curve and saw me standing there savoring the view.

"Bora, *move*! Do not stand there!" Mother commanded.

She did not wait and kept going up in a rush while, above her headscarf, a *gardalinë* was flying toward me. It was a goldfinch, and people called it a *gardalinë* because it sat on a fence—*gardh*—and sang like a blessing—*linë*—hence, *gardalinë*. The gardalinë landed near me on the short gardh, and we both stared at the velvet-green fields that spread out below us. Our village was seated at the base of the foothills of two huge mountains, and beyond our village, a field stretched out until it merged with the sea.

"Coming," I called to Mother, but the gardh around the bend of the road was hiding her figure.

Above the gardh, the giant bodies of the mountains towered. Those mountains had fathered us with good stones, and we had leveled its foothills to build our kullat. The zeniths of the mountains touched the sky and had sired ponds with fresh water for us to drink. A long, wide river flowed from the foothills to our village and into the sea beyond.

"The sky water was a gift from Zot to help life below the mountains flourish," our geography teacher had once said when teaching about the sources of water.

This was one of the few "true facts" that the teacher had been allowed to share.

As I stood on the edge of the cliff, watching the river, a misty wind tousled my hair, reminding me I had to catch up with Mother before she reached our kulla. As I was running, raindrops began to splash on my face. If a rainstorm were to follow the showers, the river would certainly blow through its banks into the fields. Fall and spring were the times when our river swelled the most because Zot was mad and threw oceans of rain at our terrain. When the river bloated, it destroyed six months of farming, but even worse, it drowned livestock by pulling them into the current. A dog began barking at me when it heard my legs pounding the stones as I ran by its master's door. I had still not caught up with Mother, and I knew that I was going to be yelled at when I finally did meet up with her.

The rain paused for a bit, and I glanced for a second at the swollen river. Its time was slim, but it could hold a bit more if March decided not to live up to its reputation. The river passed through the left side of our village, and next to it, a road connected us with the city. A few hills shadowed the city road and obscured the next village from our sights. Mother had told me that she would take me to the city next time she went. But she definitely wouldn't take me to the city after this, I worried as I ran.

Damn it again, thorns scratched my arm, stinging me, but it was my fault because I was running fast without looking.

"Good afternoon," a man said, going down the hill.

"Good afternoon," I called over my shoulder and kept going.

I was almost home, but I quickly turned to see who he was, but he had disappeared behind the green walls of the rough road like a ghost. Then, the hills, the terrain, and the river appeared again before me. The plain was flattened out like a piece of green silk laid down on the brown soil. Its velvety color faded out into the sea, and further beyond, shadowy clouds stretched from the peaks down to the village. I pumped my legs again, flying up the road, but then I saw Mother standing on the road waiting for me.

I was about to get grounded by Mother, but another man passed, greeting us and saving me.

"Good afternoon," he said.

"Good afternoon," Mother responded, and we both kept going.

The greeting was one of many unspoken rules that everyone except young daughters performed. When daughters were accompanied by their mothers or another adult, they did not have to talk. Or to be precise, she should not talk unless a question was directed to her, and ideally, she should always be accompanied on the road by one of her parents or her husband. However, having to work every day did not make that possible. For a daughter to keep the honor of her family, she had to be cautious and follow these rules to avoid a bad name. I did not understand life and its orders, and Mother did not have the time to teach me the entire art of behavior. But she held a good name for herself, and this made me want to follow in her footsteps.

In sight of our kulla and mere steps from our *trojë* (land), we saw a neighbor walking downhill. He stopped in order to speak with us and shook our hands.

"How are your worries?" he asked Mother.

"Alive," she said and quickly turned her head to throw a glance at me. "How are your children?"

"Good, my son just had a daughter," he said.

Immediately upon saying this, it was as if a shadowy cloud came over his face, like the deep gray clouds lurking above our mountains. I presumed that Mother was already thinking about a gift for the occasion. Perhaps we had an extra soap in addition to the one we had just given, or a spare bag of coffee, and if we did not, we would have to sacrifice stamps for one or the other.

I was also guessing that, in his silence, the man was contemplating what a daughter meant in our world, and I recalled my status as a

41

young daughter. I knew that they had to raise their daughter and get her married, and until then, they had to keep her reputation clean. It was the same for me. A daughter in my time was more of a burden to her family than a contributor because she was born to be sent to another family. And another family would only take her if she had a good reputation. So, she was raised to leave, and where she would be sent, she would be reminded that she was not born there. In short, she was a body without a kulla. First with the skirt then with marriage, we daughters had to find our position in other people's eyes.

When the man closed his eyes, I assumed he had come to the conclusion that a daughter meant little to nothing in his world. Then, he gathered his face together for us. Mother's face came back too.

"I'll come for a visit a week from Sunday," she said.

"All right then," the man said, and they exchanged an unspoken goodbye.

Once the man disappeared around the curve of the road, I asked Mother why she would not go on the upcoming Sunday.

"Because we have a wedding this Sunday," she replied, "my uncle's son, your cousin's."

"A wedding, of course," I said, without actually remembering anything about it.

Perhaps I hadn't cared to retain it because my sister had always gone with Mother to weddings and family occasions, and I had never been asked. But my sister had just gotten married, so she couldn't represent our kulla any longer.

When we got to the top of our hill, Mother stood quietly for a moment alongside our entry and serenely viewed the plain below, inhaling the cool air flowing down from the peaks. I was looking at the spring water where some birds were drinking water and singing. There was a white horse dipping his long tongue in the spring and sipping the clear water, a striking contrast against the velvety, green plain. Then Mother turned her amber eyes toward me, and I knew what was about to come. I looked at the horse and waited to hear her lecture about splitting up on the road and walking by myself when it was not needed.

"You are my oldest daughter now," her elegant face with the deep lines said. "You have to accompany me to the weddings." Her small lips, which looked like ripe cherries, closed, having said their peace.

"To the weddings," I said. My tongue ran fast from surprise.

"Yes," Mother said and turned her field-twisted spine and went into our kulla without saying another word.

I hung outside the door, still not realizing what had just happened. After school, I only worked and did housework. Accompanying Mother meant I was becoming a woman, and the world could see me. The velvety, green plain and the white horse seemed surprised too. They were my witnesses to that cheerful moment.

"Sure Mother, I would love to accompany you," I said out loud, thrilled. "Hell yeah," I said quietly. I finally felt like an adult, ready to relish the few grown-up perks I was allowed to have.

"Bora, come inside," Mother shot back from afar, not hearing a word of my murmuring.

But surely the mountains had heard my joy because the clouds cleared from their peaks, and it seemed as though the fields got greener. The white horse reared up on its hind legs, neighing and happily shaking its wispy tail for me, and the trees trembled, just as my heart did. Even the bushes rustled with the good news. All life around me was endorsing Mother's words as I began to feel ready to be her oldest daughter.

CHAPTER 6

The wedding was somewhere deep in the mountains where Mother was born. The tradition said that on the first days of a wedding, a few close relatives who lived nearby should come and help prepare the house. We were close relatives, but we rarely saw them. For one, it was far enough that it cost more to go than we could afford, and also, it was impossible to fit all our obligations into one free Sunday. To be fair, our leader did not forbid us from seeing our families outright, but the lifestyle he designed for us had very limited space for joy. For the most part, relatives saw each other on rare occasions such as funerals and weddings. This was a son's wedding, so it would last five days, although the biggest day would be Sunday when the bride would come. For their sons' weddings, families were more generous than for their daughters' weddings. It was one of the things our leader skipped when he talked about gender equality.

That Sunday, we got on the road early and started hitchhiking for our first *fugoni* (van). My mother did the talking, handling the ride, and as a good daughter, I simply had to follow silently. A sharp wooden stick was hanging on Mother's leg under her long, white skirt. I knew that she always hid the unbendable wood for the unknowns of long travel, but she looked silly with it, nonetheless.

"What are you doing with this stick?" I had asked her, poking fun, while she was dressing that morning.

"Shut up dreq, you don't understand," she had said angrily, calling me evil and pointing the stick at me. "Maybe I should test it first on you."

That quickly shut my mouth. Mother was ready for a fight at all times. She did not leave things to chance, and if *dreq* (evil) manifested, she was prepared to strike.

We had to take two rides with different fugonis to get to the wedding. A fugoni was a van with eight seats and took us to destinations that we could not reach by walking. On our first ride that morning, we drove in a fugoni with a woman and her four chickens. The woman was taking the chickens to sell them illegitimately. The last row of seats was taken by the four birds, all looking wide-eyed and enthralled by the trip. The many potholes in the road made the chickens cluck in surprise whenever we hit a bump. The driver was the woman's son, and there were no other riders. I figured it was because of the chickens.

After half an hour, we got off and walked through a small town to another fugoni stop. As we were walking, I witnessed what I called "Mother's grand walk." Mother was grand in many ways, but her walk was a result of a Communist system that had bent all her wishes. When her feet pressed the dirt, they held firm, assertively owning the ground she was walking on, but at the same time, she kept quiet, as she knew that her self-assertiveness did not have a say in the affairs of her land. On the rugged streets, Mother walked briskly, but softly and steadily. She kept a balance between her speed and her determination, careful not to disturb anything or anyone with each footstep. Her walk was confident, but she didn't want to be taken for a confident woman because that might attract men's attention.

Mother disliked that kind of attention, and she showed that by sporting a tailored glance that wasn't angry, but wasn't kind either. Her amber eyes gave a knowing, unadorned look to everyone she encountered. Hence, no one dared to throw a compliment her way because, to the world, she was a very solemn woman. I never saw her eyes look feminine, even when she looked at Father. I did wonder how many times her true wishes had been thrown away to build that look. It was odd, yet clear, that she hated any kind of attention from men. Perhaps that was her way of not being taken for a weakling. Perhaps being a woman was already ranked too low, and the more feminine attention you got, the lower your price dropped.

I did not know if Mother philosophized her tailored look or even if she thought about her grand walk, but she surely knew what she was doing. I knew this because I had witnessed Mother pulling off her mask, snuffing out her amber pearls for plain eyes, and breaking into feelings. The first time I could remember seeing her eyes become emotional was when I was eight years old and had an accident with my arm. After that, my sister always said that Mother had a sweet spot for me. Perhaps Mother's plain eyes and fine walk were her way of staying out of trouble. Perhaps that was how she mastered her world. After witnessing her path, I had no choice but to follow her grand steps.

At the next fugoni station, we stood and waited patiently. There was a hush in the air that made the pavement feel foreboding. The road was empty as usual except there was a traffic policeman at each main intersection. Near us, there was one standing still in the center of the intersection. He was wearing a deteriorated blue uniform and was waiting to guide oncoming vehicles, if there were any. He was a road's width away from us, and we could see each other clearly. We had learned to avoid people in uniforms. Military and any type of police intimidated us because of their authority. One word, one wrong move could cost us our life if they were to say so.

Soon, instead of wheels approaching, we heard heavy footsteps striking the pothole-strewn road. It was an army unit marching in their secondhand uniforms, passing through the town. Mother and I stood stiffly and avoided eye contact. When the army passed the traffic policeman, he boastfully puffed up his chest and took off his hat to show respect to the military. Perhaps he was glad to see other men in the same faded uniforms that he was wearing. As the army continued across the intersection, the traffic policeman did not miss the chance to demonstrate his competence. He mechanically opened his arm and, using his hat as an indicator, pointed them in the right direction. The army officer didn't care about the traffic policeman's blue uniform nor his ridiculous show of loyalty and only acknowledged him with a head nod when he marched by with his soldiers, not even taking off his hat in solidarity.

After that, the road became deserted again, and still, no fugoni came. The wind lifted some dust from the roads, and there was an ominous silence. Mother's brown hair and mine were burning from the early sun while we stood waiting in silence. The traffic policeman moved his hand once more. This time, he was ordering us to come toward him.

"Don't look at him," Mother ordered through her teeth.

"He is a spy," I whispered, looking at the ground.

The silence became menacing. Not even a speck of dust moved. I saw Mother's hand ready to grab her wooden weapon if necessary. Then, a deep rumble shook the air. It was a fugoni. It lifted the dust from the road into the air, creating a wall between the traffic policeman and us. We choked from the dust as it filled our eyes and throats. But we were so relieved that we would have chosen to inhale the dust again instead of seeing his blue uniform.

We got into the fugoni, even though it was already full of people. One of the passengers got off long before our destination, and a young guy made some space for us on his seat. Mother instantly sat between the young guy and me to protect my honor. I saw that his nails were clean, and he wasn't looking at them, even once, which made me think he was a university student, not a field worker.

As the fugoni lumbered forward, the young guy began conversing with Mother.

"Where are you coming from?" he asked.

From hell, I was sure Mother wanted to say, but she controlled herself.

Yes, Mother liked swearing.

When she could not split a log, she would yell, "Dreqi te haje," which meant "I hope the devil eats you."

Then, she would throw the ax to the ground, giving up. She called people bitches, but then she would say that she had meant it for our dog, Lule. Out of all the ways to swear, her favorite was "dreqi," which meant devil or evil, and also, hell.

"Dreqi was everywhere," she would say. When I did something smart, she would say, "That's dreqi smart."

In the fugoni, using only her eyes and without uttering words, she said: What does this dreqi want from me now? She had sized the guy up and was warning him that she wouldn't let him mess with her daughter. Poor guy, I thought. Mother was not the person to make these airy conversations with.

"A village nearby," she finally said aloud, answering his question. "And to whom do you belong?"

"Rella is my last name," he said.

After that, Mother did not ask any more questions. Nor did he continue talking, understanding Mother's unspoken words.

As we drove up to the town, the roads squeezed and became narrower, cutting sharp corners around the rims of the mountains. Our heads bobbed up and down from the potholes, hitting the roof of the fugoni as we drove alongside an exuberant river. The further we went, the more potholes we met, and the more frightening the river became. Looping around the large mountains, the road would disappear into the mists and reappear again.

At regular intervals, we saw big rocks, which had fallen from the mountain peaks, laying on the edge of the road, ready to fall again. They were like dead bodies looking for a place to come to a final rest. I felt my stomach turning as the fugoni picked its way along the narrow curves. It was early, and the warm sun was still low, hidden in the belly of the mountains. Clouds and fog covered the road. I found some comfort in the lush pine trees at the edge of the road. If the fugoni slid, their sturdy trunks would catch us from falling into the river—I hoped.

The dense forest was green and wet, and a rich veil of fog floated through it. My window was open a crack, and I could smell the pines. But when we got higher up on the razor-edged road, it was terrifying to see the turquoise river flowing two mountains below us. To stave off these terrible thoughts, I sucked in as much air as I could from the cracked window and filled my empty stomach with the forest aromas. That refreshed my head and kept me awake, but it didn't keep me full for long.

The other passengers were sleeping, and their heads were lolling left and right, their necks slack. Mother was tired, too, and had closed her eyes, resting her head on the back of the seat. The young guy's previously talkative tongue was cut by nausea, and he lay on his seat looking sickly yellow. At several narrow curves, his hand grabbed his mouth to stop from vomiting.

After driving for an hour, we arrived in Prosek, the crown of the giant mountains. Here, the sky was closer, and the mountain peaks stretched for miles. It was my first time visiting Mother's cousins, and I could hardly fathom that our village was far below these immense peaks. It was afternoon, and as we walked, the sunlight was a soft golden color, not at all like the oppressive glare down in the country, and the air was filled with the scent of sage and other wild herbs. When I looked down, I saw stones scattered in the soil shining like diamonds. Ah—the whole tokë was godly gorgeous and took my breath away.

"Zot, there is no hell up here," I said out loud.

"Dreqi is wherever people are," Mother responded.

Give me a break, Mother, I chose not to say because she would have responded with her wooden stick.

Shortly thereafter, we came upon the foundations of a ruined ancient castle, and Mother said the castle had sheltered families when they fought the Turks, the Slavs, the Romans, the Byzantines, and so on. Now, only three columns were left on the ground. There were many bedrock fences circling the kullat around the ruins, and each kulla looked majestic.

As Mother and I walked along the trojë, the sound of women singing drifted through the trees, and I knew we were almost at Mother's cousins' kulla. This part of Mother's family was from the side of my prominent grandfather. Now that I was in his mountains, I realized that he had been a true highlander, and I understood why he had refused to abandon his codes to conform to another's ideology. As I walked on his trojë, I wondered if his deed had been worthwhile, since he had lost his children and his wife, and three decades later, his grandchildren were still just laborers for the leader who had murdered him. But on his land, relishing the soft sunlight he most surely had cherished, I grasped what I had not seen before—my grandfather had written words that had cost him his life, and even though they had not caused a revolution, it had been important to write them.

After Grandfather died, his wife, my nëna, had moved to her parents' kulla to raise their children, and now, she was living with my uncle. It was common in the villages for families to build their homes in the same *trung* (family-owned land) as their *fisi* (blood relatives). So, when Mother and I came upon many big kullat built right next to each other, I understood that here was where my mother's cousins lived.

I was wearing my pants and a golden-colored shirt with a pattern of red shapes stamped on it. My golden shirt had long sleeves to cover the scarred arm. Mother had suggested I keep the scar private when we went places because it could be perceived as a fault by people who did not know what had happened. My wavy hair covered my shoulders, and I had combed it with my fingers before we got out of the fugoni. As we walked along next to the kullat, we saw people we did not know and who didn't know us, but they looked cheerful. Mother's cousin met us halfway to the kulla and opened her arms and welcomed us. Another cheerful person in the village, I thought.

Then, a daughter about my age came running out of the kulla. She was smiling, and she ran up to me and threw her arms around me.

"You are my cousin," she said as she hugged me tight.

Such intense warmth was unusual to me. Even my sister did not hug me that way. Who are these untroubled people? I wondered.

"I'm Ela, your cousin," she said and grabbed my hand as though we had known each other for years.

Ela led me by the hand around to the back of the kulla, where the wedding banquet was already underway. The plethora of people sitting at the banquet were supposedly part of my family too, but I knew no one. I felt shy and uncertain, especially because we had left Mother behind. She had been walking slowly, talking with her cousin. I wanted to see her face cheerful for once, without a dreqi, but I was stuck with Ela, standing on the edge of a crowd I did not know. I looked away from the sea of faces and stared at Ela's smile and tried to be cheerful like her. But I couldn't. Perhaps up in the mountains you could be more expressive, but perhaps we were just too different.

The banquet tables were made of wood panels split into three long communal tables side by side. Ela and I were seated at the middle table. Before we began eating, I asked Ela where I could wash my hands. She got up eagerly to show me and threw smiles left and right on the way. Her people were looking at me because of her smiles, and it felt embarrassing, like I was walking naked in a parade. I shuttered their view with my hair and realized that I was Mother's daughter—I didn't like attention either. In a small spring, I quickly washed my nails and rinsed my face. As I walked behind Ela along the edge of the crowd and back to our seats, I thought that if I could only be as invisible as a bat in the night, my day would be saved.

Mother was still not at the banquet by the time the *miqtë* (guests) started to eat and the dancing began in anticipation of the groom bringing the bride. Once, when I glanced at the yard trying to find her, I saw a few boys peering at me. They were like carnivores, and I was their meat—their food. Or perhaps in this case, I was just their entertainment. I must be the fresh blood around here, I thought, remembering how we stared at the newcomers in our village. But food came my way, and my attention fully shifted to that.

The colors on the plate looked like a disheveled rainbow made from one fried pepper, a pickled cucumber, five fried potatoes, a piece of cheese, and a piece of a pork chop. I could tell that the pork chop had been expertly charred on the fire since it looked very juicy. I hadn't had pork in a long time, so long that I couldn't remember the taste. We ate meat very rarely and only on special occasions like weddings. When my sister had returned from weddings, I had always asked her to describe the taste of the meat. Left eating only her words, I would dream about it later. This time, I was there and needed no description.

I began by working on the piece of meat. My sister would approve because it was perfectly seasoned and charred. I crushed its fat between my teeth, and my taste buds exploded. Then I ate a pickled cucumber and an actual piece of cheese, not just the crumbles we were used to at home. Next, I tried another piece of meat, which looked just as heavenly. It was a piece of cured pork, and the salt made my mouth numb. I rinsed my mouth with their fresh mountain water, refreshing my taste buds, then I was ready to get back to work. I tasted the charred, fatty pork again to bring the good flavors back.

All the while, Ela was talking to me and smiling energetically, expecting me to do the same. I had decided to stop trying to understand her and let her see that we were just too different. All I wanted was to eat my plate and watch the brand-new assortment of people at the banquet. Only Ela kept talking to me, and she was beginning to get on my nerves with her cheerfulness.

I stopped mid-chew when she said, "A guy would like to meet you."

"What are you talking about?" I said, still holding on to my fork. My mouth was full and in paradise, and not a single word of hers would make me leave my food.

"A guy would like to meet you," she repeated.

"A guy wants to meet me?" I mumbled and bought time to think with a sip of fresh mountain water. "What does that even mean?" I asked, turning my attention back to my plate.

"Ouff—why don't you get it?" she said, annoyed.

Because, I wanted to say to her, the only thing I care about is my plate and watching the crowd. But she wouldn't understand.

"Zot, why are you so slow?" she sighed with mock drama.

Perhaps she had meals with meat more often than I did. Perhaps not having to fight for food left her time to think about other things that I did not think about.

"What do you mean?" I said to her.

Exasperated, she jumped up and grabbed my arm just as I was about to eat the roasted pepper, which I had not tried yet. My fork fell in the dirt with the roasted pepper still speared in its tines. I shot a cursed look at her as though she had killed someone. But she didn't care for the roasted pepper or my serious face and tightened her grip on my hand before dragging me away from the kulla.

A few steps beyond her kulla, there was a stretch of rugged fields.

"Whatever," I said to her when I saw the airy view of the mountains.

I inhaled a fresh breath and closed my eyes to enjoy those regal peaks. When I opened my eyes, a young highlander was standing near Ela.

"You are so stupid," I exclaimed to Ela, but she hurried off toward the banquet. She had successfully delivered her product, and her work was done.

As the young highlander said hello, the afternoon light fell on his milky skin like a leaf on a still pond. The sun might have conspired with him, but I still responded to his hello very curtly. Considering the codes for women, I should have talked properly and been more soft-spoken, but I was angry at Ela and couldn't hold my irritation.

"I just wanted to get to know you a little bit better," he said.

"I'm sixteen," I lied.

I was eighteen, but I just wanted to shut him up. Not that girls did not marry at sixteen, but it could still be considered early.

"Good," he said and paused for a minute. "Do you want to go for a walk?" he asked, breaking the silence.

Back in my village, we couldn't walk alone, let alone walk with a guy over the mountains. Who are these mountain people? I thought, getting more upset.

An alpine wind, less whiny than ours, pushed my hair back, letting me see him more fully. I questioned his blue eyes because they smiled at me kindly. He looked untroubled, and his milky skin glowed. I noticed that his face had the same cheerfulness as the rest of the mountain people. I stared at him in the same way Mother had stared at the guy in the fugoni so he would leave us alone.

"Thank you, but I think I'd prefer to go back," I said.

He was cute, but he and I lived by different rules as far as I could tell. He smiled again and didn't seem afraid. In fact, he seemed rather amused by the situation.

"Don't be scared," he said as I was leaving. "No one will say anything, and nothing will happen."

Don't be scared—how dare he? I got upset again and wished to have Mother's stick to break a couple of his bones.

"And who are you?" I said out loud.

"No one," he said, "until you get to know me."

"Look," I said, "up here in your mountains perhaps you are freer but down in the country, things run differently."

He retained his bliss, and his blue eyes did not blink from my harsh words. My hair was flying from a gust of wind, and he seemed to be looking at me with a sense of wonder. The view of the mountains was still mesmerizing and the warm sunlight still soft. Perhaps I overdid it, I thought.

"The mountain looks nice," I said, "and so do you, but I'll pass for now."

And with that I headed back toward the banquet.

"It was nice meeting you, field girl," he said and stayed there.

Likewise, I thought, but I didn't say it. I walked back around their kulla, surprisingly not thinking about the pork chop or the roasted pepper I had not tried yet. Instead, I was amazed at how different these people were from the rest of our country.

When I stepped into the yard, I saw Mother seated at the banquet, and I happily went to sit next to her. Immediately, she snapped at me.

"What are you doing here?" she said.

I looked at her in surprise, and she looked at me in amazement too.

"Go and sit with your age," she said tersely.

"Fine," I said, not having a choice but to go and sit next to Ela since I didn't know anybody else.

Ela had what I called the "mountain smile" on her face and was waiting to hear what had happened with the blue-eyed guy. I did not understand what she was expecting to hear, but she would not like what I had to say.

"I didn't like what you did and don't do it again," I said sternly.

Her eyebrows frowned, and she began shaking her curly, black hair, annoyed. Fortunately, at that moment the *nuse* (bride) showed up, and we both forgot about our argument.

The nuse's face looked wet from crying, but her dress was filled with colorful threads and rhinestones. She was probably around nineteen. She sat down at the banquet with her eyes to the ground, and her head never lifted for the rest of the day. Without conversing, but thinking the same thought, Ela and I stared at her and delved into her movements, knowing that soon we would be in her position. After a good staring at the nuse, we finished our meals and went to dance for the young couple until we were ready to drop from exhaustion.

Later, as I fell asleep on the wood floor underneath my wool cover, I thought about how nice it felt that the mountain people were freer and danced more than us, but I was glad I had not risked my day for a boy. My blanket was sheep's wool and made my skin itch, but it warmed my toes, making me further enjoy the fine air of the mountains and giving me a good sleep.

A mountain goat bleating her guts out woke me up the next morning. She was pregnant and ready to give birth. I found Mother drinking coffee with her cousins and waiting for me to rise. She was ready to leave but hadn't woken me up, in part because she was cherishing the last bit of time with her family, knowing how long it would be until she would see them again. I said goodbye to Ela, thinking now that I would miss her joyfulness and her mountain smile. Mother said goodbye to her family, and we left to take the first fugoni home.

It was a Monday, and the fugoni was full again with riders going to work or to the next town. My grandfather's mountains felt more familiar to me as the fugoni drove us down the mountain. But this time, the driver twice threw the wheels briefly off the edge of the road, making me sweat from fear. The pine trees will hold us, I kept thinking while the fugoni's tires wrestled with the loose gravel on the shoulder of the road. Mother slept the entire ride, resting before work.

She had told me that I had to take our bags and go home and not work that day. That meant one less stamp–meal in the family, but that was what she wanted me to do. My sister was coming to visit, and I had to prepare dinner for her new family. She would stay with us for a week.

When you were freshly married, you could spend a week at your parents' house quite often. After that, you'd have children, and then the visits would become few and far between. My sister had been married six months, and already she had stayed a couple of times with us. She looked different as a nuse, but she never said much about the change. They had said she was an exceptional student, and she had wanted to go to university. But the state didn't allow her to do that because the second criteria, our grandfather's record, got in the way. At least they let her finish high school, which in my case they did not. She graduated high school with straight As, and then she had to get married.

As we headed down the mountain, I became terrified about

getting to the station and seeing the traffic policeman again. Monday morning's dirt roads were always busier than Sunday's, and I hoped that there would be more people waiting with us this time. As we got off the fugoni at the station, we did find more people waiting, and a different traffic policeman was giving directions. But like yesterday, the secondhand green army came through. We did not wait long for the second fugoni, but once we were inside, the driver had to wait for the march to end. The second ride ended quickly because the driver drove fast in hopes of going back and getting another round of the morning rush.

"Cook some rice," Mother said to me after she stepped out of the fugoni.

After pork chops, we are going to have rice! That is fantastic!

"Rice is great," I said to Mother, feeling very cheerful.

I was in the country again, where cheer did not fit into our days. But somehow, the mountain air had stuck with me, and its smiles no longer felt silly. Mother was too occupied to see my mountain smile and left in a rush for work. It was still early, and people were floating down our muddy roads to the fields.

"Good morning," I said without a smile multiple times as I was going up to our kulla.

Field people were reserved and did not smile at each other like the mountain people. That was one of things that the blue-eyed mountain guy did not understand.

"How did you rise?" Kol said as he came around a curve in the road.

"Good morning," I replied, pleasantly surprised. "I rose good!" I said, the mountain smile on my face. I was rather excited to see him, as it had been quite some time since our paths had crossed. "How about you?" I said and touched his shoulder.

Oops, I don't know why I touched his shoulder—I shouldn't have touched him, I thought. The skin over his cheekbones filled with color. His shoulder had felt firm, and his face looked ripe like a peach ready to be eaten. He glanced at me with a humble smile.

Mustering up a firm voice, he said a misplaced, "Nice."

"Nice, what nice?" I asked, catching that his emerald eyes were lost in my mountain smile.

"I meant good," he said shyly, blushing more.

He was an absolute dream, and I couldn't take it.

"Are you going to work?" he asked, continuing to peer at my smile.

He could not restrain his curiosity toward my new demeanor, and I could not restrain myself from falling for his dreamy peach face. He was late for work, but he stood across from me as though he wanted to say something. But he did not say it. Kol had never looked at me like that before. Look what a mountain smile can do, I thought. Tempted by a smiling Bora, he moved a couple of steps closer to me. In his eyes, a green valley rested on his pupils with layers of yellow, sparks of brown, and pieces of gray on top of the lush green.

"My sister is coming home, and I have to prepare dinner," I said, panicking after melting into the depth of his eyes.

They were so lucid that I could see his heart beating through their green-yellow hue. I lowered my plain, amber eyes and moved a couple steps away, this time blushing my heart out.

"I see," he said.

His shoulder moved closer again, but this time, I didn't touch him, although I wanted to. I wanted so badly to plunge my fingers into his golden hair, which seemed to be calling out for me, but I did not do that either. I was being tortured by his breath tickling my cheeks and making me feel drunk.

Who is this man? I thought.

Who is this woman with a new smile? Kol was probably thinking.

"And where are you coming from if you don't mind me asking?" he said, his nice uneven lips searching for an answer.

"I was at my cousin's wedding," I said and moved a couple steps further from his firm body.

"I see now," he said, as if he had found an answer that was good enough to make sense of my mountain smile.

"Have a good day Kol," I said, leaving his enamored face but longing to be with it more.

"You as well Bora," he said.

He lowered his mossy eyes like he was yearning for a word to say. But still, he didn't say it. I turned my back, and we both parted ways, each of us carrying a mountain smile.

Without a doubt, if Mother had seen me smiling that much, she would have killed me. We were lucky that no one was crossing the road either. And with my touch on his shoulder in the open? Oh, that could fuel gossip for a month, I thought. But Kol's green eyes were worth all the yelling in the world and every one of my mountain smiles.

The sun was creeping shyly up my legs as I climbed our hill. I opened the wooden door of our gardh and went into our yard. I was still giggling, thinking of Kol's face. Beneath our yard, I saw the white horse drinking fresh water from the spring. The white horse noticed my mountain smile, too, and stared up at me, motionless.

"Shut up," I said to myself, "Mother would kill you."

I tried to wipe any excess joy off my face and bury my celebrations down deep.

Even though the white horse was not ours, he was often present because he was attracted to the spring. We didn't have a horse, but we had a bitch, as Mother liked to call our dog. Our dog's actual name was Lule, which meant flower. Kol and I had picked the name Lule together when she was a puppy because she was pretty. I got Lule when I was eight years old, and when we were kids, Kol and I played a lot with her. But one day, Father told me that we had to toughen her up so she could bark if wolves came close. I felt sad for her, but Kol told me that was normal for dogs. Later on, while I was staying in our capital for seven weeks, Lule became aggressive, and she was put on a leash.

When we were young, Kol and I spent a lot of time together. But now that we were not in school anymore, Mother warned me that people could misjudge our relationship.

"Those people are *bitches,*" she'd say, and I couldn't agree more.

Since then, Kol and I rarely saw each other, only conversing here and there and exchanging amorous eyes. Even so, I knew Kol very well. I grew up seeing his legs getting longer and his arms firmer, and I liked the handsome young guy he had become. He was the only one in the neighborhood who I let loose with and shared my mountain smile with. He knew me well, too, and he wanted the best for me, just as I did for him.

Wanting to or not, the mountain smile stayed with me while I was doing the housework, and fortunately, no one was around to see it. But as I was putting the wash on the rope, I saw my younger brother coming home from school, so I sent my smile back to the mountains and, perhaps, to Kol, since he was one of the only ones who could read it.

The winds were flowing sporadically around our hill, buffeting my brother's body as he cartwheeled his way up to the kulla. In the distance, behind his flips, the sunset was closing out the day, splashing an orange light across the shimmering water, the lowlands, and all the way up to our rugged yard at the base of the big mountains. It reminded me of the warm sunlight from the peak of the mountains. I stood still and breathed in the fresh air and thought it would be nice if Kol were to come to fill water from our spring.

Mother came on the heels of my brother and pulled my mind back from the mountains.

"It's late," she said from the door of our gardh.

I diverted my attention from the sunset and quickly finished putting the wash on the rope to dry. She was holding logs, so I moved fast, soon finishing with the clothes and rushing toward her to help.

"I don't think your sister will come," she said as I grabbed the logs from her hands.

"Maybe she will come next week," I replied.

We both felt disappointed about not seeing my sister, but in the back of my head, I felt happy. We had only had enough stamps to buy the *mik's* (guest's) meal. But tonight, we could eat the food we had bought for them.

I put my knees on the floor and inserted the logs into the stove to warm the kitchen. When we had *miqtë* (guests), Mother, my siblings, and I would sit close to the table, but we would never eat, pretending that we were not hungry. These miqtë who we would save our precious stamps for were always men. We were cooking a delicacy that night—rice—because we had expected my sister to come with her husband. When she had brought her mother-in-law, we had offered whatever we had that night because it was not necessary to go out of your way for women. Perhaps with just a piece of cornbread and some oil, she would be happy. My younger brother was nodding his head happily too, thinking of eating the rice.

Mother, my younger brother, and I ate the visitor's meal and sat in the warm kitchen for a while. The three of us were the only ones left living in our kulla. My two older brothers were finishing their military service, my sister was married, and my father came home once a month. Afterward, Mother was knitting while she rested her back on the stiff sofa. My younger brother was trying to catch a fly on the wall. He loved catching bees too. Mother and I were waiting for the day when he would get stung so he would stop doing it. He was cute, but so dumb that it was adorable. He had fair skin with straight, black bangs, which sat like a cap on his forehead. Each day, his white face had a new red scratch, and bumps never left his head.

"He is a small dreqi," Mother would say.

He was wearing a sweater that I had worn when I was his age. Mother had knit the sweater, and it had a red eagle on the chest. As for me, I was sitting next to the stove, looking at the sparks of the orange fire. I was thinking about how a wedding in the mountains can change a person. I had discovered a smile I did not know I had, and it had gone to the right person. A new Bora was breathing out of my tiny chest. In bed later, smiling in the dark and reminiscing about Kol's face, I closed my eyes and slept soundly.

CHAPTER 7

My robe got cool when I got out of bed the next morning, and I grabbed the washed clothes from the rope to wear. The pants hugged my skin, their coldness preparing me for the harsh workday. I combed my hair and tied it stiffly at the back of my neck, then I indulged myself by remembering the last two days of mountain smiles and Kol. I moved to the kitchen to find some warmth.

Mother was there drinking her coffee before work, seated on the sofa Father had made. The sofa had a thin tapestry on top of its harsh wood, which made it tolerable to sit on. The long tapestry was red with black-and-white patterns and had been knit by my sister. My younger brother was standing close to the stove, mesmerized by the fire. The stove was old and scratched, but its fire was like a heart for a body. On top of the stove, a teapot was whistling. I put some more sticks into the stove and held my fingers above the flame.

Across from the stove, there was an old, walnut cabinet with two shelves, two drawers, and four slim, worn legs. This was where we stored our food, glassware, dishes, and silverware. The kitchen was always dim since the window was tiny, but the cabinet drawers and shelves looked even darker from being empty. We had more people than plates and food in our kulla. Only a few spiders honored the cabinet with visits. Blurry light shone through the rough glass of our one window onto our bare walls. Icons were forbidden and pictures were too costly, so a flower made of cloth was the only rosy thing adorning our walls. I had made the flower with the help of my sister in one of my early attempts at learning how to sew.

A piece of dry, tasteless cornbread was waiting for me on the table below our blurry window. That cornbread was my breakfast, and I despised it. But my stomach felt relieved, knowing that I had enjoyed a fine meal last night and did not need to eat it. On the days that I didn't have food to take with me, I fed my stomach early in the day with wild berries from the thorn bushes on the road and left the cornbread for lunch. Out in the fields, I would be so hungry by midday that the taste of the cornbread was much more palatable. In spite of my preferences, my younger brother ate his cornbread happily, his black bangs tangled in with the crumbles.

Then, Mother grabbed him by the hand and sprinted toward the road. When I washed her coffee cup, my pants touched the cold stone sink, and the fabric of my pants felt thinner than it had in the past few days. Mother would have to buy the cloth to make my skirt soon because my pants could not take any more mending and needed to be covered by the skirt. I mused about going with Mother to choose the fabric for the skirt, and from that idea, the pleasant smells of the ration supply room quickly seduced my brain. But shortly, I got my work bag ready and headed out too.

Daydreaming about fabrics and fragrances, I headed to the fields, but a neighbor with a pale face joined me on our road, diluting my reverie.

"How are you doing?" he said.

"Fine," I responded dryly and without a mountain smile, of course.

His pale face brought me back to earth, readying me for the hard work that was about to come. We both continued walking in the same direction because we worked in the same field, but our tongues were numb and kept quiet. But boy, our legs were brisk and drove us quickly through the cold, gray morning to the fields.

The spring rains and damp days were still tyrannizing us, and I held on dearly to the image of Kol's smile to warm up my flesh. Soon I will see him again, I fancied as I strolled right into the muddy field. In no time at all, muck covered my pants, but I would make sure to scrub it out on my break. All of us were obsessed with keeping our garments as spotless as possible, a never-ending battle since we worked in dirt all day. Even if the mud was inevitable, on the roads we tried to step on the rocks to keep our shoes, skirts, and pants neat.

In the fields, we would gather around the well twice a day to wash up—once before lunch, when we were hungry, and once after finishing work, when we were exhausted from spreading manure all day. We cleaned the soil from our faces and rubbed our clothes obsessively. If the stains were hard to get out, when we got home at night, we would make sure to boil our clothes until they shined. But that obsession was not even close to the cleaning of our nails. Thick, rough hands with permanently brown skin around the cuticles was among our greatest fears. Seated on the white sheet during our breaks, we would absentmindedly pluck particles of dirt from our nails. And, each day, there was a point when both men and women would hold their hands up to the bright sun to see the soil beneath their nails and then vigorously dig it out.

You could spot a field worker out of the crowds in hospitals, weddings, roads, and fugonis just by seeing how they looked at their fingers. Transfixed like a killer who wants to erase the evidence of the murder scene, we pulled off the field's marks by scrubbing the soil from our body and clothes like it was a stigma we needed to be cured of. When I was young, I had named it the field's syndrome. After I began working, I caught the field's syndrome too. Our hands were weirdly shaped enough from clutching the shovels, but the dirt under our nails established our low position.

Out of all the people, the field worker was the lowest in rank. There were doctors, nurses, teachers, officers, and office employees—and then us. Although every person was ruled by the state, the field workers were ruled by both the state and the common citizens who felt the urge to differentiate themselves from us because of our occupation. Remarkably, all of us were forced into this trap, but people still loved playing against each other. The assumption was that anyone could work in the fields, even a junkie, a mental patient, and above all, the impoverished. In short, the field worker was the person who none of the upper classes wanted to be associated with.

Perhaps we didn't save lives or create weapons and underground battlements for attacks, but we alone cultivated and harvested grain and vegetables to feed their bourgeois bellies. However, fieldwork was considered unskilled labor because anyone could work in the fields, and therefore, the upper classes did not reserve much respect for the proletariat. So, we kept ourselves bright and clean.

In the summer days, we left our whites out until the heat made them bone dry. Below the headscarves, we kept our freckled faces clean, washing them in streams and over wells on every break. We cared what the upper strata thought about us and were desperate for their acceptance. We became maniacs about cleaning to try to gain their respect or, in the very least, to keep up our pride for our own sakes.

CHAPTER 8

All the pants I ever wore were my older brothers' pants. To make them mine, I would cut the waists and sew them tightly, so they fit my smaller frame. We rarely bought new clothes, but when we did, they would be three sizes too big so they could fit us in the coming years, just like the shoes I had been wearing since I was fourteen. Our clothes were passed down to us from our older siblings and were made by our mothers when they had free time to do *pun dorë* (handiwork).

Mother taught me and my sister how to sew and knit because young girls were mandated to learn the art of stitching at a young age. It was as important for girls to learn to sew as it was for boys to learn to become good soldiers. When I started my first piece, Mother said it was terrible, but she made me keep going because "flawed but finished is better than perfectly half done." Later, whenever I would make a piece she liked, she would be pleasantly surprised and say, "*Shife dreqin*" (Look at the evil). I liked that dreqi version more, so I kept knitting to hear her calling me dreqi again. I knit my first sweaters when I was thirteen, all in a plain black color. After knitting only black sweaters, I first sewed a flower on a pillowcase, and that looked good—enough. Later, when my skills got better, I tailored garments, patched rugs, and anything that was needed. I knew

Mother was very proud of me because I kept hearing her calling me dreqi. I was surprised and amused to hear her express herself that openly, and that was the warmest she got.

Black was cheap to buy because it was a color people did not prefer, although many had to wear it. You wore black when someone died, but if you were a woman, you had to wear the color of mourning longer. When a relative died, women wore black for months to a year. In a bigger loss, such as the death of a husband, wives were required to wear black for the rest of their lives. Nëna had not even buried Grandfather before she had to don dark cloth, and she never wore any other color again. Like the skirts, the black clothes conveyed a message about status, declaring a female body to be a widow for life. This was another rule that applied solely to women. A man could wear a white shirt below his jacket at the funeral of his dead wife, and if he wanted, he could look for a new wife the next day. Because that was acceptable to his fellow men. Besides, who would marry a woman who had been left with children to raise? The answer was *no one.* That would bring shame and rejection to the aforementioned men.

The competition for a spouse favored men far more than women, so men had more options. There were countless daughters who had never been married and were desperately looking for husbands. A typical family in our village had three to six children, and at least half were daughters who were on the open market after finishing middle school. If a young woman passed her twenties, it was even harder to find a husband. It went hand in hand—the older you got the less of a man you got. One of the most prominent fears of families was *to ngel ne der,* which meant they were afraid of their daughters being left unmarried and still on their father's doorstep. With that fear in mind, parents were in a rush to get their daughters out their doors. The faster we were out, the better. It was like our fate was thrown into the trash, and it did not matter what kind of bin. "Her husband is awful but at least she is married, better a miserable wife than a miserable daughter," the saying went. That was how low the standards were for the beginning of my life. That was why Mother had married off my sister right out of high school. She had been about to turn nineteen, and people had known her "expiration date" was near.

I enjoyed working with my hands when I was sewing, and it gave me pride and satisfaction because of the process of figuring out the measurements, calculating the lengths and widths, drafting the design, and even putting the thread through the eye of the needle. There was only one thing I hated doing—cutting off the thread. Women used their teeth to cut the thread, but it gave me goosebumps and made me cringe to hear it slipping on my teeth while I ground my teeth together. Since I couldn't tolerate the sound of it, I kept a sharp rock in my pocket to smash the thread on a stone until the thread broke. The best part of tailoring was when I would find old pieces of clothing and create a whole new thing out of it like when I made curtains from old sheets. Mother called me a super dreqi then. Like the long-lasting pants I wore, repurposing clothes was what we were taught to do. Stitching and patching were among the few activities where a daughter could express herself freely and relish in it.

Just like clothes that we could not afford to buy, common commodities were rare in our households. It was hard to choose between a bar of soap and a glass of rice in the ration supply store. When Mother would have to give a bar of soap to a family who recently had a daughter, it would cost us a meal. For that reason, things like soap were used sparingly for personal needs and saved as gifts for special occasions, such as weddings, engagements, and births. I did feel sorry for Mother when she had to make these difficult decisions in the ration supply room.

To make the most of our means, we relied on Mother Earth as much as we knew how. We were the most innovative when it came to keeping our clothes bright. When we washed our clothes, we would first take the ashes from the fire and throw them in a big pan of water, letting it come to a boil over the fire. Once the water was boiling, we sank the dirty clothes into it. Afterward, we left the clothes in the rolling, ashy water, which worked as a cleanser for the stains. To make the whites even whiter, we took even more time and used more techniques because that's how desperately we field workers wanted to look good.

After boiling the clothes, we left them to soak for a day in the ashy water. Finally, we rinsed them, scrubbed them by hand, soaked them again, and ideally, finished up by drying them outside on a hot sunny day. Even if the sun made them bone dry and destroyed the quality of the fabric, it made the clothes whiter. And oh Zot, we loved white.

In the fifth month of the year, the earth would breathe flowers, and we would explore the foothills of our mountains and pick herbs and flowers with inviting perfumes. That was the most adventurous technique we used for creating pleasant scents for our clothes. Although it was a female thing to collect herbs and flowers, whenever I hiked with Kol, we would both pick up aromatic leaves.

Kol's favorite flower was a yellow one that lived on top of the hills. It resembled a sunflower but was smaller with a tiny sunburst in its core. My favorite one was a flower that was more common in the fields. We called it *lulekuqe* (red flower) because it had chili-red petals with a dark core of inky-black seeds. When we were young, Kol would often pick up a lulekuqe and bring it to me. As we grew up, he had to hide the red flower in his pocket, giving it to me with fewer red petals each time. One day, only the stem with the black seeds was left in his hand, and since then, he stopped bringing them to me.

When Kol and I were young and did our carefree exploring, we would bring back flowers and herbs and drop them in the hot water to boil with the clothes. We also used fruit skins for nice aromas, and we sometimes held orange or clementine peels preciously in our pockets. When we had them fresh, I loved squeezing their skin and breathing in the zest, which many times got in my eyes and made them sting. Although it was as rare as roses in the desert, there were days when our stamps could afford a couple of oranges or sometimes pears like the ones that hung from the tree in our yard.

Regardless of our means, freshwater was plentiful throughout our land. For nice textured, silky hair, Mother taught us to wash our heads with rainwater. Since we were blessed, or cursed, to live in a land with heavy rainfall, we had countless chances from September to April to collect rainwater. The sky's water made our hair soft, and the sun made it glow. To complete the full treatment after doing the wash on a sunny Sunday, I would sit outside on a flagstone and bask in the sun while I brushed my split hairs. Mother would come outside and cut my split hairs, and I would cut hers too.

Most of the women had long hair, and some wore headscarves. In the fields, wrapping a piece of fabric on your head became popular because it protected your hair from too much of the tokë's oppressive sun. Only the old women wore headscarves all the time, keeping tightly within tradition, and they carried the most old-fashioned hairstyles underneath. Often their scarves were black, and under it, there were two braids of hair that looked just like two horns on top of their heads. It looked funny, but Mother said not to laugh at traditions.

Nëna had these same black horns, and I liked to watch her braiding them. She started by dividing her hair into two parts. Then, she constructed two long braids, weaving in a thin string to each braid, and then she knotted the braids together on the crown of her head. She finished by putting her scarf over her horns. She preferred me to make them for her, but whenever I did, Mother yelled at me because I liked to accentuate her horns. Nëna found her larger horns funny too, but Mother did not.

There was a time when I made Nëna's braids that I will never forget. After I finished with her braids, she put on her scarf and told me to put my head in her lap. I did so, and then she began combing my hair with her wooden comb. But the comb caught on my ear.

"Oh, your ears are virgin," she said. "Nëna will give you a nice piercing."

It was as simple as laying on her lap while she bored a needle through the lower part of my ears, both left and right. She left a thin stick inside the new holes to keep them open. I kept the sticks until I got my first jewelry.

I was in seventh grade when I got my first earrings, and it felt weird wearing them because no other girl in my class had such an expensive thing. When women wore jewelry, they were either married or engaged. Father brought the piece of silver for my earrings from his mining job. I'm pretty sure that was against the rules, but for once, he apparently found the guts to do it. Father gave the silver to a man in the village who hand-carved metal under a table in his bloody basement, and he smelted jewelry too. A pair of earrings lasted a long time since it was hard to make them to begin with, but essentially, that was the only piece of jewelry you got in your entire your life.

Earrings typically came later than ear piercing, but Mother gave me the earrings much earlier than was usual. She looked at me and said that I deserved the world. Well, to be honest, she did not say it, but I could read it in her amber eyes, which then were overly expressive and watery. Although she did not mind it, my sister would say that Mother had a sweet spot for me long before the earrings came along. I felt no guilt about this because she was the oldest, and for so long, she had gone to the weddings with Mother and had enjoyed the privilege of eating pork chops. Nonetheless, owning a pair of earrings and having red flowers accompanied by a blushing face were pleasant enough things to live with.

CHAPTER 9

Mother's sweet spot for me was rooted in the guilt that grew over the years. My first trip to our capital city, Tirana, was linked with that guilt, but it had all begun with the pear tree. In our yard, we had a pear tree older than our kulla. It had a big, wide trunk rooted deep in the soil, and its branches opened up broadly, shadowing the untamed ground. There were also cypresses and a couple of tall pine trees in our yard, but the pear tree was more memorable because of its fruit.

When the children of the neighborhood would get together to play hide and seek in the late afternoons, the trees were the first place we would choose to hide. In the dusk light, we blended with the leaves and branches, our silhouettes camouflaged by the shadows, making it impossible to be found. If suddenly we were discovered, we could jump down and run to touch safe before the seeker got there. We had a few bunkers to hide in, but the older we got, the less we preferred them. If we got caught hiding in a bunker, there was no way to run from the seeker, so we were trapped and "killed," losing the game.

I remember playing a lot under the pear tree when I was young, in part because its low branches made it easier to climb. I liked to swing on one strong branch and watch the green, velvety grass beneath my feet. Sometimes, I would sit in the pear tree while

I waited for Mother to walk me to school. Mother and I would walk part of the way together in the mornings, then she would head to her field, and I would go to school. When my younger brother was too young for school, a grandmother in the neighborhood took care of him while Mother was at work. Whenever Mother had to leave for work early, I would walk to school with other neighborhood kids, sometimes Kol or Maria.

One day, when I was eight years old and finishing second grade, I was sitting on the gravelly stairs of our kulla, waiting for Mother so we could walk together to school. It was spring that day, and across the yard, I saw that the pear tree had a fresh green color glowing from its young leaves, and I could not resist walking toward it. Just a few days away from bursting with blossoms, its branches were packed with dense, brown buds. I climbed up to a lower branch than usual, sat down on it, and swung on it while I waited for her. I was just going to swing back and forth a few times and jump down once Mother called me.

But I heard Mother yelling, "Get out, little dreqi!"

And then I heard Lule crying. Father had brought Lule home only a few weeks before. She was still a puppy and loved to be cuddled and take naps inside, but Mother did not like her napping in the kitchen. When I heard Mother yelling, I got all fixed up to go and save Lule from Mother's wooden stick. I jumped off the branch, but my feet clumsily caught one another, sending me crashing to the ground. I did not make a sound, but Lule saw me and ran toward me. I was behind the big trunk with my elbow buried in the soil. Lule came and began whining quietly as she licked my arm that was jabbed into the dirt.

"Bora," Mother called, but she could not see where I was.

I looked to see if my legs had any scratches, and when I moved them, they felt fine.

"Bora," Mother yelled again.

My elbow was feeling cold from the wet soil, so I pulled it out. Lule moved away when she saw Mother coming, cowering with her tail between her legs. Suddenly, my arm felt sweaty and hot, as if the bones were bleeding, and pain shot through my whole body. Mother rushed toward me and found me in a mess of pain. I was wailing on the ground and holding my arm. Distraught, she hugged me and began drying my face with her skirt, but I could not keep tears from pouring out of my eyes. Mother lifted me from the ground and stared at my elbow. We both saw that the skin around my elbow was unnaturally swollen and turning to a blend of blue and red. Mother tried to move the arm, but I winced as though a lightning bolt had shocked me.

"We have to go to the doctor," Mother said.

She seemed more frightened than Lule, but at that moment, I couldn't care less about either of them because the pain was bigger than my body.

Mother and I both walked in agony toward the fugoni stop, but for different reasons. Halfway there, she lifted me up and carried me on her back because I was walking so slow. Once we got to the stop, Mother set me down on the grass. I had never seen her so worried. She was so desperate for the fugoni to take us that she went over, stood on the road, and raised her hand in the air, ready to signal the next fugoni to stop for us, even though she knew it would not come for another half an hour. There were two fugonis that ran their wheels around the potholes of our road—one in the early morning and another in late afternoon. We were lucky because it was still early morning, otherwise, we would have had to wait for hours until the next fugoni would pass.

As we were waiting, Mother saw a neighbor friend passing through toward the fields and told her that we were going to Tirana to see a doctor. When I heard the name of the capital, I thought that it could be exciting to visit it—if I were not wailing because of my ruined elbow. Mother's friend said that she would take care of our kulla without a problem. Then, a beige fugoni saw Mother's outstretched arm and picked us up.

It was my first trip to our capital, even though it was only an hour's drive from our city, but I knew it was where our "supreme" leader lived. Before that, I had heard our leader's voice only from the radio at school, but I knew that he and his important people lived in the Blloku neighborhood of the concrete capital. Our teacher had told us that Tirana was beautiful and had the biggest buildings in the country and big hospitals.

As we drove to the capital, a searing pain shot through my arm every time the fugoni hit a pothole in the broken roads. I recalled a neighbor who had broken his arm. Rumors had it that when Edi went to the capital's hospital, the doctors cut the flesh and bones of his arm, stuck the two bones together, and sewed the skin. Then, they used two wooden planks to stabilize the arm, wrapped the planks with a cloth, and hoped the bones would glue together. Rumors also said that the arm Edi broke was shorter than the other after that because of the bone the doctors had taken out. Ever since he broke his arm, it was said that Edi was the kid with the weakest hand in his class.

Riding to the hospital in the fugoni, my shattered elbow was throbbing and swelling up bigger and bigger, and I became terrified that my arm might have the same destiny as Edi's. Mother looked terrified too. I thought Mother was worried because she did not want a daughter with one shortened arm. I was sure that she had definitely heard the cut-and-glue story of Edi's arm. I also knew she was worried about taking the entire day off work. It will just be a few days, I thought after I remembered that it had taken Edi only a day or two to come back to school. I also thought I should tell her that I would stay away from the pear tree, but the pain beat away my words.

That hour ride felt terribly long, but we finally made it to the hospital. Mother waited in the reception area while a nurse took me into another room, helped me undress, and gave me a long shirt with buttons down the front to wear. I laid on the bed, holding my arm stiffly at a ninety-degree angle, my elbow resting on my stomach. The nurse gently told me that she wanted to straighten my arm.

"No!" I blurted out, tears flooding my eyes.

The nurse looked knowingly at me and took my arm away from my stomach, laid it down along my side, and carefully touched it with her fingers. The pain was fierce and came at a lightning speed as she felt the bones. Another nurse came in, and they talked for a bit before the second nurse shot an injection into my other arm. After that, I fell fast asleep. I recall waking up once and seeing the darkness outside the window. I thought about Mother for a spell, but then, too tired, I fell asleep again.

It was the next morning when I finally woke up. I saw a cast on my arm from my shoulder to my fingers. My arm did not hurt as much, but it felt distended like a sack filled with flour. My eyelids sank occasionally, heavy from the medication.

The iron bed was big, and the covers were laid evenly over it and were keeping me warm. Across the room, a portrait of our leader was hanging on the wall. We had pictures of him on our school's crumbling walls, but the picture on the hospital wall was newer and made him look more fashionable. Perhaps in Tirana the leader and his people had to have up-to-date things. Over his picture, light was sprinkling in from the window, which was covered by austere curtains in a blanched, sanitized beige color. The room was stark white with two beds and a screen as a divider. There was a chair across from my bed with a shiny plastic pillow embedded in the seat, but no one was sitting on it. Where was Mother?

I got out of the bed and walked barefoot into the hall to look for her. Even though it was heated, the hall felt icy because it was so extremely clean. My arm felt heavy from the cast that was carrying my useless arm. I thought about Edi's story and realized that the doctors might have to make my arm shorter too. I lifted up both of my arms and carefully compared their lengths to see if the injured one was a pinky or a thumb shorter than the other, but it was hard to tell because of the cast. Edi's story was haunting me and invoking glimpses of last night's dreams.

Two nurses found me in the hall while I was measuring my arms.

"Here we are," said one nurse to the other.

She had a shrill, high-pitched voice, and I recalled that she was the nurse who had injected me.

"I told you that we would have issues without her mother here," she said, her voice extra shrill.

The second nurse stood quietly, looking at me with gentle eyes. But I was startled by what the shrill-voiced nurse had said.

"Where is Mother?" I asked, frozen.

As I was waiting for an answer, the gentle nurse knelt down to my level, next to my encased arm, and kindly asked how I was feeling.

"Did Mother leave?" I said to her, panicking.

"Yes, your mother had to leave because we have to keep you for two weeks to see how your arm is coming together."

I crumbled to the sterile floor. The bleach on the linoleum began strangling my tiny chest.

"But she will come back soon," her gentle voice continued as she came close to me and stroked my head.

"But why? Why for so long?" I asked, knowing full well that two weeks was too long a time for Mother to stay away from work.

The gentle nurse did not have an answer and gave me a sorrowful look, which made me realize that she was the one who had straightened my arm.

I headed to my room, hopeless. I had to spend two weeks in the hospital room. My body felt flimsy from both the physical pain and the pain of being left alone. The nurses followed me into my room. The nurse with a gentle voice helped me get into the bed and tucked me in. The other one told me to be ready at midday for the doctor's visit and stormed out, saying that she had more patients to see.

Later, they came back together with some food, took my vitals, and wrote them on a board hanging from the foot of the bed. When the doctor visited me, he did not say much and left quickly after checking my chart. I slept through the rest of that day, and I slept through the next, and the next, and the next, and so on, aching for the two weeks to pass.

I longed and waited for Mother's visit, but she never came.

By the end of the second week, the gentle nurse felt guilty about Mother not coming, but I knew it wasn't her fault. That day, the doctor opened the cast and examined my arm. His face was troubled, and he went to get another doctor for a second view. It is shorter, I thought to myself. But that was okay by then— I just wanted to go back to my hills. While we were waiting for the doctors to come, the gentle nurse held my hand while the other murmured unhappily. The second doctor came, and both of them agreed on some matter. Then, the shrill-voiced nurse left upset.

"We are stuck with this child here," she said as she left.

The doctors followed her. The gentle nurse once again tucked me in and told me in a melodic voice to get good sleep.

The next day, they put me in the surgery room for the second time because, as it turned out, my bones had fused wrong. I had broken my elbow, and the first attempt to re-attach it had not worked. The gentle nurse was there preparing me, and the shrill one injected my arm multiple times. Shortly after, the sterile walls faded from my sight, and I was gone until the next morning. That second surgery was longer, but the melodic voice said it went well. I remember my body feeling beaten up while the nurses changed my robe.

Weeks traveled by, and still Mother didn't come. For seven weeks, neither Mother nor any other visitors came. To say that I felt forgotten is justifiable and not unexpected. In daylight, I got used to it, but when darkness came, I missed Mother more. For days, I looked out the window at the terrain across from the hospital to pass the time.

When I first saw Tirana's private houses through my window, I realized that our kullat were very, very, very, ugly. Up until that point, I had never seen new buildings—other than bunkers—but in Tirana, I saw that bunkers were not the only cement in our country. The capital was in a fine valley enclosed by mountains, and pristine roads and manicured properties hosted its upper-class citizens.

When Mother finally came one Sunday, she found me standing

at the window. I turned and saw her at the door, but I did not feel much of anything. Her face looked just like any other woman's face to me. Perhaps it is possible to forget your mother's face, I thought. Perhaps a dear one's face, when unseen, gets washed and folded and then locked in some secure safe beneath the wound. Blankly, I walked over to her and hugged her because she was crying profusely. Mother did not like crying, but she was feeling sad, and I understood. She asked the doctors if she could take me home.

That same day, the doctors took off my cast and released me. One of my arms was thoroughly scarred, but—amazingly enough—I had two arms of the same length. I left the icy hall, waving at the gentle nurse with the melodic voice and having gotten used to the smell of bleach. Mother held my other hand tight. She did not speak, but her hand trembled as she squashed my fingers. I did not tell her to free my hand, nor did I ask her the reasons for not visiting me once. I imagined there were many I did not want to hear.

For seven weeks in the hospital, I had locked Mother away. Some days I had thought I would never see her again. But then in the fugoni, second by second, she began to look more recognizable and familiar. She had been locked in my safe, and there, her face was washed finely, shone smoothly, and was tucked away sweetly, echoing euphoria. But in the fugoni, her face looked worn and woeful. She never told me her reason for not visiting, but I realized years later Tirana's important citizens of the Blloku had kept Mother away from her eight-year-old daughter.

So many scenarios ran in my mind, like the brigadier not giving her a day off because he could not afford to show his paper at the party office without projects being done. Or Mother, tight for money, could not afford to take the day off and pay for four fugoni rides to visit me. As for Father, he was probably held up for two months straight digging a tunnel, and perhaps, he did not even know that his daughter was in the hospital.

Mother looked sad and worn because she knew that even human life was not more significant than the projects and the plans of our

Communist leader. Our leader's ideologies could kill your father and your husband, make you abandon your child, jail you for twenty-five years, and so on. On our ride back, every few miles the fugoni passed banners with *Rrofte Partia Komuniste* (Long Live the Communist Party) on them, imploring us to cheer for the Communist Party and reminding us who our chief was. In that fine city, our leader painted his banners and drew up his plans while spreading suffering around the rest of the country. Tirana was the capital of our hell and inextricably linked with guilt.

When I returned home, I saw that Lule had gotten bigger and more aggressive. I understood that Mother must have beaten her to toughen her up. When Lule was a puppy, Kol told me that I had to kick her away because that was the best way to make her stronger.

Kol came by a while after I got home and found me cuddling Lule, relishing in her company. She barked at him twice, and then left us alone. We sat out in the yard, glancing at the plain and the calm sea beyond. I was afraid to do anything because of my arm.

"Does it hurt?" Kol asked, his face looking like an unripe white peach with green eyes on it.

"Not anymore," I said.

"I found a thornbush full of berries, and I was waiting for you to come so we could eat them together," he said, blushing joyfully.

"Sure," I agreed, and we marched off.

We hiked up a small hill at the back of my kulla, kicking some rocks along the way. There was a plethora of wild herbs and flowers perfuming our path. Kol held my other hand, softer than Mother had, when he helped me to cross a coulee. Then, we sat and enjoyed the blackberries, feeling liberated by the adventure. When we got back to my kulla, Mother asked Kol to keep an eye on me and to walk with me to school. There was less than a month left of school before summer, but he and I had been glued together all that year. Our bond was even stronger than the one the doctors had created in my arm because it wasn't forced, and while we didn't know its future, it felt great in the moment.

CHAPTER 10

The pear tree in our yard witnessed the challenges of our household. My mother planted it before I was born, and to this day, it stood watch next to our kulla. Every year, Mother would struggle to keep us away from its fruit. But all standing and buried titles belonged to the state, so we were not allowed to eat the fruit from our trees. Instead, we had to harvest them and bring the crops to the ration supply room. Indeed, we watched as oranges, apples, and pears grew on our trojë only to become deliciously juicy fruit we could not eat. If we ate the fruits, we were denied the piece of cornbread we were entitled to. How would the state know? With the large number of government-sponsored rats around to accuse us. The price was too harsh, and in the long run, it was not worth creating a poor rapport with the state for a few pears.

I remember once in December when I was thirteen and Mother took our pears to the shop, the store worker told her that it was assumed that while you were harvesting the fruit you would eat some. So, they were deducted from our food stamps. Mother stared at him with a look that said she would like to chop off his head.

"These are the orders from above," the store worker said apologetically.

I looked above his head, as I saw something fluttering. It was the banner saying *Rrofte Partia Komuniste* (Long Live the Communist Party), which made it crystal clear who made the harsh rules and reminded us to cheer them on. The store worker used a big scale on the counter to precisely measure each ounce of our fruit. That time, our paper stamp bought us a glass of sugar, a palmful of beans, and one scoop of cornmeal—instead of two—because of the pears. As we left, I bid our pears farewell without tasting them. Perhaps, if you lived high up in the mountains you could evade the insanity that gnawed away at our stomachs in the lowlands.

Some country men played the law by hiding pigs or chickens under their sofa or in the cellar. On cold winter days, they would cut up the animals, staining the basement with blood, and hang the meat to cure. A pork chop or a chicken wing could cost the men their lives, but ending their family's hunger was worth the hanging. When we had traveled in the fugoni with the chickens to the wedding, we had been the only passengers because the driver, the woman's son, had been afraid that a spy would see the chickens and inform the officials, getting him arrested for four chickens.

It seemed that few rats lived up in the mountains, but they were legion on our streets. People never stood around along our rugged roads for more than a minute because rats were lurking in the shadows, greedily taking bits and pieces of whatever word they could find to feed their insatiable appetite for satisfying the state. Knowing that, our streets stayed hushed and empty, and people's legs kept on the move because they were afraid of accusations that could lead them into the concrete jails. Thoughts, opinions, and concerns were red flags.

You absolutely could not laugh in the open.

Even simply being happy was not right to the filthy spies. I once heard the story of a man who was laughing too loud on the road. The rats rushed in and silenced his tongue forever. My Uncle Llesh, who worked high up in the government, was not afraid because he knew that he was too much of a necessity to them. But for the rest of us, fear closed our mouths, and we didn't dare exchange even the bare minimum out in the open—yet another unspoken rule that we all conformed to without ever discussing it. It was fair—that's what our leader with the nice costume told us. From his black, shiny car, he waved proudly, reminding us that we were created by his fair hands.

Perhaps we did not have churches or streets to gather in, but surely we had the ration supply room. There was always a long line outside of the monochrome room, but each of us loved going in. Visiting the ration supply room was like going to church and seeing the entire community. It was the place to see and be seen. I truly enjoyed going to the supply room, even if it meant dropping off our fruits.

One day, when Mother and I were waiting to go inside, I was not excited to be seen because I was still waiting for my skirt.

"*Je gati per burr,*" Mother said, which meant I was ready for a husband.

"I don't even have my skirt yet," I replied, frustrated.

"You have a pair of earrings," she responded.

I was still eighteen years old, but in her mind, I was a year older. Mother's practice of living ahead was a trait of the poor, like buying shoes three sizes bigger than my actual foot. But I loved the smell of the ration supply room, so I did not mind Mother's remarks.

That day, we saw my friend Maria buying yet another skirt with her mother because she was already engaged. For the second skirt, I assumed that her mother had sacrificed a week's work. But, if that was what it would take to get her daughter out of the door with honor, it was worth the sacrifice. Maria was my age, and we had known each other since before school, so we chatted warmly as we waited to get into the store. Maria had a fiancé and was cleverer than me, and through her, I would learn the limitations forced on me because I am a woman.

As if the ration supply room was meant for people who lived in the free world, it smelled nice inside, and the goods were plentiful. Light-blue tiles dressed its walls, and it looked flawlessly clean. There were lots of fabrics to catch your eye and admire. There were also fruits and vegetables in all shades of bright colors, but we couldn't afford to give up the stamp. The ration supply room was designed by our leader to only stingily fill our needs, just as our schools, hospitals, and our lives were planned to give us just enough to survive, but no more.

Still, we cherished the visits to the ration supply room because there we were invaded by the figments of our imaginations. In that room, each of us privately gave in to dreaming of a fictitious life baptized with the ration supply store's goodies. Seduced by the smells emitting a heavenly ether across the room, we couldn't help but daydream. The dream would last right up to when a field worker's hand would sneak across the lavish fabrics to pull dirt from its nails, turning us 360 degrees and back to the ground. And there, at the counter next to the scale, we were suddenly wide awake.

Despite that, we cherished the air of the room, as it allowed us some whiffs of indulgence. Perhaps it only takes brightly colored fruits and vegetables to dunk the poor into a false dream. Standing in that rectangular room, people were permitted to envision a life of prosperity and a future with plenty of color. That dream was a man's own journey; the state could not control it. In the end, "these bitch stamps," as Mother would say after having only a few more to pay, would force us to forget the nice colors and the abundance of the room.

The same day that Maria bought her second skirt, I felt bad for Mother because she had to decide between my fabric and a loaf of bread, and she bought the loaf instead. Food was her primary concern, but I had been out of school for more than a year and was still wearing my worn pants. Even so, I was convinced that before I knew it, Mother would be back in the store and buy a piece of fabric that I could sew into my first skirt. Presumably, I could sew it and wear it on the same day, depending on the fabric that Mother could afford.

Once we had left with our goods and crossed the long queue

outside, Mother promised to buy the fabric on our next visit. I looked down at my pants, trying to estimate how much time was left before they completely tore apart. I put my hands inside the pockets to explore the thin fabric. My fingers found a few seeds, and I took them out and saw that they were the poppy seeds from Kol's lulekuqe. Then, I wondered how long I would be allowed to keep loving his peachy face.

CHAPTER 11

A few Sundays after I had seen Maria in the supply room, I woke up with the sun and opened the curtain to pull some light in. Since it wasn't Pascha Sunday, it was our day. I dressed and sat outside on the stairs, admiring the clear sky before the bright sun would impose itself on my sight. I was still barefoot, and I attempted to feel the chill of the stone staircase attached to the side of our house that faced the sea. Our kulla was constructed on a flat-topped hill below the mountains and faced west. It looked like a dark spot against the lighter mountains due to its rough-hewn stone sides, unfinished surfaces, and gray grout. Its square, rigid form dominated the trojë like a monolithic cave. There was a line of grout on the outside wall between the first and the second floor. The kitchen was beneath the line, and the bedroom and the *odë* (living room) were above it.

Upstairs in the odë, we had a single bed, a couch, and a table with a carpet underneath it. It was a cold room and only used for a formal *mik* (guest) who was not one of our *fisi* (relatives). When it was time for the daughters in a family to marry, an odë functioned more like an open door for men asking for the hand of their victim.

In our kulla, Father's bed was in the odë, as he did not sleep with Mother, since . . . I didn't know when. In my parents' time, adults felt ashamed to sleep with their partners. I didn't know why, but I knew that Father slept alone and lived alone. He worked in the state mines, and we rarely saw him. He felt like a stranger, but somehow, he was our father who we loved without question. I slept with Mother in one of the three beds in our kulla's only bedroom, which was on the second floor. Mother had a bed dedicated to her, and not too long ago, there had been three sons and two daughters sleeping in that room with her. My sister was married by then, and when my older brothers were home from the military, one slept on the stiff kitchen sofa, and the other slept on Father's bed when Father wasn't there, leaving only me and my younger brother in our bedroom with Mother.

As I was sitting outside on the stone step, Mother called me from the kitchen window, but when I got inside, she rushed out of the room. I perched next to my younger brother, who was playing with the wood next to the stove, and put my hands above the flame to warm up. Like thunder, Mother came back and tossed a piece of fabric at me.

"Here, you can make your skirt now," she said.

The fabric fell on my face, flopped down to my chest, and landed on the floor. I stared in disbelief at the fabric, then I grabbed it as if it were a piece of gold. I was eighteen years old, which meant I had been working among the adults two whole years without proper clothes. I brought the fabric close to my cheek. It felt divine, like the back of a baby lamb's ear. It was white-colored cotton with blue dots and was thick enough to last for a long time. White was my favorite color, and I glowed beneath my coffee-colored hair while thanking Mother. She looked touched, saying without speaking that I deserved the world, just like when she had given me the earrings.

I had never been more excited to do the wash than on that day. I took the fabric, my pants, and my brothers' clothes, and I went to the back of the kulla. I blew on the dry sticks to rouse a fire, and soon the cinders were glowing and a flame rose up. I went to the spring crooning with joy and filled the big pan with mountain water. After I brought it back and landed it on the heat, I boiled the clothes. Later, I rubbed them with my hands. As a field girl with the name Bora, I liked everything to look white, just like Mother, who had named me after the word "snow." I kept rubbing until Mother called me for lunch. I left the clothes to soak in the hot water and went in.

As Mother, my younger brother, and I sat quietly together and ate bean soup, I saw Mother's mid-brow wrinkle moving delightedly, acknowledging that her daughter had grown to be a young woman. At that moment, without a word from Mother on how to behave or what to await while wearing a skirt, I opened the door of the woman's world.

In our family, you were expected to understand and learn by yourself, as we never talked much about dos and don'ts. I learned what to expect in life and what I could and couldn't have by hearing real stories and by watching other people's lives. After the dishes, I put the clothes up to dry, knowing that I was ready to sew the fabric that would make me a woman. By late afternoon, the fabric was ready, and that evening, I owned my first skirt.

The next day, I put on my skirt and went out into the rough lands for my debut. Under the white fabric with blue dots, my frame didn't look as bony anymore. I floated elegantly when I walked, like I was born with the fabric around my waist. It was a glorious day. I finally was part of the other women, and each woman who I saw complimented my new garment. In the field, I saw eyes widen and cheeks smile at me like never before.

I walked home from work with Maria that day, and we saw Kol at his kulla working on his lawn. The good weather had finally made its appearance, and Kol was wearing a light T-shirt. My mountain smile appeared instantly.

"How are you, handsome?" Maria shouted.

Maria was always more brash than me and knew Kol did not take her seriously. Besides, she was already safe because she was engaged, and as long as she kept her loud mouth only between us, she did not risk being misunderstood. Kol strode slowly toward us, mopping sweat from his forehead with his arm. I once touched his shoulder, I remembered. He walked toward the gardh and answered with a plain "good" to Maria. Then he looked at me and I looked back at him with my mountain smile, but he did not flinch.

He stared at my skirt and said, "Wow," and couldn't help but blush.

His golden hair flopped carelessly as he moved his country man's body closer to me.

I continued smiling as he uttered, "One engaged and one wearing a skirt."

I detected a faint whisper of trepidation.

"You both are almost out of our doors," he said plainly.

"Hallelujah! Almost there," Maria quickly responded.

My smile shrank abruptly. I didn't know how to respond to what was just said.

"It was good to see you," I uttered to Kol, and then I mumbled to Maria, "I have to go."

Then I left. Not understanding what Kol had seen from my skirt, I tried to walk fast to get out of their sight, but the whining wind was descending from the peaks and forced me to slow down. I felt bothered by Kol saying the words that were still swirling in my mind. Eventually, beating the wind, I arrived at the top of our hill, still brooding, and turned to stare at the blue waves, which blithely joined the azure sky. There and then, the pear tree shook its leaves, telling me that Kol was right. My time was running out. Soon I had to leave my door for good, and the skirt was nothing more than bait for my potential husband.

CHAPTER 12

Maria and Kol were the two closest people to me after my family. For eight years, Maria and I had shared the same desk in school. Later, when we finished middle school, we were separated because we were sent to work in different fields. After that, we sewed and knit clothes together in our free time, but that was fleeting because Maria left our rugged roads and rough fields not long after finishing school. Maria got married at eighteen on the dot, and after that, her clever face dropped for good. Through her, I learned that my face would look constantly tired when I got married because of how yellow and washed out she looked. My oldest sister also looked tired once she married, confirming my assumptions. But most importantly, through Maria I learned why Kol and I didn't stand a chance.

It all began with Maria liking a guy from our village and wanting to marry him. The guy was proper and respectful and loved her too. But her family didn't agree to the marriage, nor would most families. By some measure, it was shameful to marry someone from the same village. Even if he were the most admirable guy in the town, he would be passed over by the daughter's family. Plainly, marrying a man from the same village meant that perhaps you had dated him before. Just the idea of a daughter having the guts to date and find her husband was revolutionary and did not fit right in any father's kulla. That modern mindset was a pure threat to people's—men's—rules and morals.

When Maria had asked her mother, her mother said: "How dare you talk about a man? Have you seen him privately? How could you have done this to me? Did I raise you like that? Oh Zot, what if someone saw you, all the village is talking shit about us, your sister will never get married with this reputation you have given to her"—she started screaming—"Your father will kill you! Your father will kill me, what will people say, Zot, what have I done to deserve—this?"

Bitches, as Mother would say, talked a lot, and families could not bear the expense of having a bad name. And boy, what could be worse than a daughter linked to a man before marriage? Daughters were not allowed to walk by themselves, let alone find their own husbands.

And above all, we lived in a country in which men shouldn't love. Period. Because love could bring cheer, proceeding to laughter, and resulting in hope, and you know how bad it is for a dictator to let his people hope. A man was not allowed to show signs of affection to his wife because that could make him appear vulnerable. And who wants to look vulnerable inside an authoritarian nation? Maybe a few, but our men were raised to know that expressing love was a weakness.

Furthermore, love, as a complex thing, destroyed the gender inequalities between skirts and pants, posing another threat to men. Let's suppose that people began marrying for love. Suddenly they would soften up, and then what would happen to all the unspoken rules between men and women? No, no, no. No one wanted to dig into that. Women, afraid, did not want to marry for love because they were raised to obey a ruler, and men were content with the ruling. So, no matter how much a daughter's family wanted to get her out the door, she was still not allowed to fall in love and pick her husband because her name would go running around the fields stigmatizing her entire family.

Therefore, Maria did not last long because her mother went

nearly insane trying to track down a son-in-law who her people would accept. And in the end, a cousin of a cousin of a cousin found an unrelated cousin and arranged an audience with Maria. That day, she kept her clever head bowed and said yes because no other answer was accepted, and she got married to the unrelated cousin of the cousin of the cousin of the cousin.

For all the above reasons, Kol and I did not stand a chance. No matter how much Mother liked him, she would never agree. As for Father, he would've killed me if he had seen my mountain smile when I was talking with Kol.

A few days after Maria's wedding, I was coming from work when I saw Kol. He had seen me from afar and was standing against the bushy, green gardh, waiting for me to walk with him to our kulla. My mountain smile had dried up since the last time we spoke because of his comment about my skirt, and so had his.

When he said "Hello," I heard a doubt in his voice for the first time.

When I had seen him at Maria's wedding, he had showed some muted, vaguely blushed glances, but nothing more. Without understanding the cause of the change in his voice, I was modestly relishing the walk with him. Kol was twenty years old then. His stride had grown decisive and confident, but he did not seem in a rush to get married. For men, however, it was different. Men could marry at any age, and they could even flirt openly, while women would get the blame just for looking. However, I knew that Kol was different. His genuine manners never left him as his body got taller, and despite his age, he was respected by everyone.

It was a nice day that afternoon, not too hot but comfortably warm. A perfect, soft late afternoon before the evening pulled in. Revived by the pleasant weather, the bushes along the road stood at attention. Kol was hopping on the rocks, and a pleasant wind made my skirt dance and touch his leg, although he did not seem to feel it. His mind seemed occupied, but his peach face prevented me from caring about his dour presence. He and I knew that we were born to love each other from afar, but on our rough road, we could not lock down our adoration.

After his countless blushes, he spoke.

"Bora you have changed," he said, his emerald eyes longing to say something else. But again, he did not say it.

"We both have," I admitted.

"You know soon you will get married," he countered.

That was not the conversation I wanted to have with him at that moment, and somewhat defeated, I said, "I know."

Silence followed as I got despondent about his words, which had tasted bitter, like eating raw coffee beans.

Before we passed a curve on our road, he turned left and right looking at the yards and checking beyond the gardh, his cheeks still blushing. At the top of a hill, the natural gardh receded, permitting a seductive view of the plain. We halted and stood gazing at the terrain, which seemed starved for water. Kol was still blushing, and his white neck moved again as he thoroughly checked up and down the road. Then, his attention loomed back, blushing at the highest level as he turned toward me and came close, close, too close—and shot a kiss on my lips.

The road seemed to slide as his uneven lips met mine, and I fell right into the bed of the dried field. I lay there dizzily with his taste in my mouth, not believing we had touched.

His lush, green eyes escalated the moment, and he said, "Perhaps I will never be able to give you something else, but I will always care for you," and put his hands in his pockets.

Then he brought up one of his hands, which was clenched, to his face. A red color splashed across his green eyes as he opened his hand, and I saw a red flower in his palm. It was a lulekuqe, a red poppy flower, covered in black seeds. His fingers were struggling to hold the lulekuqe, as its dark seeds began falling while he delivered it to me. The few red petals left were tired from hiding in his pocket and were falling, roaming free.

Then, we both saw that our love, like the untamed lulekuqe, had gone unabashed into the wilderness, as it was never meant to be.

After a year, Kol became a great man, a married man. The day that he had kissed me, his hesitation had come from the voices hidden within him that could not tell me that he had become engaged.

I was barely into my nineteenth year when I first saw his *nuse* (bride). It was at their wedding. She was in her late teens too. Kol was bursting with pride, handsome as ever, as he stood next to her at the altar. His bride looked shy and sat with grace and elegance beside him. I avoided making eye contact with the groom because it was his day, and I did not want to pull clouds across it. Mother saw the blank smiles coming from my crushed lips. I was striving to be cheerful for him, but she knew that my jolly spirit had turned off forever.

At the banquet, Mother sat with me, loathing her awful world. She did not say it, but I could see her face fuming because her daughter was being denied happiness, and without uttering a word about Kol, she got redder and redder. After the wedding, when we reached our kulla, her mouth erupted, calling everyone but Kol bitches because she knew he was not to blame. I was incapable of talking with her. I could only breathe out despair. So, I went upstairs to our bedroom and changed from my skirt into my worn pants. And then, I put my hands to work. I stoked the fire and boiled the clothes and hung them on the rope to dry and swept every corner of our kulla. I grabbed some old sheets, tore them, and made pillowcases and rags. I went to the pear tree and ripped off leaves that didn't seem in great health. Then I showered my brother for the day. All the while, I dreamed, daydreamed, and dreamed even more about living in a world where love can flourish.

That night, I dreamed of summer. In my dream, a red sky was giving my red skirt a radiant glow. I was walking home from the fields in my stylish skirt, and Kol was there on the road, waiting for me. His firm body was pressing against the gardh like a sophisticated man from the city. When I got to where Kol stood, he grabbed my neck and kissed me against the gardh in the open. After he pulled his lips away from mine, we both stood there laughing so hard that our souls began to shake, and tears slid through our eyelids from joy. Then, as we stepped onto our rugged road, we saw that it was paved and had a modern, level surface. We walked along, seeing many vibrant flowers blossoming. It was like a path in a garden. At the crest of the hilly road, we stopped to gaze out at the plain, our stylish garments illuminated by the sun. I lay my head on his shoulder and looked out at the lavish, green fields. There, we shared a fresh kiss, and afterward, Kol's face was serene.

A neighbor wearing a hat came along, and he smiled at us. He then shared some good wishes, including *"Ju rujt zoti te dyve"* (God bless you both). As soon as the man turned and continued on his way, Kol put his hands on my cheekbones and turned my lips toward his. He was longing to say something, but my eyes were turning to look at the neighbor. My cheeks slipped from Kol's hands as I turned away from him and started to walk up the road, following the man with the hat.

"Bora, don't leave me, I love you," Kol yelled.

But I could not attend to him any longer; I had to follow the neighbor. Before the neighbor rounded the curve, he stopped walking and turned around to face me. Then, he took off his hat and transformed into my Uncle Llesh.

I woke up from this dream bewildered. I remembered that it was the morning after Kol's wedding, and recalling Kol's nuse dancing with him plunged me deep into the bitter sea of my reality. His wedding day had brought such sadness into the air around me that it was unbearably heavy to try and breathe. Laying in my bed, I wanted to get sick so I could defer my reality and hallucinate and dream more about a life in a better world. That magic state, though delirious, rescued me from a void that was unlike anything else that I had experienced.

There, I thought about the gray zone, the nearest exit, and the hasty escape that Uncle Llesh had performed. He was the only man I knew who had successfully left our awful nation and was testing the free world. In my delirium, I imagined a new nation beyond the borders of our geography books, a nation with bountiful space for love. That was my hope.

I knew how inaccessible the gray zone was, especially for a woman, but that couldn't stop me from yearning for it and longing for a different life. It would have been crazy to think that a woman could ever manage to actually escape this country. That would have been an absolutely insane dream. It was unheard of for a woman to have the ability to escape, and our regime treated any type of runaway with death. But, what else could I wish for when I had to see Kol with his wife every day? It was truly awful how my life had turned out. There was only one real thing left to do and that was to get out the door.

CHAPTER 13

A baby's cry had not let us sleep all night. My sister's two-month-old daughter had polluted our ears every two hours.

"Martë, Martë, Martë zgjohu," Mother was shouting, telling Martë to wake up.

My sister, Martë, had come home for a visit after becoming a first-time mother. Kol had been married about three months by then. It was dawn, and Martë was exhausted and sleeping soundly next to me with her baby fastened to a tiny wooden bed on the floor. She had wanted to name her daughter Donika, but her husband had wanted to call her Teuta, his mother's name. Since it didn't work for this daughter, my sister would name the next one Donika because that name was significant to her. She claimed it was her favorite teacher's name. I knew my sister would have another baby because her first child was a daughter, and until she managed to have at least one son, she would continue giving birth.

"*Çohu o dreq*" (Get up evil), Mother barked, commanding Martë to wake up.

I shook Martë's arm and noticed that having the baby had made her face look even more pale. She sluggishly got up, and when she lifted her shirt up, a breast the size of a healthy melon came out. She began massaging her breast with her palms, pressing and pressing for the milk to flow, her face contorting from the pain. Then, she shifted and bared the other breast, pushing on it even harder. After letting some milk flow, she let the baby seek out the nipple. My sister was skinny before the baby, but now she was rounder, had matronly cheeks, and smelled of her baby's odor with a dash of soured milk.

It was six a.m., and I had to go to work. I put on my skirt over my pants and walked down the stairs. I stopped and sat down on the middle of the stairs, or as I called it, the waist of the rough stone dress. The morning air of the kulla was so delightful that I would often sit there breathing it in. That morning, the early light was falling shyly on the sea, shimmering like the glances of a young lover. The blue sky was still tangled with the night above the land. It was summer, and the morning breeze was flipping my earrings and tickling my cells one by one, waking them up with the chills.

"Ta pe mardhif" (You will catch a cold), Mother said as she came down the stairs and ushered me inside.

"Si ke njeft" (How did you rise)? I asked.

She answered with a good, *"Do me bash kafen?"* asking me to make her coffee.

"Po" (Sure), I said and followed her into the kitchen.

I heated some water and made coffee for her and my sister. We didn't have enough to make some for myself, but when I washed Mother's cup, I drank the last sip, gulping down some sandy coffee grounds with it too.

When my sister came down with her baby, Mother said, *"Martë, gato grosh,"* telling her to cook beans, and with that, we both left for work.

Mother and I did not have the same walking speed, and she was always in front of me. It's not that I walked slow, it's that she walked unreasonably fast. As I hurried to catch up with her, a woman carrying a baby bed came out of her own gardh and said good morning to us. While they conversed, I watched her infant sleeping tightly in the bed. I asked myself if I wished to be a mother. Hmm.

I recalled my sister's distorted face when breastfeeding. Absolutely not, I concluded. It actually looked very painful to have your breasts smashed like that, and I imagined it must be torturous smelling like milk while having to listen to your baby's cry all day.

Then I thought about how Kol's babies would look. I wasn't thinking about what *ours* would look like, just what his would look like, because ours was impossible. I hoped his babies would look exactly like him. Not that his wife wasn't attractive, but Kol was cute from childhood all the way to becoming an adult.

"Where is your mind?" Mother asked.

I saw that the neighbor had already left without me uttering goodbye.

"I'm thinking about Martë and her baby," I said quickly.

But Mother was skeptical, not believing my words. "Bora, don't worry," she retorted.

"What . . .?" I said, not understanding what she was saying.

"Don't worry," she repeated, "you will have yours soon."

"Aa, po po" (Yes, sure), I said, not knowing how to respond.

A few neighbors crossed us on the main road, saying *"Punë te marë"* (Have a good workday) as they passed, bringing to mind that we had to split up for work.

"Shnet cuc" (Goodbye my daughter), Mother said, bidding a sweet goodbye before heading to her field. *"Shnet,"* I replied.

I stood and watched Mother go for a moment, thinking that her nature was changing. She was becoming softer as I grew up. But I didn't know how to handle that side of her, so I shoved it aside and headed to the field.

It was Saturday morning, military training day, and it seemed that we were the first field to start the training that day because a secondhand, army-green vehicle stopped at the field entrance at seven a.m. on the dot. Three military men marched toward the head of the field. There was one officer, who was wearing his hat and, behind him, were two soldiers with shaved heads. We dropped our farming equipment and promptly gathered at the front of the field. We did not wait for our brigadier to notify us to gather at the front of the field because we knew that the officer's higher rank was more important and demanded our utmost attention.

The soldiers handed over fatigues just like theirs for us to wear, and in two minutes, sixty scared workers transformed into a secondhand unit. The target was live, the oath was said by one of us, and we lined up ready to fire.

The officer called out to the front line.

"*Ndalo, prap, shejn, ngarko, pushoje, vazhdo, ndalo, vazhdo, vazhdo, vazhdo, vazhdo, vazhdo,*" he shouted, ordering us to halt, mark, fire, and depart as the gunshots echoed off the mountains.

Then he shouted the same orders to each line in turn, advancing the lines one by one.

When I was younger, I could hear the rifles firing in the distance as I sat on the stone stairs of my kulla. I could always hear the mountains shattering in tears while the sky swallowed up the cries. That's how war must be, I had thought then, full of unexplained sounds and blasts.

"*Ngarko prap*" (Reload again), the officer yelled at a sixteen-year-old boy who had recently joined the work brigade.

The boy paused, shaking. The officer once more ordered him to shoot. The young boy put the rifle against his tiny shoulder again and pulled the trigger. The force of the weapon firing swung his body to the side, and his bullet strayed wildly, endangering our lives and missing the target once more.

But the officer just repeated "*Ngarko prap,*" commanding him to repeat.

Third, fourth, fifth try, and then on the sixth time, the boy's rifle finally hit the "enemy" on the right side of its ribs.

After the shooting, they separated us into two squads and made us crawl on the ground to duck and evade the enemy.

"Down, cover, dead space, double action, snap, reverse," the officer catechized us with his orders.

We dragged our bodies through the terrain, snorting in the soil. The pregnant ladies were left behind in shock. Not the shock of shooting but the shock of their bellies suffering in distress from seeing the rest of us crawling on the ground like bodies cursed to live in a battle without a war. After almost two hours of hell, they left us in peace until the next week. To insulate ourselves from the rape of our souls, we rushed to erase our memories of their orders by getting back to our work. Our entire field grew watermelons for the summer months, and twice a week a truck would come to pick them up. On those days, we needed another hour to fill the truck carefully enough to not smash the produce. The flawless watermelons went to Tirana, and the faulty ones were left for our supply rooms. I went to my row and looked for a mature watermelon to pick. Seeing the big fruit sitting on the soil was how I overcame their war that morning.

My job was to collect the watermelons that had grown from the seeds that I had buried. The sun was burning, so I put on a headscarf to keep my head cool. It was easy to tell when a watermelon was ripe by its hairy, itchy tail. If the stem was dry and the leaf had burned, I hit its belly twice and listened for a nice *plup* sound. If I heard that sound, then I knew it was perfect.

With the harvest starting a week before, I had to go further and further to find ripe fruit. The row was so long that I couldn't see the end. The further I went, the more dysmorphic the watermelons were from baking in the heat. Cracked with flies hovering, burned yellow on one side, too small, too green, rotten, small, tiny, small, and one, two, three, four, five, six . . . twenty-nine steps it took me to find the first ripe one. Counting was a good way to not get bored while looking. I severed the dry stem, heaved it up, and carried it back to the head of the field.

"This is yellow, put it on the other side," a lanky guy with skinny legs said to another worker, a young girl, while I was dropping my watermelon.

"Which side?" the young girl asked.

"Open your eyes," the guy insisted, pointing to where the

disfigured watermelons were.

The young girl could not see very well. Why don't you open your eyes? I wanted to tell him, but daughters did not talk. So, I picked up her ugly watermelon and dropped it on the right side.

"Thanks for your help," the guy said sarcastically.

I ignored him, and since the young girl was next to my row, I helped her by signaling to her when I saw a ripe watermelon. Then back and forth we went all morning, carrying the heavy fruits as the soil got baked and our throats became parched.

At lunchtime, we went to the well, pulled a bucket of water out, and cleaned our hands and nails. I shared lunch with the other women, then I sat quietly to rest. I wanted to lay down from the exhaustion, but I couldn't, so I sat. I felt two eyes watching me, and then I saw the lanky guy's face again. If he had been nicer to the semi–blind girl, I might have liked him, but he wasn't. So, I went back to my row without acknowledging him.

One, two, three . . . thirty-six steps to the next acceptable watermelon. I carried it back, and headed down for the next one. Thirty-eight . . . forty-five . . . fifty-four . . . fifty-seven and I found another good watermelon. I was so far away in my row that I couldn't see the field entrance behind me.

"Do you need help?" a voice asked behind me.

I turned, holding only the watermelon in my hands, not a shovel or a wood stick.

"No," I responded, seeing the lanky guy in front of my eyes.

"You could use some help," he said.

The assurance in his tone reminded me of the mountain guy at the wedding but without the smile and the serene look.

"Don't you have your work to finish?" I said, annoyed.

"So you aren't that polite," he said, raising his eyebrow.

I didn't answer. I stared at him blankly, saying nothing.

"What is your name?" he asked.

I was tired and standing still made me even more fatigued, but I couldn't leave because he would think I was afraid.

"So, you aren't going to talk now," he said. I stood there, holding the watermelon, not moving. I didn't even blink in order to prevent any glance of dismay from coming out. Then, he walked toward me. My long legs stayed firmly planted in place.

"Come, I can carry that for you," he said and took my watermelon.

I couldn't go back with empty hands and accompanied by a thick-headed man, so I decided to find another watermelon and hoped that he would leave me alone. I walked softly to hear if his steps were following me. Fifty-seven, fifty-eight, fifty-nine—

"Bora," he yelled.

Oh, apparently, he knows my name, I thought. Sixty, sixty-one, sixty-two, sixty-three, sixty-four, sixty-five—

"Aren't you coming?" he shouted.

After not hearing his voice for a while, on the eighty-second step I found a good watermelon, and I headed back with it. On the fifty-seventh step back, I saw him standing ahead of me, waiting for me. In a sweat, I searched through the rows to see if another worker was close by. The field was exposed, and I could see the others, but their bodies were flickering away like the last flame of a candle. There were no long plants to hide us, but it was hard from afar to understand if two people were in the same row, let alone if they were a man and a woman. I didn't stop my march and continued walking toward the lanky guy carrying my watermelon.

If he touches me, I thought, I'll drop the watermelon and run. But where would I go, what would I say? No one would believe me. People might say it was my fault for luring him and imply that I had some story with him, and that could ruin my name. Would the brigadier care? Absolutely not. Even if the lanky guy were to lay in my row the whole day. The brigadier only cared about my worksheet and my duty to finish by seven p.m. I looked for a wooden stick, but the grounds were stripped and barren from only growing melons.

"Why are you so difficult? I just want to talk to you," the guy said when I was a few steps away from him.

"I don't know you," I tried to explain.

There were sixty workers in our fields. It was impossible to know everyone, plus I was a daughter and not allowed to talk to strangers.

"Where is your kulla?" he asked.

"I have to work," I said.

"I'm persistent," he shot back.

If he really wanted to find my kulla, he could ask acquaintances, just as he had asked for my name, and then he could come as a real man to ask for my hand. But he was one of them—the ones who used and fooled young daughters with false promises of marriage.

"I have to go," I said and marched forward to pass him.

"Don't you care to at least learn my name?" he asked audaciously.

I was but an arm's length away from him by then. I did not respond. And as I passed his skinny body, he grabbed my scarred arm.

"Whatever I break I take care of," he said.

I held my head straight, looking forward and clutching the watermelon tightly in my hands as I waited for his hand to free my arm.

"What are you doing?" a gruff voice said from behind me.

"It's not your business old man," the lanky guy responded.

"That's my daughter," the gruff voice growled.

And then, I felt the skinny body of the guy getting shoved away from me. I turned, and I saw the old, wrinkled, twenty-five-year prisoner standing behind me.

"Are you going to hit me?" the lanky guy taunted the old man sarcastically, flashing a scowling smile.

"Dare to come close to her again and I will gladly go back to jail," the old man said.

That wiped the sneer off the lanky guy's sarcastic face.

As the guy slunk away through the rows, the old man picked a watermelon from my row and walked toward the field entrance. I followed behind him without saying a word. I didn't say thank you because it was shameful to even acknowledge the behavior of the lanky guy. But I truly wanted to thank the old man because he had saved my skin and dignity from getting damaged, and we both knew that pride and honor were very important in our field's land. It was almost four o'clock, and between the military training, helping the blind girl, and dealing with the lanky guy, I had lost at least two hours of work. I ran fast up and down the rows, grabbing rotten and unrotten fruits and bringing them up, trying to get ahead. Some women held the melons with their skirt so they could carry more than one at the same time. But ever since I had gotten my skirt, I only carried the watermelons with my hands, even though I could only carry one at a time and had to make up the difference by moving very fast. I did not want to destroy my only skirt. It had taken a while to get it, and I was not sure when or if I could get a second one.

By the time I was far into my row, I spotted some watery, red fingerprints on a rotten watermelon that had split open. It seemed that a hungry worker had pulled out whatever good fruit had been left. If the brigadier saw that, he would shame us in order to find the one who did it. So, I broke the watermelon with my foot to make it easier for the insects to get inside and erase the marks. Working in the fields that were cultivated made it even harder to not be corrupted by hunger.

It's been a long day, I thought as I was carrying my last melon. I had walked up and down the rows from seven a.m. to seven p.m., and with the summer days being more exhausting, I could not wait to go home. I avoided crossing paths with the lanky guy when I was waiting in line to clean up, and without the strength to clean my nails thoroughly, I washed my hands quickly and left.

Heading home, the sunset was beginning to drift from the sky. It was a hot evening, and the closer I got to my kulla, the merrier I felt. Then, I heard someone shouting my name. "Bora!"

It was Kol calling. I had successfully avoided seeing him for more than three months, since his wedding in May. I pretended that his voice hadn't reached my ears and walked faster to get out of his sight.

"Bora," another voice yelled.

Damn it, I thought. It was a woman's voice, perhaps Kol's wife, and I had to turn for the sake of good manners and respect. I rotated my head and saw Kol with another worker from my field. The woman waved at me impatiently, signaling me toward them.

"Hi," I said to Kol without looking at him.

"We have to go and fill the truck," the woman said.

"Hi, Bora," Kol said, greeting me with a kind voice.

"They came late without telling us," the woman said.

She seemed tired and frustrated that we had to go back and rightfully so, but orders were orders.

"Sure," I said and peeked at Kol's sunburned face.

"I can come and help," he said to the field woman.

"That would be great," she said.

"No," I exclaimed firmly.

"What, why not?" she replied.

No because I really like him, and it hurts me to be so close to him. No because I am trying to forget him. No because he looks so good and I look so exhausted. No because I can't resist loving him. No because of so many reasons, I wanted to shout at her.

"Because it's not his job," I said instead.

"But he wants to help."

"Yes, but he is not working with us, he wouldn't get paid," I stated, annoyed that she was insisting.

Kol was staring at me, his face blushing from the heat of the argument.

"Bora, that's okay, I don't mind helping," he said, his green eyes spraying spring and flowers.

I pulled off from my battle and said, "Yes, sure, fine," and headed down with them, defeated.

"Did they have to come at eight o'clock?" the field woman kept saying, cursing over and over again.

It wasn't eight, but it would be past eight by the time we finished and got home.

"I know," I said.

I felt uncomfortable walking with the two of them. Kol was silent and I was too. I couldn't spare a word for him.

When we got to the truck, a few other workers were gathered around. All the other young workers were already at their kulla because they had finished earlier and had gone home without knowing about the late truck. Kol and I were the youngest left.

"Daughter, you have to get in the bed of the truck to arrange the watermelons," a middle-aged man said.

I can't get up there in my skirt, I wanted to say.

But he turned to Kol and commanded, "Young man, lift her up."

Kol and I stared at each other like we were about to perform a misdeed, but without showing any signs of wavering, Kol brought his body close to mine. Oh Zot, my heart started burning in my chest. I lifted my arms up as he looked at my waist. Then he exhaled, blushing, glanced at my eyes, and hoisted me up. Midway up, he faltered for a moment, dropping me down a bit.

"Ouch!" I winced as my chin hit his collar bone and my face fell onto his neck.

He quickly regained his grip and lifted me up. In that nanosecond, my nose registered his smell, and from the touch, my body soared like a kite in the air.

"Are you okay?" he asked when he set me on the bed of the truck.

I nodded a yes and noticed five workers holding watermelons, waiting to hand them to me. I stretched my hands down to grab the watermelons and began arranging them.

Somehow, on top of the truck bed, my exhaustion from the long day switched to euphoria. When Kol brought his watermelons to the truck, I just took them without daring to look at him. It took us an hour to finish loading the truck. It was the first time Kol and I worked together and, perhaps, the last. He lifted me down when we finished, but my kite didn't soar that time because I resisted falling and touching his neck.

Then the three of us left the field and headed back to our kulla. The woman who had brought us back to load the truck was drained by the long day and quiet on the way back. I could not muster up the energy to speak, and Kol did not attempt it either.

"Good night," the woman said as she separated from us when we got to our rugged road.

"Good night," we both replied demurely. In the early, tranquil dark, Kol and I were left alone. We shyly hiked up the road. A loaded silence descended. When we arrived at his gardh, I bid him good night.

"You as well," he replied. And then, after I had only moved a few steps, he added, "It was nice seeing you."

I guess it was nice seeing you after all, I thought.

"Likewise," I responded.

Then, after two more steps, I heard him utter, "I apologize for hurting you."

I stopped as my heart got heavy hearing his remorseful voice, and I turned and looked at him.

"Don't worry you didn't," I said. "It was just me, my bones are heavy." I was trying to make a joke and leave.

"No," he uttered. "I apologize for hurting your feelings, I didn't want to, I don't want to, I loved you, and I always will. We didn't have a choice, or a chance . . . You know it too."

I held my place, star-struck in the early dark. My entire life, I had waited to hear him openly say that he loved me. Yet, I wished he had said it when he was free.

"I know," I said, thinking how badly I loved him. "Have a good night Kol."

I'll always love you too, I wanted to say. But I kept silent because it didn't matter anymore. In real life, he could not be my other half.

"You as well Bora," he said and waited to go in until I had disappeared around the curve of the road.

I was not allowed to have the only man I adored. And now I knew he loved me too, perhaps as much as I had—or did. How rare and beautiful was our love. How pure and honest what we felt. How could the earth have given me so much affection to have to bury in my heart? And yet, despite my heartache, I forgave him because it wasn't his fault for hurting me. It was the fault of our bitter world. It had divided us with its norms and customs.

"Bora, is that you?" Mother was washing clothes in the yard.

I walked toward her feeling tired and ill after a day that from the beginning had cruelly showed me that it wasn't mine to live.

"Why are you so late?" she asked.

"The truck came late, and I had to return to fill it," I said, desperately wanting to fall into her arms.

"I see. Don't worry about the clothes, go and eat *grosh* (bean) soup with your sister," she said. I forgot that Martë is home, I thought as I watched the orange ball of the sun dip into the sea. I heard the baby's cry and went inside. Martë talked to me, but I was too tired and heartbroken to eat the bean soup, let alone hold a conversation. I laid down on the bed long before Mother and Martë and recalled the good deed that the old man had done by saving me. Then, I fell deeply asleep.

CHAPTER 14

After Kol got married, the husband arrangements began to smother my door. I would have no choice but to say yes to someone, but I couldn't care less who that yes would go to. I began to prepare my dowry, and it was light as a feather because I didn't have much to take with me. Surprisingly, it was not Mother who was trying to push me out the door. It was various villagers who thought I would make a good wife. Instead of marrying me off quickly, Mother was rather difficult with the potential husbands, only fueling my sister's vocal opinion about Mother having a sweet spot for me. Mother made many excuses.

"He doesn't look right."

"He lives far away."

"He doesn't have a kulla."

"He got burned in the face in the military."

"He is poorer than us."

"He has five sisters."

"He is not as good as you."

"He looks like a dreq."

"His ears are too big, think of the children."

Her reasons may not have been sound, but at least they were

funny. Perhaps, after Kol, Mother knew there was no right husband for her daughter and was hesitant to throw my heart away. Mother also knew that, once I got married, there would be no coming back.

But all her reasons fell apart once Ben's name came onto the table. Ben was a psychiatrist, an only child, and was living in Manati, another village right next to Lezhe, our city. It was just one fugoni to Lezhe from our village and only one more fugoni from Lezhe to his village, three stations in total. Was Mother ready to have a doctor for a son-in-law? I didn't know, but she never opposed it. My aunt said that she knew his family well, so she talked with Ben's mother and arranged a Sunday visit.

When that day came, we had washed the kitchen, the dining room, the clothes, and our nails by early morning. Preparing for any *mik* (guest) was a lot of work, let alone getting ready for a suitor— and a doctor at that. I had already washed my white skirt with the blue dots, and my sister had given me a clean, long-sleeved, beige shirt. After I put them on, Mother walked into the bedroom. I was watching out through the window.

"What are you doing there?" she snapped.

"Waiting," I said.

"It's shameful to watch through the window. You are a daughter, for Zot's sake," she said, rolling her eyes.

I was aware of my limitations, and she knew it, but somehow, she had to say something *"per syt e njerzve"* (for the people's eyes) or just for the sake of saying something.

"Don't worry, I'll be careful," I said softly to ease her wrath, but I was unwilling to move.

As she was leaving, I pulled up a stool and sat next to the window. She murmured that I was a little *dreqi* (evil), but, you know, a good evil. I checked my nails again for any trace of dirt that would show I was beneath the doctor's status. I had done a good job. There was no dirt, just some specks of blood left from cleaning roughly. I preferred blood over the dirt rank. I opened the blurred glass to have a better view.

It was a steaming hot, sunny day, and I lifted my skirt to splash some light on my pale, thin legs. Then I touched my palms to the burning window until they were hot and put them on my bare legs to enjoy the heat. The light was shining so strongly that it blinded my eyes. I drew a brown curtain of wavy hair across my face to save it from freckles. Despite the strands of hair over my face, I would be able to see the miqtë well when they arrived. That was how I had snuck a peek at every one of my potential husbands when they had arrived for an arrangement visit.

This time, more than the others, I was curious to see my suitor. He was a doctor, and his name was Ben. I had thought a lot about him, specifically about things that could be wrong with him. Otherwise, why would a doctor want to marry a field girl? It would be understandable if he were old, or a widower, or had lost a limb, but my aunt had told me that none of those things applied to him and that he was in his late twenties. I speculated that he might have delayed getting married to become a doctor. That would be a valid reason. I thought about Kol, too—how would he feel seeing me marrying a doctor? Perhaps jealous, like the first time I wore a skirt and he had realized that the world could now see me as the woman he saw. I have to admit that recalling his jealous face was very gratifying, and yet, I knew I had to replace him with a real husband.

I examined the idea of my visitor again and wondered who would be coming with him. He will probably be accompanied by his father or his uncle, whoever has a better reputation, I thought, just as three figures arrived at the top of our hill.

It was a radiant day, and I could not see clearly too far in the distance because the sun was shining right at my window. I could tell that an arm was moving toward the wooden door of our gardh and that the thinnest person was opening it. That must be Ben, I thought. I could feel bumps growing on my cheekbones from pressing them so hard against the bars of the window as I tried to see better, but the pain did not deter me from spying. The blazing sun was behind them and shining right into my eyes, so I could only see the three of them in silhouette as they were marching toward our kulla. As they were walking across the yard, I began looking at one of the guests who seemed to have quite long hair for a man. I could not see his face yet because they stopped at the pear tree. I assumed that they were amazed at the beauty of our pear tree, although its branches remained indifferent to them.

Then I saw an unthinkable sight—a woman. It was something that could only happen in fairytales about these visits, and my jaw fell wide open in surprise. It was hard to believe that the potential husband was accompanied by two people—a woman and a man. I knew that he was a doctor, but what the heck was that woman doing here? It was bold and unheard of.

Mother came outside, acting not at all out of the ordinary, even though there was a woman at her door requesting her daughter's hand.

"*Mirë se erdhët*," she said, welcoming them, but with her feet firm, holding her ground.

"Thank you," the woman said.

Both men had not yet said a word. How on earth is that woman talking before her husband or her son? I was shocked. She was quite audacious since we were not even permitted to breathe before our men breathed.

I assumed that the potential husband was her son, otherwise she would not be allowed to journey to our kulla for this kind of occasion. I shifted my attention to her son. Ben. He was a tall man with a proper build and pitch-black hair. His clothes blended well with his light-colored skin and his dark, lustrous eyes. He was wearing an expensive charcoal-gray suit, and his glossy hair laid on his head neatly from his forehead all the way back to his long neck. The doctor looked flawless, everything on him looked ideally put together.

"*Mirë se te gjetëm*" (Thanks for having us), he said to Mother, his teeth gleaming under his lips.

I wondered again why a doctor—especially a good-looking doctor—was at my door. It's not that I believed I was appalling, but realistically, I was the earth and he was the sun. Two completely disparate entities, and the sun was way more powerful. I had learned these things in my physics and chemistry classes, which I really enjoyed because these were the only subjects that were taught without limitations. The state deemed it necessary to take some students, make them good scientists, then demand that they use their knowledge to create weapons. They did that with Uncle Llesh, but that's a story for another time.

Anyhow, Ben's father headed inside first, then the bright son walked up our stairs and into our kulla. We used our odë only for serious *miq* (guests), and obviously, Ben was one of them. Father was not home, but his bed was well made in the corner. I pulled my head away from the bars on the window when I saw them come inside. My gut got strangled when I heard their heels hitting the stairs, and it only got worse as they passed my bedroom door on their way to the odë. I would be lying if I were to say that I wasn't also feeling butterflies in my stomach after seeing Ben. He was indeed quite an attractive man. I started thinking about him as my husband and about the audacious woman as my new mother as their footsteps headed to the sofa. One of them had a noisy gait. Once they sat down, it was my turn to impress them.

With the other suitors, my only job had been to enter the room, bring coffee, shake hands without looking directly in their eyes, sit down, listen to the conversation, and suddenly—leave. Then, I had to go to my room and, with Mother's help, decide whether that man was worth spending my entire life with. But with a mother-in-law in the room, I would be walking on eggshells too.

I left the bedroom and went down to the kitchen to make the coffee. When it was finished, I stepped into the odë with a tray and three coffees. My aunt, her husband, Mother, an old man from a kulla nearby, my younger brother, and some neighborhood kids were all in the room. There were always children at these events, in part because it was a kind of introduction for boys and girls to what life would be like when they grew up. That's how parents taught us without using their tongues. It was big news in the neighborhood when someone came to a daughter's door. Perhaps even Kol knew that a doctor was coming to ask for my hand, something that he had not been welcome to do. As joyful as it was for the neighborhood to have men at a daughter's door, it was disappointing if you didn't produce good news.

The three of them stood up as I gently put the coffees on the brown table. Then, I straightened my field-curved spine, making sure I kept my eyes lowered, and thought for a moment about whose hand I should shake first. The other times, I had shaken hands from the oldest to the youngest, but this time, a mother was there, altering the norms. I was confused as to why the hell she was there and annoyed at the possibility that their lack of conformity was a way to assert their elite status over us.

I stood still, my head bowed, because I knew it could be a fatal to look at them and equally fatal to move to stretch my hand out to the wrong person. They broke the rules, let them deal with what to do, I decided. That's what Mother would do. I stood there like a statue. At least they've got the chance to take a good look at my body, I thought.

"Nice to meet you, Bora," the father finally said.

The long-sought dilemma was resolved. I nodded my head, agreeing without looking, and shook his hand. His name was Leke. Then his wife stretched out her arm, leaving her son for last. I don't know if I was chilled from the situation, but when I touched the new family's hands, I felt nothing but cold skin.

I sat down next to my aunt, crossed my hands uncomfortably and stared at the carpet. I was not allowed to look because that could send the wrong message. "She is an audacious future wife," they might say, "not subdued enough for our son." My place was to sit quietly and listen, like a mute, and possibly exchange a few shy glances with the potential groom.

Once they began talking, it was disappointing to discover that we did not have much in common. But after all, they were a doctor's family, and we were field workers. I had nothing of interest to listen to, so I moved my eyes from the carpet to the kids.

Finally, his mother spoke to me.

"How are you, my daughter?" she asked.

Since traditional norms did not apply to her, I decided to dare to lift my head to make eye contact. She was wearing city clothes, had shorter hair than the field women, and was smiling excessively. She didn't seem bothered that I was looking at her.

As a good future daughter-in-law, I quietly replied, "Good."

I truly did not know how to interpret her. Her name was Linda. Was she a brave woman who I should admire, or was she a classic mother-in-law who would make my life hell? When it was time for me to leave the room, I got up and gave my hand first to the father, then to Linda, and then to Ben. I gave Ben a brief glance when he touched my hand. Ben looked at me and smiled politely. I bowed my head shyly when I saw his smile and left the room amused. I had yet to hear him utter so much as a sentence, but he seemed well composed and assured and struck me as a good man. That's how a doctor should be, I thought. I liked his clothing and his air, even if they seemed too refined for a girl who only owned one skirt.

Once I got out of the odë, I let the air out of my chest and walked to the bedroom. Then, I waited for Mother to come. But first, my aunt came along and restated that Ben was a good man and from a good family.

"Am I good enough for him?" I asked her. "Why is such a man in our odë?"

"Take your luck, stupid," she said eagerly.

Mother came into the room looking skeptical. I knew what she was thinking as we were both thinking the same thing—why would a doctor come and ask a lowly field worker for her hand in marriage?

"What? Why aren't you jumping from happiness?" my aunt said, upset seeing us both reserved.

"You understand we have nothing in common?" I said.

"So, if it's not a problem for him, why is it for you?" she said.

"Maybe it's not a problem, but it's odd," I said.

"Bora is right," Mother blurted. "A family like his at our doorstep is very unusual."

"Exactly, he is unusually good, you can't refuse him for that," my aunt said.

Mother could not disagree with my aunt, and neither could I. We both unequivocally put our trust in my aunt's judgment and agreed for Ben to be my husband.

Mother proceeded to the odë once again, heavier than before. This time, she was about to hand her daughter's future to someone else. I watched her as she walked down the hall, and her body looked as if it was shrinking with each step, since one step after the other was taking her closer to the moment when she would lose the baby she had carried for nine months inside and nineteen years outside. From that moment, as she was mouthing out the good news, she must have felt naked in their gaze and heavy in her heart, as she knew that she had given away her rights to my skin. The next time that I would see Ben and his parents, Father would be in the house, and then everyone would get a proper handshake.

CHAPTER 15

After my engagement, everything looked different to me. The mountains appeared to be less colossal and more mortal. The wind didn't whine that much and was more a tiring blast of hot summer air. The sunsets did not matter, as the lulekuqe were gone. Lule was a crummy, old dog, and I preferred not to recall my memories of her as a puppy. Kol was a sad dream because he was someone else's husband and because I was about to be someone else's wife. My mountain smile was locked inside. The pear tree was not inviting even when it bore fruit. The thorn bushes had no berries I cared to sample. The supply store visits held no excitement, and my skirt didn't either. The white clothes metamorphosed into a gloomy color. I knit and sewed only if Mother asked me. My eyes were indifferent to Mother's grand walk. The leader felt the same day by day and murder by murder. Even the bloody basement had stopped frightening me and was now just eerie. The fields became unmemorable, and its people seemed undistinguished. The shovels did not tire me as much, as they relieved me from my mundane day. And to tell the truth, even the songs of the *gardalinë* (goldfinch) rang vacantly.

Ben went to finish his military obligation after we got engaged, and I prepared to be a good wife for the doctor. I thought about the small things that would change in my daily routines like having to always keep my nails clean since his and his family's nails were neat and clean.

The *shenj* (engagement) happened when Father was home. His presence was required to formalize the agreement.

"Bora Zefi is given to Ben Doda," they said.

That was what shenj was about—to cut the deal. And with that, I got some blessings and bonus clothes from my new family. It was embarrassing, but at my shenj, I wore the same skirt and the same beige shirt that I had worn for our first meeting. Those were the most distinguished clothes I possessed. If Ben were a field worker, I wouldn't have cared, but on the day of our engagement, he came wearing a new blue jacket instead of the charcoal one and a fresh shirt with dark-gray pants. It was unmistakably clear that we were in a different class.

Father attended our shenj along with my two older brothers, a bunch of old men from the surrounding kullat, and a few children from our neighborhood. My older brothers and I had a five and seven-year age difference and did not talk that much, partially because they knew I would be out of their kulla soon. Shortly before dawn on my wedding day, I would be as foreign to them as a person who lived on some other trojë. I knew my fate's journey, and it did not belong to their house. I was acquainted with the fact that a kulla without daughters would give my brothers better prospects of finding a wife with a notable reputation. That was not to say they did not love me. They loved me as much as a man could love a sister, a daughter, and a wife in our days.

At my shenj, it was odd to sit on the sofa among the men of my bloodline since Mother, Martë, and I usually sat in the kitchen. The three visitors and the rest of the old men were on the couch with me. Ben was sitting with Linda and Leke at the other end of the couch. The children sat cross-legged on the floor, glancing at the future nuse. I was quite uncomfortable sitting there at the corner of the sofa, so I stared at the carpet, listening to the women's feet rattling up and down the stone stairs to the hall and the occasional clanging of a plate on the table. I didn't lift my head to see what food they were serving since I was afraid of meeting others' eyes. For once, I was the center of attention, but I couldn't wait for the day to end because it was quite unpleasant.

During the entire shenj, I spoke no words because it was not necessary and a bit prohibited.

"*Per hare*," Ben's father toasted to the couple's fine future.

Each time they cheered, I had to touch my glass of liquor to the glass of someone near me then put it back down, still full.

"*Per te mëra Mik*" (Cheers to good things), Father responded to Ben's father.

"*Faliminers*," Leke said, toasting with a thanks but not a cheer.

Leke was well behaved, but he seemed too reticent for a plain miner's kulla. Perhaps as a lifetime teacher, his prowess and manners had manifested in his real life too. However, compared to his wife's conduct, he seemed like a saint. Linda sat quietly at the table, behaving like a woman of our world, but later, in the suitcase she left for me, Mother and I discovered that she had done her damage with the clothes she had bought for me. When I heard Ben conversing with the other men at the table, I relayed to the carpet that he seemed to be a well-spoken, composed, and well-dressed man.

Once the lunch was finished and toasts were given over coffee, I touched Ben's hand for a goodbye. He held my four fingers tightly, and our thumbs lay alongside each other peacefully. His palm was cold like a dish, yet his skin was soft and clean and felt unlike any other hand I had touched before.

Later, when I opened the brown leather case of my shenj, I understood that the blessing and bonus clothes were analogous to Ben's sharp taste. I assumed that Linda had chosen them and was waiting for me to match his good style. For all that, I wore only one of Linda's skirts, the least modern one, on the following days. As for the shirts, they all sat in the suitcase because they were too vibrant for our hills.

"At their kulla, you can dress as they want," Mother said vehemently, noting that Ben and his family appeared to be clueless about our codes and our lives.

During the following months, Ben held my hand a couple of times when he visited. Linda was with him each time. He never came by himself. It seemed unusual, but I thought that perhaps this was how a high-status family operated.

One visit, they found me putting washed garments on the rope.

"Hello, my lovely daughter," Linda said, greeting me warmly.

I found her smile too forced or perhaps even insincere. Then, she cheerfully went inside to meet Mother.

Ben did not know what to do with himself once we were alone that day. He stood there for a moment, then he put his hands in the bucket and began helping me with the clothes. It was a shame for a man to touch any housework, but I let him help. His hands were cold but felt gratifying to have them helping me. He looked atypically charming for our unembellished hills. His white teeth glinted in the sun as he asked how my day had been.

"Good, working," I said and immediately spotted the dirt in my nails, which I hadn't had the chance to clean up.

He saw me, and when I saw that he saw me, he smiled at me kindly, indicating that he was not bothered by my field nails. From then on, he knew that I knew, and I knew that he knew, the different social levels between us.

After he let go of my hand, he turned and became glued to the view of the sea.

"How are your patients?" I asked, trying to understand his enigmatic gaze.

"Difficult," he said conclusively.

He is a man of few words and even fewer emotions because his eyes do not reveal a shred of feeling, I thought.

"What exactly is it that you do?" I asked, since psychiatry was rare in our country, if not unheard of. Also, he had an audacious if not loud mother, so I figured he would expect a curious wife.

"I work in a hospital in Tirana diagnosing mentally ill people."

Tirana, I thought, and mentally ill people. Hm. Neither of those sounded good to me. What was mental illness in our country given that you could be considered ill if you did not conform to the interests of the Communist Party? I wanted to ask him if he had diagnosed our psychopathic leader. But I couldn't because he was a doctor and what did I know? I was the field girl who somehow had the chance to talk with someone at his level, and soon, oddly enough, I would be his wife.

He saw my brain getting lost in the waves but didn't ask about what whitecaps I was confronting. Unflinching, his eyes remained shielded, and he stared at the azure sky without letting a spark of ardor out of his enigmatic face. I kept composed and tried to enjoy looking at the green fields blending with the sea. Then, he left, and I began waiting for his next visit.

I saw Ben's neat hands three times in total before our wedding. But that was enough, Maria assured me, who was pregnant and looked even more tired than before. I told Kol about Maria after exhausting all the means of trying to avoid him.

"Maria is pregnant," I said when I met him on our road one day and did not know what else to say.

But all I was thinking about was how long it would be until we could change paths because what the hell was I going to chat with him about?

"Nice," he said, his green eyes melting softly in the light. "How are you? I never see you anymore."

Yes, you haven't seen me because I once loved you, perhaps I still do, and you are married. And I can't forget the day I touched your shoulder, and the ones when we held each other's tiny hands. I often still dream of us living in a free world where you bring me flowers and we watch the sunsets. I still remember how your blush goes from pink to red to purple to light pink and, in the end, settles to a fine salmon. Lastly, I still recall your kiss, and how tender it was, but do you remember Kol, *do you?*

I wanted to yell all of this, but instead, I said "I have been busy."

I still had a full ten-minute walk to bear with him. He blushed, which displayed all the colors of his face around his green eyes, making him look even more handsome. Wonderful, I thought, these ten minutes will transpire like the twenty-five years the old man spent in jail.

Then, Kol's voice bent like our spines in the fields as he said genuinely, "I wish you the best in your married life, and forgive me if I haven't come for a cheer coffee yet."

I acknowledged his apology with a cloudy and monotone, "Thank you."

Then, I realized that I had to return and ask about his wife, but it was almost the end of our walk, so my pain was nearly done.

"How is your wife?" I asked.

As I crossed in front of his body to take the path to my kulla, I saw his face darken in hesitation and looking awfully red.

"She is pregnant," he said.

"Oh good," I said, "I meant nice."

I shook my head like someone had stung my tongue. I could not comprehend what he had just spoken.

I finally managed to utter a congratulatory *"Urime,"* my voice sounding like a cold engine on a winter's morning. Staggered by the news, I followed up with "Good night," and turned my tail and left in a hurry.

Kol never came to drink the engagement coffee, and I never went to them for the *urime* (congratulations) of his child. We both knew we could not cheer for fates we had not chosen.

CHAPTER 16

I draped my twenty-year-old body in a white dress on a Sunday morning. Although it was a summer day, my skin was cold from the mist of my thoughts. If Ben had visited more than three times, if Ben's touch were warmer, if Ben were not a doctor, if Ben were Kol—I would have worn Mother's traditional red wedding costume, and perhaps, my wedding day would have felt more intimate.

When Mother saw me in the white dress, she told me that I was the most beautiful nuse she had ever seen. But I felt uneasy seeing her amber eyes watery and weak. Her warm words kneeled down my soul with the pain of separation. It was known that every bride had to leave her home on her wedding day and move into her husband's house. I had never seen their kulla before, but that morning I was saying goodbye to mine.

Mother and Martë sat me in the odë to wait for my groom while family and friends walked in and out to say goodbye. Our odë looked no different that day than it always did, except, of course, for the nuse in her wedding dress, mourning mutely under her veil for the lonely journey of her life that was about to commence. My sister clutched my hand all morning, as she knew the emotions that were tormenting me.

Soon, my husband was standing next to me, holding my hand with a detached, controlled face. My wedding veil was hiding mine, but I could see his. Not a glimpse of a feeling escaped from Ben's black eyes, and his flawless skin did not twitch even once. As he held his cold composure, not a single glossy hair moved on his head. I quit holding his hand because it was too cold, and I so much needed his warmth that moment to solace me from my mourning. I took his arm instead. I never lifted my head to see who attended my wedding because I was afraid that I would cry more if I saw any green eyes.

The closer we got to the time to leave, the more my pain grew, mounting a heavy knot in my throat. A few minutes before we left, my family members came one by one and gave me a kiss on the cheek, which soaked my veil with my tears even more. It began with my younger brother, then my older brother, then my sister, then my other brother, then Father, and last, was Mother. It was like the kiss you give to a dead person before you put them in the casket.

I walked down the hill to my groom's car as my family lined up at our gardh door and shouted goodbyes and waved. I hid my tears because it was a happy day for the others, "a daughter out of the door" as they said. Trying to be brave, I thought about how this was a voyage that had been taken by every woman, and now, it was my turn. There were neighbors and relatives gathered for a small banquet in the yard to feast my day. It was a poor lunch feast to celebrate the daughter leaving the house.

After I was placed inside the car and the car was pulling away, I watched the loyal shelter of the large mountains receding. They were saying goodbye, too. My mountains and my hill will not protect me anymore, I thought; they cannot be my comfort. I felt like all my bones and limbs were being thrown across the countryside into an unknown territory. I could not hold my rivers in my throat anymore, and even though Ben was in the car with me, I found the space to cry it all out. Every nuse cried as much as I did because we knew that, from the moment we stepped out of our birthland, we were alone to battle with the beast of life. From now on, my husband would

125

own my life. A body without a kulla, living the fate of not belonging anywhere and at the mercy of my Zot, I thought, trying to come to terms with it. But when I thought that even Mother would not be around to call me dreqi, I wept even more.

As we drove toward Ben's village, we picked up the road that went to the city, crossing the desiccated river, which hardly resembled when it was swollen with fresh water from the mountains above. Ben held my hand, but his grip was motionless and cold like a thin coating of ice on tree leaves. As my life was shipped in a vehicle to his house, I needed his body to be warmer and more caring, so perhaps I could rest my head on his shoulders and drain my tears. But it wasn't, and I couldn't ask for comfort from a frigid and unknown man.

When we reached Ben's kulla, I looked out the car window through my veil, and I saw people waiting in the streets ready to celebrate. Everyone was well dressed and flying in and out of the entrance of his kulla, waiting for a woman in a bridal gown to be put on display. Ben opened the door of the vehicle and pulled me out with his polished hand. I stood still then, in order to display the flowers sewn to my white gown and allow their miqtë to take a good look at the nuse. My posture was reticent and shy, as I was being eaten by so many eyes, and I glued my jaw to my neck to avoid seeing anyone's glance. Although Mother had never instructed me, I knew what a good nuse should do from seeing Martë, Maria, and other brides.

I waited for Ben's arm to direct me, and we both began to cross the crowd. People were lined up on each side of the path, singing and welcoming us as we walked. Little children were holding the tail of my dress, and because my head was bowed, I could see their pure faces staring up at mine with loftiness and awe like I was a myth. I was their amusement and the playing field of their day. Our feet came to a halt when two women cheerfully cut in our way and forced a spoonful of honey in our mouths. I swallowed the sweet, viscous liquid and set my jaw back to the nuse's position. On other occasions, eating honey would have been a delicacy, but this time it tasted bitter, as it was not consumed of free will.

After the tasting was done, the two women pointed at the banquet tables, while in my left ear, two other women were deafening me with their piercing voices. They were from the kullat close by, and their job was to sing for the new nuse who had joined their neighborhood. When I had been a guest at weddings, their songs had been entertaining and had not irritated me, but now, I found them agitating because all the songs applied to my life, my husband, my mother, my father-in-law, and my beauty.

"*Nusja e bukur, vjerra me e bukur*" (The bride is lovely, yet the mother-in-law is more lovely), they sang in my ear.

As Ben politely pulled the chair out for me to sit, a middle schooler raised his arm, and with his chest straight up and bursting with pride, he bellowed, "*O malet' e Shqipërisë, e ju o lisat' e gjatë*" (O mountains of Albania and you, tall oaks)!

All at once, the women stopped singing, and the men quieted. His youthful voice continued, shooting like an arrow into our collective hearts:

O malet' e Shqipërisë, e ju o lisat' e gjatë!
Fushat e gjëra me lule, qe ju kam ndër mënt dit' e natë!
Ju bregore bukuroshe e ju lumenjt' e kulluar!
Çuka, kodra, brinja, gërxhe dhe pylle të gjelbëruar!
Do të këndonj bagëtinë që mbani ju e ushqeni,
O vendëthit e bekuar, ju mëndjen ma dëfreni!

(O mountains of Albania and you, tall oaks!
Wide fields with flowers, which I have in my mind day and night!
Your beautiful shores and your pure rivers!
Peaks, hills, cliffs and verdant forest!
You sing to the cattle that you carry and feed,

O my blessed motherland, you delight my mind!)

The boy went on to recite Naim Frashëri's poem, and I
lifted my jaw from my neck to watch him, knowing that, for
the first time, no one would be looking at me. Fragment by
fragment, as his young voice delivered the familiar words, my
veil began catching tears.

Kur dëgjon zëthin e s'ëmës qysh e le qengji kopenë,
Blegërin dy a tri herë edhe ikën e merr dhenë,
Edhe në i prefshin udhën njëzet a tridhjetë vetë,
E ta trëmbin, ajy s'kthehet, po shkon në mes si shigjetë,
Ashtu dhe zëmëra ime më le këtu tek jam mua.
Shqipëri, o nëna ime, ndonëse jam i mërguar,
Dashurinë tënde kurrë zemëra s'e ka harruar.

(When the lamb hears its mother's voice,

oh how it leaves the flock,

Bleats two or three times then with its feet runs the
earth,

And even twenty or thirty of its kind cut in front of its road,

And if they scare it, it doesn't turn,

Yet it flies through their middle like a sharp arrow,

That's how my heart is left in my motherland.

Albania, my mother, even if I am an exile,

Your love, the heart never forgets.)

As he finished, my veil soaked for the second time as I thought
about Mother, my kulla, my hills, and each thorn and tree I had left
behind. As my tears fell to the earth, I stared at its particles, soothed
in thinking that each that stepped on its surface shared their own

losses and gains.

Linda came and hugged me, and my moist chin had to rise from the ground and look at her excessive smile as she wrapped her arms around my bony shoulders. After Linda, Leke came, welcoming me, but more restrained, and then he sat down next to Ben.

Unable to control her elation, Linda stood beside me and said in my ear, "Welcome my daughter," like an enthusiastic child.

She was the antithesis of her son, I noted. To my right side, I had a detached, emotionless man, and to my left, I had an overcharged, emotional woman. I did not know how to respond to her over-expressive nature, and since being a good nuse was already a lot to manage, I shifted my eyes back to the ground. Shortly thereafter, she got up and disappeared with her miqtë, and soon I saw her dancing.

Everyone felt jubilant after the poem, having released all their heartaches for the day and replacing them with food, drink, and merriment. On my plate, a pork chop spoke a delicious language to my empty stomach, but I pretended that I didn't understand its juicy voice because a nuse never ate in front of her miqtë. I sat at the banquet without even using the bathroom for four hours straight. Although, there would have been no need to, since I had cried every drop of liquid out of my body. Nonetheless, my legs sparked with pain as they went numb from sitting for so long. My scarred elbow felt stiff after being immobile for four hours, so occasionally, it involuntarily jolted itself to a new position. My neck was hurting more than any other part of my body, from having my jaw glued to it at an awkward angle for others to see me without me seeing them. It was hard to be a good nuse, I realized. Perhaps it is even harder than being a good wife, I thought, staring at my plate.

At twelve p.m, a daughter. At one p.m., a nuse. At four p.m., a veteran nuse. At five p.m., a wife. I had changed status three times in half a day by the time some miqtë began to leave. By six p.m., I was exhausted, hungry, and still did not feel in love with my husband. Ben had spared three sentences to me all day. The first one had been directional.

"This way," he had said when he had pulled me out of the car.

Before that, he had said, "Oh Zot, too many people," looking at his miqtë.

By four p.m., he had said, "It's almost done," not to me, but to himself.

I excused him, thinking that he was a doctor and that he stood proudly next to me, although not delightedly. But I was surprised by his lack of warmth when children came nearby and sent cute smiles to him.

Just after six p.m., my mother-in-law and her creepy smile, grabbed my arm and told me that we were about to go to their odë and that it was nothing like my odë. Perhaps Linda's joy was masking Ben's stillness. Perhaps she was the most passionate spirit in the Doda's house. That was Ben's family name—Doda. Ben was an only child, and maybe that had made him reserved, if not cold. It was hard to weigh which was worse—spoiled mother or spoiled son. I was more afraid of the prospect of a spoiled mother. There would be no other woman in the household to talk to about my relationship with Linda and how she treated me. As I followed Linda's loud steps, I knew I was at her mercy now.

"We will go to the main room first," she said, her pitch-black pupils fixed on me.

Linda had Ben's eyes, or better yet, my husband had her glossy black eyes. She took me to the odë and sat me on the couch. The inside of their kulla was overwhelming. The odë had two big sofas, an armchair, a table, a red carpet, two windows shining plenty of light through bright green curtains, and a bookshelf—more furniture and things than I had seen in the kullat of our entire neighborhood put together.

"Do you like the curtains?" Linda asked, coming back with a glass of water for me.

No, I thought, but I said, "Yes."

"It cost me a fortune to get this color," she said, standing still and looking at them with admiration.

"I understand," I said without understanding why she would pay a fortune for a piece of flashy fabric.

Yet, the bright green curtains certainly were interesting, and the bookshelf facing the sofas was even more so. I had never seen a bookshelf in a house before, only in schools, and unlike in my school, these shelves were filled to the brim with books. The entire family must be very studious, I thought. A drawer with a key fueled my curiosity too, and I wondered if there were any illegal books locked in there that I could read.

On the right side of the bookshelf, two curtains of a modest ivory color hid a tiny room.

"This is Ben's father's bedroom," Linda said.

I watched her from the sofa like a good nuse as she disappeared behind the ivory fabric and turned on an oil lamp.

"Come in, don't be shy," she said, "this is your father's room."

I guess he is my new father, I thought, not sparing a word, in accordance with Mother's lesson: If you don't know what to say, say nothing. Inside, there was a single bed with a small mirror and a nightstand. Leke sleeps alone just like Father, I thought, observing that some things do not change even when in different classes.

Linda then sat me on the sofa again.

"I'll bring some food," she said avidly and headed toward the kitchen.

There was no question that she was very pleased with our wedding. Her accomplishment in getting her son married was done indeed, and it could not be undone.

While Linda's heels clacked out, Ben came into the odë. He opened his dark-blue jacket and sighed with exhaustion. He was wearing a white shirt that contrasted gloriously with his black hair and eyes. He looked like a divine groom, but still, I couldn't feel his warmth.

He went to the window and sucked in the fresh air blowing from the sea. He seemed glad that his wedding ceremony had ended, and he leaned his body in relief against the window. I heard him murmuring words, but I could not make out what they were. Perhaps, I thought, that's how men behave when they get married. Or perhaps he is unhappy because he loves someone else. Maybe he desires another woman who he could not marry. But what family would reject a doctor for a son-in-law? At least not any family that I knew. Soon I got mad at myself because what kind of wife would think that way about her husband and on their first married day, no less? Conceivably, I was a terrible wife. But I heard Linda's heels coming back and saw her skirt dancing while she brought plates piled with food, and I forgot about everything.

My new father came in after Linda, and the four of us sat together. There were four knives on our table, and I did not understand what we were going to do with them. I began picking at the food like a bird. Ben began eating by using his fork to hold down his food and his knife to chop his food. There was rarely enough food on one plate at my household for anything to need chopping, but after watching my husband, I used the fork to cut a piece of cheese to eat. I felt embarrassed, like a stupid field girl who didn't know how to eat with a knife. And Ben sat like a privileged, high-status man who did not have a clue how those below him—like his wife—ate. As for Linda, she was in her own world still cheering for our marriage. Only Leke let the knife lay undisturbed and used his hands while eating, understanding that I understood, and that I understood that he understood, and then, we both understood each other.

After dinner, Linda and I cleaned the table, and afterwards, she showed me the rest of the house. Their kulla was in a flat area close to a ravine that drained down to the sea. You could hear the stream from the three stairs in front of the kitchen door. A dense forest of native oak and pine trees surrounded their house, isolating it from outside eyes. Perhaps the plethora of water from the ravine had caused those trees to triumph and rise up in between the kullat.

The Doda's house was something between a new kulla and an old one. It had one floor, and it had ceilings inside. As you entered from the yard, you met three stairs, which led to two doors facing each other. The door to the hall was on the left and led to the odë, bedrooms, and bathroom. The kitchen was to the right. Linda's bedroom window was in front of the three stairs and had a good view of the sky.

The showing of the rooms began with the kitchen, and I saw that its door latched perfectly with the wall, leaving no space for the whiny wind to enter. I had never seen a door made so precisely and in such a lustrous mahogany color. Then, I noticed a sofa made of polished wood with a sheepskin cover. It was not like the six planks of wood that Father had put together to build our kitchen sofa. Even with the long rug that my sister had sewed, our butts got sore in a few short minutes. However, it had been made by Father, which made the sofa prone to unconditional love.

In Linda's kitchen, one wall was bare except for a window made of clear glass, which was dropping light on a square, white table. The white table was right next to the sofa and had a jar holding two fresh flowers on top of it. A yellow fabric with a sewn red flower will be just perfect laying under the jar, I thought. Across from the wooden sofa, there was a metal stove without any scratches. On the left side of the sofa, close to the mahogany door, there was a hutch filled with glassware, which reflected my face. Linda's kitchen was well furnished and had more stuff than more than five field kullat together.

When we left the kitchen, we crossed in front of her bedroom window, and I saw the three stairs again as I followed her to the hall. The hall was a rectangular shape with a door at each end. At the near end was the odë, and at the far end was the bathroom. On the side walls, there were two doors that faced each other. Linda's bedroom was on the right side, closer to the bathroom.

Ben's kulla was the first house I had seen with an indoor bathroom. Usually, the lavatories were constructed outside of the kulla, hidden somewhere in the back. I was very impressed by the indoor bathroom, but I was more stunned by Linda's bedroom. When she opened the door, the first thing I saw was her bed, which was one of the fullest full-sized beds that I had ever seen. It had an actual straight mattress covered by smooth blankets. At home, we made mattresses from sheep's wool, and they were never straight and never comfortable. I had seen a mattress like hers only once, in the hospital in Tirana.

On each side of the bed, there was a nightstand with a green oil lamp. Seeing the green-colored lamps, I was certain of Linda's favorite color, and then I began wondering if I had a favorite color. She walked across the room and opened her closet.

"Here are my clothes," she proudly declared.

The closet was trimmed with hand-carved, light-brown wood. All this closet space just for her clothes, I thought. In my old bedroom, I had shared one cramped cupboard with my entire family. The inside of Linda's closet confirmed that the vibrant colors of my shenj clothing had all been picked in accordance with her palate. Linda became extra jolly as we stood admiring her clothes, obviously liking that the field girl was impressed by her room. I was still debating which color was my favorite as we left her clothes. I was in between two colors, yellow and red, and since I was unable to choose, I concluded that, perhaps, I had two favorites.

The door across from Linda's was my bedroom.

"Let's see if I have done a good job with your room," Linda said enthusiastically before we went inside.

I was quite surprised and thrilled that she cared so much about my feelings. She opened the door, and I gaped in wonderment.

"That's your bed," she said.

The bed was made of iron, and it was covered by a silky, red blanket. I was stunned. How does she know that red is one of my dearest shades? I thought. There was a long mirror on the other side of the bed, and I could see myself standing in the doorway in my wedding dress. That's my bed and I have a mirror, I thought to myself, amused.

"Get inside," Linda said, pushing my twisted back.

Next to the mirror, there was a fancy piece of furniture that I didn't know the name of.

"This is a dresser," Linda said, understanding that I was lacking the capacity to mouth out its proper title.

I didn't even know that dressers existed, and now I had a flowery, hand-carved one.

Nightstands with oil lamps stood on either side of the bed, and mercifully, the lamps were not green. It's not that I disliked Linda's favorite color, but light brown seemed a more soothing match for a lamp. Then, I noticed the elegant wooden closet next to the window. It was so big and so beautiful that I felt lightheaded, until I thought about all the clothes I didn't own to fill it. The windows in all of Linda's rooms, including in my new bedroom, were larger than the windows in our kulla, and they were situated at the center of the walls, instead of in random corners. The window in my new room looked out at the pine trees.

Linda was smiling, waiting to hear my approval, but I couldn't articulate anything to her.

Finally, she said, "I'll leave you alone now," grasping that I needed time to comprehend all that was being given to me.

"Thank you," I said in a daze while I walked with her to the hall.

Then, I turned back toward my room like a bird heading toward its cage. I stood at the door, across from the mirror, and I saw that my shoulders were carrying feathered wings above my white dress, and my neck looked like the neck of a white pigeon. I like my cage, I thought, and went inside, closing the door.

CHAPTER 17

The brown leather suitcase next to the closet was waiting for me to unpack my life. It was past seven in the evening, and the early darkness had begun to leak into the yard outside. By the time I finished placing my clothes in the elegant closet, I saw the dark creeping like a dreqi through the window. The night had fully conquered the azure sky, and I tore my eyes away, making sure not to look again.

I lit one of the oil lamps on the nightstand that was next to the piece of furniture that I didn't know the name of. The dresser, oh yes, the fancy dresser with six drawers, all vacant, waiting for me to fill them. It was a large territory to take over, especially combined with the closet space. I wondered if Linda had planned that much storage with potential children in mind. Then I became sure that she and I both knew that I would have a baby soon, and then all that space would have a purpose and be taken. How many grandchildren does Linda want? I thought. I'll be content with three, and she'll probably be fine with that. But what about Ben? He's an only child, so maybe he'll want just two or even one. Whatever he thinks about it, with Linda by my side, I'm sure I can convince him to have at least two.

I was ready to take care of a child even though it looked painful and exhausting. I had gained experience from looking after my younger brother and my sister's daughter, Teuta. Martë was pregnant again, perhaps with Donika, if it was a girl. I had watched Martë's belly button grow, and sometimes, I would envision mine pushing away from my spine like hers. I hoped my hair would stay the same, a shiny, brown velvet, but I knew my face would probably become rounder and hide my sharp cheekbones. I hoped, too, that my husband would hold my arm as Kol held his wife's, not too lovingly, but not heartlessly either; and Linda would smile even more cheerfully at the joy of being a grandmother; and Mother would proudly say, "*I ke kalamajt te shëndetshëm*" (My children deemed a great health), implying that I was a good mother; and my children and Martë's children would play together, and her children, being older, would keep an eye on mine; and in their first years, they would all play hide and seek in the bunkers, and then, they would move on to hiding in the trees, and if they were boys, they would climb the pine trees.

As I sat on the edge of my new bed, still in my wedding dress, I thought about the children who would one day fill my belly and my life. If I have a boy, I thought, I want to name him Gjon, like Father, but perhaps Ben or Linda will object. I will name my daughter Linda to smother my mother-in-law out, I thought. I had no problem with her name; it even seemed modern for her age. I wondered if my children would inherit the black eyes and cold soul of their doctor father. I didn't like his glacial skin, and I still couldn't immerse myself inside his glassy eyes. As for Linda, her nature was a bit rocky and hard to grasp. Although Leke was a teacher and I didn't quite appreciate his profession, I thought he might have good qualities that were being smothered by his wife's loud character.

My new family seemed like a stunning chair with only three legs. So, I decided that I would be the one to work on the inner spirits of my children. I was confident that I could make sure they were not taught by the Communist ideologies alone. It will be me, I thought, who will tell them the importance of learning independently, not solely from the state. And it will be me who will not let them be indoctrinated by other people's lives and become conformists. Instead, I will support them in finding their own journey.

And then, I thought, I will teach them the gravity of conveying love, even under an oppressive regime. I will touch them often so they will not feel abandoned in a wooden baby bed. I will blind them with affection so they will not see the unfairness of their world. I will kiss them at every age so they will never doubt they are loved. I will ask them not to strive to make me proud, only to make themselves content.

I will raise a son to be a kind human rather than a good man for his fellow men. But above all, raising a daughter without fear is of primary importance and a thing that can't be stressed enough. For her, first I want to give her a kulla that no man can possibly give to her. It may not be a house made with a bedrock base, but it will be made of the skin and bones of her mother, and I will always have my arms open to welcome her unconditionally. Then, I will knit her feminine soul inch by inch with thread made from pure stars and remind her that she is part of a bright light that no one can darken, and like the sun, she is undefeatable. I will burn all the terror that others insert into her and give her a world in which she is not afraid to be a daughter. Ah, and what a supreme world that will be, I thought. And then, I will stand proudly next to her as a mother who has given her child the life she is entitled to live.

At their bedtime, I will teach them both that there are two classes of humans, the upper and the lower, but underneath their clothes, they are both the lower. For a goodnight, I will close our heart-to-hearts by letting them in on the secret of happiness and the higher purpose of our kind. I'm not sure if they will believe me at first, but nonetheless, I will utter it. I will tell them that there is one thing that feels unlike anything else, that satisfies you more than food and status, more than furniture and material possessions, more than adventure, and even more than love. I will tell them that and hope that very soon they will witness it with their hearts, too. They will not believe me, I thought, but I'll continue and tell each of them that your best day will lay in the small interactions, when you give, when you serve, and when you help the other man. I will bet to them on my being that nothing will make them feel better than when helping others.

"Listen," I will say, "no job title, no accomplishments, and no wealth will fulfill you like that moment when you have served another human who is in need."

I will stare at their eyes and write into their minds that to give is your purpose.

"Believe me," I will say, "when Mother took our only scoop of sugar and gave it to a widow who was left alone to raise five children, even as a child I felt good. And when I donated the sweater that Mother had made for me to the woman's daughter, a masterful feeling of undefinable elation showered me. That storm of euphoria is like the sunsets that the supreme sky displays for you."

After I finish, I will let them sleep, holding back in anticipation of the moment when my children will become helpful to their world.

But that night, my wedding night, I knew that the delivery of all those insights would have to remain paused until I, Bora, became a woman. It was strange how, only a day ago, I had been a fiancé; a year ago, I had been a daughter; and two years ago, I had been just a field worker; but now I was ready to take on the fate of a mother. I was still a nuse wearing my white dress, but my bridal obligations had finished for the day. I was left only with the night duty, and that was my husband's concern.

Ben knocked on the door before he opened it and found me like a bird in a cage. He stared at my white dress in wonderment. He did not know that I had just gone through the life of raising our children. He also did not know that he now entered this vision too. His white shirt was untucked, laying over his pants, and a lock of hair had fallen over his forehead. That was the most reckless that I had ever seen Ben. Nonetheless, his face still looked like that of a scholar. In his eyes, I saw a glimpse of melancholy like you see on a seaman who has lost his boat. I wondered what he was going to say or do. We were in an alluring bedroom on our wedding night, but we were both staring at our silhouettes as they met on the floor.

I waited with bated breath on fire until he finally said, "I'm going to grab my cigarettes."

I exhaled, saying in my head that I had no idea Ben smoked, but I said not a word to him. He opened the drawer of the nightstand that was next to him, but the cigarettes weren't there. Then, he stared at me with his black eyes while his brain seemed to be thinking about where he had left his package. I stood still, as it was my first day as his wife, and I didn't know yet where he kept his things. He moved toward me to check in the other nightstand, and as he passed in front of me, he stepped on my white dress. He paused, and we both stared at each other while another lock of hair fell toward his eye. My body exhaled serenely as if it could hear his heart. This is the closest our skin has ever gotten, I thought, breathing in his scent.

Mesmerized, I inhaled and brought my palm to his cheek then moved it up to his eyebrow and lifted his enchanting hair. I closed my eyes and stretched my neck out toward him, longing for a touch.

"I'm sorry," he uttered, repelling my sensations and stepping away from me.

I opened my eyes while my thirsty lips were marched back into the solitary desert. Like a boat leaving without its captain, I exhaled as my heart sank. He found his cigarettes in the nightstand close to my side of the bed. Then, he walked out carefully, not letting our silhouettes touch, and just like that, our shadows separated into two while he closed the door.

I sat down in my white gown on top of the red blanket. I was tired and confused. Why would a man avoid kissing his bride? I wondered, my head a jumble, and how did I not know that he smokes? I saw my puzzled, black eyebrows reflected in the mirror. Ben is shy, the mirror responded, so why didn't you ask him? His fingers are not yellow; he never smelled of tobacco, how should I have guessed that he smoked? I replied. Ben is a doctor, and you look exhausted, the mirror reflected.

I picked my body up off the bed to take off my wedding dress.

My arms maneuvered around, managing to get it off without tearing it. As I hung it carefully in my new closet, I knew what garment would follow next—the satin slip that they had brought to my shenj. It was white with lace finishes. I knew that it had been bought to wear on the night of my first union.

I stepped in front of the mirror and saw that I was ready for him with a proper garment, and that he wouldn't have to worry about stepping on it when he came back. But then, I looked beyond the slip, to the rest of my body. It was the first time I had seen my entire body all at once. I saw the scars running on my pastel skin with the biggest scar on my elbow. My legs were long and slender, standing like reeds on a pond longing for the fresh water to come and touch them. Stretching the fabric, my hips were scorching the laces of the slip. My stomach, forever starved, was hidden, touching my spine. Next to my thin arms, two rosy apples lay over my chest. Along my skin and in between my limbs, I saw a few freckles. A lock of hair draped itself gently around my firm breast. I saw that my hair resembled Mother's brown waves, and my amber eyes were covered by her straight eyebrows as well. I inherited every angle of her face. My deep cheekbones shaded the sides of my face and pointed to my tiny chin. My lips were small and a deep red color like ripe cherries ready to be picked. From longing, my flesh and bones were simmering, calling for a storm to cool me down.

I was the contemporary of Mother's visage, and she was the vintage of mine. On that thought, behind my brown hair and my shoulders, I saw a flower reflected in the mirror. It was a lighter color than the red blanket. I left the mirror and went and touched the flower. It was a pink blossom sewn onto the scarlet, silky blanket. I wondered if Linda had made it, and if she had, I knew she must be very talented. I got under the covers, stretched out my tired body in the lavish bed, and felt with my feet to find its edges. With my satin slip under the cotton sheet, I felt like a woman, a fulfilled one, waiting for her husband to discard his worries and fill her more. But I failed to keep my legs open, just as I failed to keep myself awake before Ben returned.

CHAPTER 18

The daylight woke me up. I had plunged peacefully into sleep under the milky-white sheets like a seashell rolled along the sand by gentle waves. It took a moment to recognize my new window and the pine trees outside of it. But once I did, the reality of my new life washed over me. I felt stunned and scared and excited and peaceful all at once. I was married now. I was a nuse. I felt the lace of my slip scratching my leg and touched the smooth silk with my fingers. The sheets seemed all on my side, and I looked over to Ben's side to find him. He was not in the bed. Where was my husband? I must have been so tired and sleeping so deep that I had not heard him come in last night.

"Dreqi," I uttered, upset with myself.

I got up off the bed, opened the dresser, and wore the first skirt I found. As I walked through the hall and crossed the three stairs, I saw that the skirt was a white one with a print of tiny flowers. I opened the mahogany door and saw Linda.

"Good morning," she said, sitting refreshed on the sheepskin cover.

"Good morning," I quickly replied and grabbed the coffee maker to make her a coffee.

"Don't worry, I already had coffee," she said.

Damn it, that was terrible news. What good was I as a nuse if I didn't wake up earlier to make coffee for my mother-in-law?

"But make one for your father," Linda responded, understanding that I understood that I had screwed up.

Shortly after, Ben's father walked in. I brought him his coffee, and he began drinking it while he was reading his newspaper. I wanted to ask them where Ben was, but I couldn't bring myself to because that might reveal that I had failed to keep myself awake on our first wedding night. I made a coffee for myself and sat quietly in a chair below the window. I did not have much to say nor did either of them have any desire to ask. After all, they knew everything about the life that I had led. It was obvious that I stood out in their family kitchen. I was an outsider, but I was their outsider now.

Linda had disheveled morning hair, and her glossy black eyes were sending me creepy smiles. She seemed pleased with herself, like a woman who had just accomplished building a tunnel through a mountain. Perhaps it was because she had a bride seated on a chair inside her four walls.

I stood up immediately when Ben opened the door, but he went and sat on the couch next to Linda. He didn't say it, but Linda did.

"Ben wants some coffee," she said, attesting that she knew better than anyone what her son needed.

Linda owned my husband, but I had known that since I had seen her climb our hill on our arrangement day. However, I took no offense to it because, just as in most arranged marriages, the truth was that I knew nothing about my new husband, like the fact that he smoked. Yet, I truly hoped that we would both give each other a chance, and perhaps he could love me as much as a man could love a woman in our cold times.

Ben was wearing a blue shirt, and his face looked even more sophisticated in that color, the same sophistication Kol had in my dreams. But Ben was actually worldly and a city guy, and he carried the cold air of the Communist capital. Yet, there was no question that he looked more attractive than ever. His skin was looking pure like heaven. His glossy eyes were sunken like black diamonds in a fine sand, and his neck bulged irresistibly every time he swallowed his thoughts. He was an undeniably gorgeous man.

I was standing at the counter stirring his coffee, and I started thinking about how lucky I was to be his wife. But all of a sudden, the foam blossomed up out of the coffee pot, cascading over the sides and forcing me to swiftly pour it into a mug. Mortified, I quickly mopped up the foam as best I could and put the mug down on the table in front of him. Then, he said something that I was not expecting.

"Thank you," he said.

I did not respond in kind, instead, I sat down and was silent, thinking about what he had just said. Why did he thank me? I wondered. I am his wife, what does he have to thank me for? I was taught that a woman does not receive appreciation for anything. She was born to serve her man. Am I in a different world than he is? I knew that he was a doctor, but still, he shouldn't have felt obligated to thank me because, regardless of appreciation, I would do anything to make him happy. For better or for worse, he was my mate for life.

I remembered that I had only heard that thank you from one other mouth, and that was Uncle Llesh's. He had said it to Mother during a couple of dinners, and she had responded: "It's our duty." That was before he left our country, and after that, we never saw him again. It's my duty, I wanted to say to Ben, too, but I was too shy to open my mouth. So, I sat there, intrigued by his manners and glancing at him while he drank his coffee, attempting to read his emotionless face.

His face conveyed multiple lines of words, yet each of the lines were encrypted. I began decoding, starting with his eyes.

They were saying: "I can't face you. It's futile over here, don't look at me please. I had to cut myself off. It's hard to live with it. You can't see it. You can't see me because I have a sponge in my depths that sucks up my dirt. Don't ask me, I can't tell you how I feel. I have a worm in here that I can't kill. It's dark and small. It's a threat. Beneath it lies another one. It's atrocious, I can't show you.

My clouds hide it. My white robe covers it. And my suit jails it. I can't feel it, but I have an itch that I can't scratch. I'm afraid. I'm numb and I'm tired and I'm small, don't look at me. It's not right but I can't see you. I can't let you in. Because—please don't look at me."

In reality, Ben was having a conversation with his father, airing a few educated sentences about his workload, while I was reading his eyes. I listened to him for a moment, as he went on to talk about one of his patients, a young man who saw a vision every night above the horizon of a brown horse galloping without a rider. Did he care about the patient? I couldn't tell. But, as I listened, I remembered that I didn't know Ben yet. We had been married less than a day. Why had I presumed that I could read in his eyes what he could not say? Maybe I was just afraid he would not love me, and I had gone too far.

Then, his eyes glanced at me and back to his father. And in that one, brief glance, I recognized that what I had seen in his eyes was not wrong. He was a perfect-looking man who was frozen like an ice cube. He stood as if there were no sunshine that could fall in our country that could warm his heart and liberate him. Like a Communist book, he was completely closed to outsiders. He had sketched his borders, and any other element beyond the lines was a gray zone. He was shielded like a soldier waiting for a bullet.

My body felt like it would sink through the floor, but I held it up and looked beyond the window glass to the oak and pine trees outside. Their leaves were moving calmly, and the sky was heavenly blue. I was determined to hope for us, to wipe away the cold darkness I'd seen. I am his nuse, I thought, I will be the one to break through the bricks surrounding his heart. I will be the one to shine a light inside of him. I will know him and find his love.

I hoped to exchange a word alone with him before he left for the day. But he didn't bother. As he was leaving for work, I reminded myself that he was the sun and I was the earth, and I sat quietly in my chair like a good wife.

Now that I was married, I could take some days off from work because my new family could afford it. Linda was a retired teacher, and her husband was still teaching. Leke had gray hair, and his face was washed out from his job. He forever looked like he was about to confess. Yet, like most of our teachers, he was afraid to get his confession out.

I knew all about this kind of a man. For Leke, it went like this: Throughout his years of educating, the pen in the pocket of Leke's suit had been poking him to write facts on the board that were actually objective and truthful, yet he never found the courage to write them, leaving his students unenlightened. Leke's forehead showed that he struggled to hold the chalk, yet he conformed and let his soul wash out instead of risking his family's lives. I could not blame him. I knew that it only takes thinking of one of your loved ones to make you start complying with inhumane rules.

And to some extent, we all did it—even us, the field workers. But the impact of the field workers' labor in our society was minor since our job was to take orders and perform without touching the intellect of other people. Actually, and rightfully so, we were entitled to blame the higher-ups for our misery, and that gave us some relief. Even if our bodies held a long-lasting grudge, our consciousness was left at ease.

The higher you were on our authoritarian ladder, the more it challenged your morals. Leke had been molding the intellects of countless children for at least twenty years. So many minds had passed through his door, and he, like many other pedagogues, had been opening the gate of agitprop, the art of propaganda through literature, to each one. Leke took hold of his students' heads and began his teaching by blacking out the light of curiosity, blinding them with disinformation, and shoveling skewed political views into their minds. By first installing fear, the youth did not question the drill. Not a piece of furniture in Leke's splendid kulla could support that wrongdoing. However, one thing was certain, the upper class had more chances than the rest of us.

CHAPTER 19

One of these days, Linda, Leke, and Ben would have to decide if I should go back to work in the fields.

"Bora is our daughter, she will be well taken care of," Leke had said to Father on our shenj.

Other than that, in the three times I had met Ben and his family prior to our marriage, they had never mentioned what I would do for work at their kulla. Perhaps it was embarrassing for such an established family to let their nuse be just a farmer. I wouldn't be surprised if they were opposed to it, but I didn't go to university like them, and our leader told us that hard labor was for the rest.

After Ben and Leke left for work, I was left with my mother-in-law for the rest of the day.

"We have to go to the ration supply store," Linda said while her back was cherishing the sheepskin on the couch.

"Yes, mom," I said shyly, calling her "mom" for the first time.

I didn't call her "mother" because mother was a strong word that I reserved only for my mother, and "nenë" was too old-fashioned for Linda. When I had been in the hospital in Tirana, the gentle nurse had asked the nurse with the shrill voice, "How is your mom?" Since then, I understood that people with good jobs called their mother "mom," instead.

When I got ready to escort Linda to the ration supply store, I put on my yellow skirt and one of the new vibrant shirts that were brought from our shenj. It was a cool, dry summer day with soft light, and while I waited for Linda, I was mesmerized by the leaves of the oak trees and the pines branches moving softly in the warm wind.

"I'm ready," she said from the hall because she assumed I was still in the bedroom.

When she found me on the stairs, I could see that my mother-in-law was indeed prettier and more stylish than her nuse, just as the song said.

She took a bag, and I followed her through the bare yard, where she took my scarred elbow and tucked my scarred arm under hers, showing me how she wanted me to walk with her. Even if her shoes added some inches, we had a fair height difference, and at that angle, my elbow hurt. But I didn't want to tell her that I had a bad arm, and I suppressed my thoughts about her nature and behavior in hopes of getting used to her oddities.

Linda was unusual, and it's not that Mother wasn't. But I was raised by Mother's peculiar acts, not Linda's, so Linda's idiosyncrasies were foreign to me and seemed particularly odd. Also, since I was Mother's child, I could shoot back at Mother when she would call me dreqi in front of other people, yet as a daughter-in-law, my mouth had to stay sealed. For all nuses, perhaps it was less that the new mother-in-law was bizarre, and more that, all of a sudden, a nuse had to be a daughter to a woman who she didn't know before, like moving to a foreign country and pretending you are from there.

I heard the ravine singing calmly and fell for Linda's cheerfulness as we walked. Just yesterday, when I had moved into their trojë, I had my jaw stuck down on my neck and hadn't seen much of the earth around their kulla. Just like their home and their family, their tojë was unlike any other ground I had seen before. Every part of their trojë was flat and covered by oak, pine, and a few horse-chestnut trees. Here and there, a maple grew too. A few brambles, hogweeds, and plenty of thorn bushes stretched out toward the ravine.

Unlike our bold hills, the land surrounding their kulla was dense with plants and trees that camouflaged their kulla. The mountains were so far away that their peaks seemed mixed with the sky's colors, and they seemed to glance arrogantly and indifferently from above, not sheltering my new tokë. It did not please me to see the mountains from afar that morning, but the ravine poured melodic voices into my heart, substituting for their loss.

"I have to stop for a second," Linda said when we were in sight of the main road. "I have a stone in my shoe."

"Okay," I replied and let go of her arm.

She leaned her body on a small bunker that was built at the corner of the two merging roads, took off her shoe, and started to smack it on the surface of the bunker.

"Do you need help?" I asked.

But she didn't answer. It was just a rock—it would have fallen out without her having to hit the shoe—but it seemed that she was enjoying the act. So, I held on without saying anything, watching her. Once she was done, I grabbed her arm again like a good daughter-in-law, and we continued on.

When we arrived at the ration supply room, Linda asked me what I fancied. Had I ever been in a position to think about what I liked in a ration supply room? Oh Zot, no. I had dreamed about it, yes, but as soon as Mother would give the paper stamp to the store worker, I would abruptly wake up. Linda had many paper stamps and was telling me that she could afford to spend them on my wishes.

I was confused and trying to process my new world, so I said, "I would like whatever we need." And ideally whatever is the cheapest, I thought.

Her face flicked off like a shoe flips in the air and lands back on the ground saying, "Oh don't be shy," and waited for me to point at something.

"I really don't need anything," I responded genuinely.

"You don't work in the fields anymore, take whatever you fancy, what's ours is yours now," she stated boldly.

"Okay," I said, feeling obliged to find something.

If those words had come from Mother, I would have treasured them, but I was too shy with Linda to use her stamps for my wishes. Perhaps, having one child instead of five makes a difference, I thought. And boy, that "You don't work in the fields anymore" really stung me. Zot. Perhaps that means they have decided that I will not work in the fields anymore, I thought, but if not there, where will I go? Oh Zot, am I supposed to stay home all day with Linda? I'd rather work in the fields than die from boredom.

Aside from Linda's strange manner, I liked her, but I did not know what I would do at home with her all the time. It would be fine when I began to have children, but we were still nine months to a year away from that. It would be stifling to sit around for that long.

I found a white scarf like the peaks of the mountains on top of Mother's hill, and I gave it to Linda to buy for me.

She was talking to another woman like her, and with exhilaration, she said, "Here is my nuse," displaying the piece of flesh that she had acquired a day ago.

I was almost getting used to Linda's creepy smiles. She was proud of me, I realized, even if my name was just "nuse." And even when she had said that I was no longer a field worker, she was still proud. That's how good it gets for a wife in her new tokë, I thought.

The ravine sang for me again on our way back. It sounded quiet and melancholic from afar, but as we got closer, it became louder and louder until we closed the mahogany door of our kitchen. I dropped our shopping bag full of vegetables on the white table. I pulled out four potatoes and two eggplants and rubbed them with some sunflower oil and sprinkled some salt, preparing them for lunch. We also had bread and cheese to complement the dinner meal. It was midday, so I began doing housework to pass the time until Ben came.

By late afternoon, Linda and I sat down on the couch to wait for our men. Leke came home first, bringing some more bread with him. I was amazed by the amount of food that was circulating in my new house. Yet, I quickly tried to wrap my head around it, recalling Linda's statement that I'm not a field worker anymore. Not that I knew how to be any other Bora, but still, I strived to persuade myself that I was an upper-class wife now because I wanted to please them.

Soon Ben came in, and we all sat down at the table and began to eat. During dinner, Ben somehow managed to not meet my face even once, and I felt ignored one more time. Perhaps that's how men treat their nuse, I thought, and waited for the night to come to see him in our bedroom.

Ben looked at me when I said, "Mom, if you don't mind, I'll get to my room now."

That was the longest sentence I had said all day, and that was the second time all day that Ben had looked at me.

"Of course," she replied, smiling excessively.

Ben stayed in the kitchen, drinking tea and conversing with Linda and Leke, giving me some time to get ready for him.

In our lavish bedroom, I changed into the satin slip from the night before. It was not our first night, but in my heart, it was still our first. I turned on the oil lamp and noticed my hip bones pressing against the white lace, then I sat down on top of the red blanket. The goosebumps on my arms were telling me to get under the covers, but I was afraid that such a comfort would pull me right into sleep again, making me a terrible wife for a second night. Only the scar on my arm didn't have goosebumps. That was the cold-blooded part of my body, and since it did not have the ordinary senses, I used it for hard jobs like killing worms coming out of the ground, shoveling, and feeling surfaces that would have made too many goosebumps if I used my other hand.

It did not take long for Ben to come into our bedroom. I was still sitting on the edge of the bed, facing the door, but he did not look at me. I watched his hand while he put his package of cigarettes on the nightstand and turned on his light. His hands were spotlessly clean, even though he was a smoker. I was still trying to process and comprehend his habit. How many things do I not know about my husband? I thought.

I watched him walk to the closet. He had not said any words so far, and he had yet to look at me, but still, I felt exposed in my white slip and decided to get under the covers. I wished that he had thrown a glance at me so he could have seen the delicate sewing work on my satin slip. The surgical precision required to trim a fine piece of satin with lace took too much thoroughness and diligence to not be admired, let alone for Ben to not even look at it. I wished, too, that he would show some care for my figure, and perhaps throw a compliment at me.

As Ben took his shirt off in the closet, I turned off my light, and we were left with only his lamp on. Laying under the red blanket in the semi-dark, I watched him. For the first time, I saw the bare skin of his wide shoulders, and his body looked inviting as he moved in the closet. His long legs held his back like an ionic column. The T-shirt that he put on appeared to be soft, like I had wished him to be on our first wedding night. He took off his pants and walked around our iron bed in his shirt and undershorts and got under the covers too.

He turned off his oil lamp and settled in the bed on his back. His body was a mere palm away from mine. Despite having cold hands on our wedding day, his body seemed warm now. I could feel his heat enter the covers. I began to fantasize about his body, and the silky, red blanket seemed to catch fire. I longed for his handsome face to meet me, but he did not turn to me. I wanted my body to brush with his and to be loved by his skin. I wanted my small chin to be caressed by his breath. I wanted to know him and taste the flavor of his heart and have him open his heart to me. But he was not moving.

There was a cold space between our bodies, and bit by bit, his warmth began to fade. Together we were floating on an iron bed in the deep night, yet I couldn't sense his feelings. I waited as he kept quiet and still. His eyes were closed, yet I knew and felt that he was awake. I wondered if Ben was waiting for me to give permission, or if I, as a nuse, was supposed to begin.

So, I took a deep breath, as if I was getting under water, and slipped my fingers under his shirt. At first, my fingers met his chest. It was soft like a feather but firm underneath. He stayed still as I extended my arm and explored his belly. Then my fingers ran along his arm and down to his hand, and then to the other hand and up the other arm. But both sides felt cold. It was the scarred arm that I used to touch him, and I thought maybe that was why I didn't feel his heat. I kept moving and went to his long legs, and I warmed my palm with the soft hair of his thighs. He did not move, but I stretched my hand further and further down his leg to reach his smooth forest.

I had closed my eyes, and flames were sparking under my eyelids. The lace was tickling my pale legs as I lay on my side, exploring him. I was at his stomach, which was flat and had less hair. He kept still, but his belly was pumping, and I could hear his breath getting hefty. His breath told me that he was burning as much as I was. I wandered again to find his shrubby land. Further and further down, my hand explored, and I did find more hair, a lot more, and my hand warmed as I envisioned where I was. But still, he did not move. He kept unflinchingly still. Then my hand slid further in his shrubby land and my fingers found a flat part, where no hair grew. It was smooth and soft.

"Please don't," he said, putting his hand on mine.

His fingers wrapped around my hand and moved it from his body, then he laid my hand on my hip and left it there.

"I can't," he said.

My palm suddenly felt spikes of chills like it had touched a dead body. I laid there, frozen. Suddenly, I understood that his entire body was passionless, cold, and unloving. He was motionless, lying on his side—stiff. He had not a piece of hair awake for me. How could this be? His presence was lifeless, even though I could hear him breathing evenly. He kept silent and had no answers for me. He stayed mute.

I shrunk under that bloody cover, aghast that his body was stagnant, not alive for mine. How could he not want this, me? My lace slip now felt ill-fitting and ridiculous as I realized it would never be taken off by his hands. I am like a caterpillar that will never become a butterfly, I thought in the dreary night. How could his body be so numb? Tears began to drop as my mind screamed, not understanding what he was. My futile satin dress was drawing out my tears. My fingers trapped my saliva and the drops that were dribbling in between my lips.

The hand of my scarred arm that had explored his flaccid penis held my mouth closed against the sobs. The same hand that held my wet lips reminded me over and over what it had felt when it had touched his paralyzed body. I was shivering and deluged by voiceless sobs, in disbelief of what had just happened. I was trapped, and my moistened fingers pressed my lips to avoid saying it aloud. My life had been put behind the bars of a wealthy kulla. My lungs couldn't let me breathe, and my chest felt like it was ripping, unable to sob much longer in silence. He heard me, he felt me, but he did not do anything. He never moved a muscle nor said a word.

I almost suffocated my heart for an entire night, cursing his unloving, dead body. I cursed him violently. I cursed with a beastly voice that terrified my heart. I cursed him until pain scratched my throat, making it hurt. I cursed him so much that dreqi woke up inside me. I cursed him because I held evidence of his darkness. I cursed his body because he was cold like a dreqi in the dark. And his cold was creeping and seeping into my nauseated soul. I could see his darkness spraying my life with unfulfillment and humiliation. I could see his secret contaminating my life. Then I could see that we would be two impaired bodies living in one bed. I cursed him until I, too, became a monster, a dreqi, a satanic daughter who would burn for the rest of her life.

CHAPTER 20

I woke up alone in the big bed with an acrimonious taste in my mouth. If my throat hadn't been feeling dry and my tongue hadn't been tasting the salt from the tears left on my lips, the bright sun coming from the window would have made me think that the night before was just a nightmare. But I couldn't deny what had happened. There was not a cell in his body that wanted to move toward me, to discover me, to know me, to touch me. The hollow feeling in my stomach reminded me that there had not even been a glance or a tender word. He had never looked me in the eye. I understood that my fate was sealed. I was a wife who would never know love.

I decided that I would not use his name again. Neither my mind nor my mouth would speak his name. He was now nameless. He would just be "he." I wanted to remove the unheard of, but in the dryness of my throat, the truth persisted. And along with these truths, shame arrived, too.

He wasn't in the room, but his pillow carried some of his dark hair, announcing he had slept there. Had he even slept in our room on our first night? A skeptical gleam came to my eyes when I asked myself this wicked question. It was embarrassing to even have to question that, even to myself. How could that happen? How and who could I ask about these things? How could I ask why my husband didn't want me? Why did he make me his wife but not want to make me his woman? How could he be so heartless and destroy my life like that? How could he bring me into this vile situation? Then, my heart became exasperated, beating ferociously.

The bedroom was vacant, but even if he were in the room, it would still feel empty. And even if he were in the bed, I would still suffer from loneliness. And perhaps, in addition to feeling alone, I would endure a dash of pity for my fate. As I pulled my untouched breast out of the cover, the flower on the silky, red blanket, which had seemed like a masterpiece of work, appeared wilted and counterfeit. Did the masters of this kulla know about their son? Oh Zot, did Linda know about him and was hiding it with her creepy smiles?

My hand pushed against the perfectly straight mattress, lifting my body from the bed, knowing that they had robbed my life. I was living in a lie. Their lavish, comfortable kulla now seemed faulty and empty of any truth. Each and every single thing there felt fake—the dresser, the closet, the nightstands, and, of course, the mirror, which had fooled me with false hopes of being a fulfilled woman. Their furniture, so meticulously made, tried so hard to imitate a normal life, but it was a sham that was hiding a well-planned, fraudulent marriage. A husband who had an empty, unloving heart. A heart that felt inhuman. My love had been a palm away as I had waited for him for an entire night, but he had stayed concealed under his shrubby land, not caring to meet his wife. He couldn't touch. "Please don't," my mind had repeated over and over, and as the stars had shone in the dark, they had said he would not be mine, and all I had felt was his chill.

I stood up feeling sick to my stomach. I pushed my hair back, frowning when I saw the white, satin slip. I took it off and dressed quickly without looking in the mirror. I didn't want to look at myself, in fact, I wanted to vanish from my reality like a puff of smoke. I crumpled the slip in my hands and opened the door. It squeaked, but no one was there to hear it. I quickly passed the hall and saw the three stairs. I was too disturbed to sit, so I walked right into the kitchen. No one was seated on the sheepskin cover nor on the chair.

I went straight to the stove and threw the exquisite slip with its delicate laces into the smoldering ashes. Then, I quickly broke some sticks to stoke a fire. The flame burned through the lace and the white silk, and I swallowed my freshness and my female side. It was bitter to see my marriage burn like that, but his body had not a speck of passion for mine. He was covered by a rime of ice that couldn't be melted by my touch.

My heart couldn't hold last night's scene anymore, so I lifted my futile body up. I filled the teapot with water and made some tea. Then, I sank my fingers into the hot tea. My skin was burning, but I had to tolerate it, just as I was being forced to tolerate a loveless husband for the rest of my life.

Linda opened the mahogany door and walked in wearing a wide smile. She was cheerful again.

"Good morning my daughter," she said, irritating me even more with her abstruse high spirit.

Why was she so joyful and so nice to her daughter-in-law? Mothers-in-law weren't supposed to be nice—was she just pretending?

"Good morning, how did you sleep?" I asked, examining her—perhaps fake—smile.

She did not respond, as she was distracted by the mahogany door opening and allowing her son in. She didn't miss a beat and, full of care and love, she went and hugged the nameless. From their warm embrace, I saw that he was still swimming in her placenta. That dreqi knew about her impotent son better than anyone else. It was so obvious that it made my stomach turn.

Once the hug was finished, Linda sat with the posture of an accomplished woman, her motherly love floating in the air like a fine mix of potpourri for her son. He sat on the sheepskin-covered sofa next to her like a sheep himself. He didn't say a word to me—not a greeting, not a blank smile. He didn't even throw an eye my way. He fully ignored me as if he didn't owe an explanation to the poor field girl. My blood was hotter than the tea mug I was clenching in my hands, and I felt angry, if not livid, that he couldn't muster even the tiniest decency toward me. I was enraged at the absence of some humility, if not a confession.

As I watched the two of them conversing and enjoying their morning as if their world were an ideal place, my anger turned to sorrow. My body began to sink in the chair from despair and disappointment. I couldn't believe how easily they were ignoring what they had done to a daughter's life.

Unable to brave it for any longer, I went in front of the sofa and blew a hole in the adoring mother-son air. I stood staring at him without uttering a word, fuming. Both of them had no choice but to acknowledge their poor field nuse, who they had tricked so well. Still looking at his mother, not at me, his face turned to a sickly yellow. I heard Linda breathe shakily and felt her glaring at me while my eyes bored a hole into her son.

When he finally looked at me, I moved my head closer to him to look straight into his eyes. A lock of my long, brown hair fell on the white table like an innocent audience.

"What are you doing?" he said timidly.

His eyes were so wicked and shielded that I couldn't see anything inside their darkness, and it frightened me. But I did not let him see the unease I felt looking at his dead eyes.

"Would my husband want coffee this morning?" I said caustically, as if I hadn't heard what he had said a moment before.

He couldn't utter so much as a vowel and affirmed only with a nod. He was limper than the sheepskin he was sitting on.

After discharging my anger on the nameless, Linda's creepy smile and her studied posture shattered. Her small body crumbled over the skin of the sofa as she understood that I knew. Now we all knew. I straightened up and drifted to the cabinet. I was ready to break the mugs, the plates, the glassware, and every fake article that they had in their kulla, but instead, I went to the counter to mix coffee for him.

If I had spoken like that to another husband, I would have been beaten to hell. Yet, perhaps that other husband would have been a more decent man, and I would have no need to talk like that.

Leke walked in, cluelessly greeted me, and sat next to them.

"Do you want a coffee, Father?" I asked.

Since I'm making one for your nameless son, I wanted to say.

"Of course," Leke said.

He looked amazed at my saccharine voice, perhaps because that was the longest I had ever spoken around him.

The blood was still boiling in my veins causing a tremor that shook the nameless' mug as I brought it to the white table. I held my urge to throw the coffee in his face when I saw that he was ignoring me again. I left it on the table instead, like a good nuse. Next, I brought Leke's coffee. As for Linda, she didn't have one, and I wasn't willing to ask her.

I sat down in the open chair, holding my mug. Leke was reading his paper *Zeri i Popullit edhe Zeri i Rinise (The Voice of the People and the Voice of Youth),* gathering opinions to drill into his youthful students. Linda was sitting quietly because the world knew her secret now. As for my husband, he was sipping the brown coffee I had made for him. I tried to see through his dark façade, but couldn't. He is impenetrable, I thought. Only Zot knew who—or what—that man had inside.

Apparently, enough time had passed for Linda to process what had come to light because she suddenly changed course. When I looked over to her, she smiled her creepy smile at me again, as if my life could change with just a smile from her. Leke got up, his son got up right after him, and they both left for work.

I was left behind with a giddy, albeit dumbstruck, mother-in-law. I left their coffee mugs unwashed—why should I care about being a good nuse when I had that kind of a husband? I didn't even look at Linda as I departed through the once nice mahogany door and went to my room.

My stomach began turning again when I saw my bed. I wanted to vomit on it, I hated it so. How could I lay in the same bed with him when I knew that he was using me and that my entire being had been sacrificed to save his? The red color of the blanket looked like the fresh blood of a slaughtered animal. I held my mouth shut and looked at the cabinet and saw that even the cabinet held secrets.

The mirror only antagonized me further, yelling "You are an unwanted woman," at the first sight of my reflection.

Oh Zot, my life was a piece of fiction, and Linda knew it. Perhaps Leke knew too. How could this be real? Did these people think that my soul was so inferior that it was acceptable to spare it? Yet, I couldn't blame Linda and Leke as much as I blamed him. My husband was wasting me. I curled my fingers into my palm and formed a fist, hitting the mattress, cursing each of them until my scarred arm throbbed in pain. It was too much to bear, and my head dropped to the bed. I felt ill trying to grasp how worthless and twisted everything was and that I lived in a kulla full of lies.

A few hours after cursing my fate, someone knocked at my door. It was Linda, of course, wearing her usual cheer, still pretending her smile would fix what she had done.

"Can you help me with my yard?" she asked.

I didn't shut the door in her face, not because she didn't deserve it, but because I needed the outside air.

"Sure," I said like a good nuse, since that was the only thing left for me to be. I dried my face with my skirt and followed her.

Outside, I thoroughly scanned her tokë to see what was needed. Then, I took a shovel and began cleaning the paths for the new plants. I sweat out my anger by watering the freshly upturned earth. After, I refined the soil and removed rocks that could kill the young sprouts. When I grabbed a hammer and broke some of the stones that were in the way, Linda found the sound brutal and went to sit on the stairs, overseeing her worker. I finished by removing the weeds in the corners of the yard, and I left the soil well fertilized.

After dropping the shovel, I asked Linda, "What are you going to plant?"

Plainly and cruelly, she said, "Nothing. I will not plant anything."

And with that, her small body climbed the three stairs and turned into the kitchen.

"All this work for nothing?" I panted to myself, out of breath.

I looked at the fruitless soil and envisioned the blossoms blooming—a sham, since the land's owner would leave it unplanted. It was odd, though understandable, that the rich loamy soil belonged to the wrong family.

I washed my hands and went back inside. Linda was making lunch, and the smell of fried onions and potatoes singed my nose. I cut some bread, and we both sat and began to eat. She acknowledged that I knew the truth by sitting humbly, without her pseudo-cheer, for once. Perhaps she had reconciled with it, but I was new to this infertile fate. My face was still burning from the memories of last night.

As I watched the spoon pierce her old lips, Linda—in an attempt to be kind—insisted I have cheese. The cheese felt good on my tongue, but it failed to help swallow my thoughts. Linda, her son, her husband, and I were all boiling in the same damaged pot. Each of us knew it, but we had no choice but to make believe that it worked. I washed the dishes and put them in the cabinet while thinking about what the three of them had done to my life. It was inescapable.

I asked Linda if she needed anything else.

"No," she said gloomily.

Then both of us, conceding the ugly truth, retired to our rooms.

I lay on the cold bed and managed to discharge my anger and sleep for a moment. The darkness had already come when I heard his null voice. He was in the hall talking to his father. As I got up off the bed, I saw myself in the mirror. The nap not only scattered my thoughts, it made my face glow. He was back, and I didn't know how to feel about it.

I went to the kitchen and put some wood on the stove. He didn't greet me or acknowledge me, and I realized that he would never reveal why he couldn't love me as a wife. It was clear that he couldn't face me and never would. He just wanted a dull wife, and what's better for that than a poor daughter. I warmed the food for them. That was my role after all—to clean, cook, and obey my husband, even though he was a heartless, nameless one.

My nerves were calm by then. Perhaps it was the sleep or the physical tiredness from the yardwork that had soothed me. I was less fueled by anger, and even though I was disheartened with the secret that I had to live with, I knew I had come to terms with the fact that he wouldn't change. Other women had an inmate, an officer, or a miner for a husband. I had the other kind, the loveless one.

It had not taken long. After just three days of being married to him, I could see that he didn't want this. Linda knew it too. She knew that her son would never blossom, and that's why she didn't want to plant anything in her yard. An impaired crop stays impaired. No matter how fertile my soil was, it was futile because he was uninterested in the entire business of marriage. I didn't need any more time to understand that his hands would never caress my body and our nights would forever be cold.

CHAPTER 21

It was still summer, the end of a season that, as a freshly married woman, I had expected to live differently. But I had not. I had been married for two months. One morning, I was sitting on the three stairs on the outside of my new family's kulla, looking around at what was now, without me choosing it, my new tokë. Straight ahead, I could see across the rich soil along the ravine. The bushes and weeds, and the oak, maple, chestnut, and pine trees had knit their roots, stems, branches, flowers, and leaves together, sealing our kulla from the outside. The ravine was singing more quietly now than it had in the springtime, as the mountains and skies yielded less water in the summer months. It was peaceful there.

My bare feet were touching the stairs but couldn't feel the chill of the floor that they knew and longed for. The leaves of the horse chestnut tree alerted my chestnut eyes and spoke to me.

"Your husband, who you wanted to love undyingly, cannot love," they told me.

The solid trunks of the trees guarded the kulla. It was secure, and Leke and Linda hid Ben within it, and now they would have to hide me, too.

Fall would come soon, and the thirst of the ravine would be

quenched again. The ravine knew that. She knew that her voice would be filled by the cold waters, letting her sing at length until she drained again. She had a circle of seasons to live for. But I, what did I have to live for? There was not a drop of change coming for me. I was the illusion of two people who had decided to dedicate me to their son. As he said thank you for every cup I made, I was aware that I had been granted a man who was satisfied with his wife giving him nothing but a cup of coffee.

A sparrow flew from our gardh to a branch of an oak tree and took up song. Then a gardalinë alighted on a dried yellow flower, and a chorus began. Almost as soon as it had begun, their great performance came to a halt when the gardalinë opened its gray wings, straightened its red neck, and flew away, its white tail bobbing in the air behind it. Unexpectedly, just like a bird—that's how Uncle Llesh had flown away. I was eight years old the last time I saw him. It was a few months before my accident. Uncle Llesh and my husband were similar in many ways. They both went to university, and they both were polite, knowledgeable, and worked for the state. But there was one major difference. One was a married man, and the other had the guts to not be a husband. It was only after I got married to the nameless that I realized the gravity of Uncle Llesh's decisions. It had taken great strength of character to sacrifice his family and himself in search of liberty.

Uncle Llesh had been convinced that the foreign sky was much brighter than ours. Escape itself was greater than being just alive for him. He was an admirable, self–made man and had lived in our country bravely, fearing not a soul. He had sparkling eyes, and his intellect was well equipped to withstand the terror of radio speeches, bunkers, military, rats, and any other fears they tried to inject in us.

"Lleshi was the only one I saw laughing in the open, and when the rats saw his smile, they shrank into the shadows. They couldn't weaken him," Mother once said.

Uncle Llesh had a crucial job, and he had been appreciated by the higher-ups, but the insanity of the authoritarian leader had made him desperate to leave our *atdhe* (homeland). He was one of the few in our family who went to university, and after finishing his studies, he was employed in the laboratories of the state. As a scientist, he was a valuable man to our paranoid leader, who saw nothing more crucial than developing new weapons. The rats kept an eye on him because it was thought that even science shouldn't be above fear.

When he turned twenty-six, the question of why he was not married began to ring louder and louder. People proposed multiple daughters to him, but he kept rejecting them, which only threw progressively darker shades on his name. If he had gotten married, he could have shushed the rats and made his escape more feasible, but as the wife of a traitor, his wife's life would have been totally ruined. So, even though a wife could have protected his plan to flee, he courageously committed to staying a single man. Perhaps he even rejected true love because of his wish to escape. However, no one knew anything about his plans, not even his mother. When he got older, her worries about her son being in danger grew, and she began begging him to find a wife. Her motherly instincts pushed her to try to save him at any cost. But he did not want to bind the life of a woman, even a field daughter, to himself just for the sake of covering his motives. He was that decent of a man.

After his mid twenties, the rats sniffed around his region, viciously trying to find his dirt, but there was nothing tangible because his escape plan was only in his head. He was well read and knew about geography beyond the leader's borders. He knew science better than our worthless teachers, and in the university, he had learned a foreign language to make himself ready for the other world. He was curious, and through books, he saw a freedom that he couldn't unsee.

Uncle Llesh escaped with a friend who had also stayed unmarried. They both had the fortitude and the intellect to evade countless disgusting rats. They escaped on a Saturday night because the next day they were not expected to be at work. They walked for six hours through the mountains to get to the closest neighboring country—a country that we were not allowed to say the name of. The two countries were joined by a huge lake. Our geography book included the lake, but everything on the other side of the lake had been erased.

We realized what had happened on Monday evening when the military came to search our kulla. They looked high and low, even in the bloody basement. Then they yelled and threatened us as if it were our fault. Before they came to our kulla, they had gone to Uncle Llesh's kulla. There, they found only his mother with her three daughters. Uncle Llesh was the only man of the family. His mother had no other son, and her husband had already died from an explosion in the mines. Perhaps it was good that she didn't have another son because the state would have killed him for Lleshi's betrayal. The state reduced his mother and sisters' wages, but the locals helped them by donating whatever food they could.

There was no plan that Uncle Llesh could have made to avoid the suffering and punishment of his family. He had known that, and he had known that his mother would be left alone for the rest of her life. His sisters would get married and move to their husband's kulla, but his mother would lose her only son and would have nothing to look forward to in her remaining years. Perhaps he had been selfish, but not so selfish that he would leave a wife waiting for the husband that he was never going to be. The price would be heavy on both sides, but freedom won in his mind. Uncle Llesh spread his white wings, straightened his red neck, and flew over the waters with his white tail bouncing behind. Then we never saw him again. After a while, he became nothing more than a myth that lived on forbidden tokë.

My bare feet were still unmoved by the three stairs knowing Uncle Llesh's story. Why had my husband not considered fleeing or, at least, not marrying? If he had made one of those decisions, my life would have been different. Perhaps I might have married a country man or a miner, both without a penny, but rich in dignity. Even better, I could have met another highlander, and I would have been ready to take a walk with him on the crown of the mountains and live a rough but cheery life. But when a doctor had knocked on Mother's door, all the other possible husbands had faded away because of his reputation. The nameless knew that Father would never question a name like his, and so, he stole my life to save his. I couldn't forgive my husband for bringing me to a marriage that had no worth.

CHAPTER 22

Tradition said the bride could visit her family's kulla after the first couple months of married life. Every day of those months, I waited, doggedly patient, to see Mother and her tokë. I knew that, as a married woman, I couldn't express antipathy for my husband and his family, even to my mother. But I longed to see the summer's parched hills where, just a few weeks ago, I had walked free, without the heavy heartache now piercing my heart. In the months since we had gotten married, I had seen his face one hundred twenty-five times. Two times per day, once in the morning and once in the evening, except for Sundays, when I would see him three times. This morning was one hundred twenty-six.

When I awoke that morning, his black hair gleamed over the pillow, and his face looked angelic above his neck. But once his dark eyes opened, I harked back to his erring act of the night before, one that had been repeated every night since our marriage began. With a light grunt, he quickly took his body from our iron bed and walked to the closet. I watched his long, white arms flipping impatiently through his clothes.

"Bora, have you seen my white shirt?" I imagined him asking as if we were an ordinary couple.

But instead, he muttered, "Where is my white shirt?"

He seemed irritated that he had to stay even a minute longer in the same bedroom with his wife. He still could not address me nor what he had done.

I got out of the bed and quickly put on a robe over my nightgown so he couldn't see my body. I was too shy to show it to the man who had already rejected it. Crossing the beam of sunlight hitting his pillow, I approached his half-naked body and went to the closet. I flipped through his shirts to find his white one. I had to look at his bare chest when I handed it to him because I was avoiding his eyes, still contemplating what kind of man he could possibly be. He was facing the mirror, and it reflected his dark self. One, two, three, four, five, six . . . one, two, three, four, five, six . . . one, two—I counted the dresser drawers until he left the room. Each day, it would take only one interaction with him for me to remember how meaningless my story was. My sheer futility would exasperate me, and I would wish he didn't exist so I wouldn't have to be there. By the afternoon, with the cicadas clattering in the core of the heat, I would get fed up enough to begin cursing his existence. By the end of the day, I was submerged in despair. From that point on, I swallowed my sanity in order to fall asleep on the same bed with that man every night.

I would be spending a week at my kulla as a freshly married woman. I was entitled to stay for two weeks, but the night before, Linda had announced that she would be picking me up the following Sunday.

Before we left for my village, Linda's heels announced her presence with a sharp staccato on the floor as she came into the kitchen.

"Here, wear this," she said, smiling and holding a shirt across my chest.

It was a tangerine color and had long sleeves and a purple collar. It was a city shirt, and I was not a city woman.

"I wish I had your youth to wear it," she said.

"Thank you," I replied, borrowing her son's cursory politeness and averting my gaze.

Leke was sitting in the kitchen, and I noticed that he was reading his newspaper *Shqiperia e Re (The New Albania)*. He was sipping his coffee, apparently indifferent to my politeness and Linda's excitement. I truly did wonder if he knew about his son, or if he was like the kind of teachers who knew nothing about their students but liked the practice of schooling. I crossed the three stairs and went into the bedroom to change my shirt. I put on the tangerine-colored one and felt no excitement whatsoever, even though the shirt looked nice on me.

On my way back to the kitchen, I ran into my husband in the hall. He was coming from the odë and holding two books. He showed no excitement about the shirt either, but that was to be expected.

"They're for work," he uttered about the books.

I nodded my head saying okay, surprised he had said anything to me. Then, he spoke again to me.

"You can read these books too," he said.

I stopped, feeling uneasy, and said, "Sure."

He handed me one of the books, and I accepted it and thanked him like you would thank a stranger. As we both walked toward the kitchen, I ruminated about his chat with me. That was interesting to say the least. But he had been too uncharacteristically warm-hearted for me to trust it. Does he want me to find a hobby because he has been witnessing my decline and is afraid that one day I will explode? "Beautiful," Linda said about my outfit when I entered the kitchen.

Sure—beautiful for other people's eyes, I did not say.

"What time are we leaving?" I asked her when he came in and sat next to his father.

Then Linda sat down on the chair next to her son.

"Ask Ben," she replied indifferently.

Mother-in-law, father-in-law, or him—who will I first visit my kulla with? I thought.

"Ask me what?" he said, relaxing his shoulders against the sheepskin.

"Bora is going to stay with her parents. She has to be accompanied by her new family," Linda said.

"I have to be at work, I can't," her son claimed.

"It's on your way," Linda promptly replied.

As they argued, Leke did not turn his eyes toward us. The writing in the *New Albania* was clearly more interesting than the conversation. I thought about how the nameless had offered his books to me just a few seconds earlier. I had felt for him, but now I was burning from anger because his response stung me like a cold-blooded bee. How embarrassing was this—he did not even want to take part in the most minimal duties of our marriage.

"Mother would like to see you," I said while I dropped off his coffee.

And I want to see you carrying your lies around while introducing me to the world, I thought, and I want to run into every neighbor along our way just so I can examine your face when you call me your wife. I want to see if your dark eyes change color, and I want to check if you have any feelings, and perhaps during our ride, you could tell me why you married me. He gave me a blank stare, understanding that he had no choice but to travel along with me.

"Here is your bag," Linda said a step before we were about to walk down the three stairs. I saw that the bag contained beans, tomatoes, peppers, and plums.

"You don't have to," I said, ashamed because I felt as if my silence was being bought by her vegetables and fruits.

"We are family," she insisted, smiling enigmatically.

How could I disagree, and yet, how could I agree to having a nameless man as my spouse? She knew her son, so why was she ignoring such a fact to my face? I couldn't understand her. I couldn't comprehend why she expected me to overlook my useless husband for a nice shirt and a bag of vegetables.

"Sure," I said, looking at her smile, which was testing my nerves, took her bag, and left.

I was going to have to walk with him for two fugonis in a row.

I let the scarred arm hold Linda's bag and held him with my good arm because the other one brought shameful memories. As we passed along the secluded road, I was amazed that no one stopped to converse with him.

"Good morning doctor," neighbors said politely and shyly, but they proceeded without another word.

He responded each time almost as if he were forced to, exposing an upper-class attitude toward other people that I had never noticed before. Most of those people were field or other such workers. His wife was a field worker, so why was he so cold with them? Was he afraid that he couldn't hide himself from people who work every day in the hard soil of Mother Earth? Perhaps he knows that we are not so easily fooled, I thought. The more I knew him, the more his once sublime face flipped over into that of a spiritless man. Yet, as his nuse, I had to keep holding his arm.

We took a small fugoni from his village to the city. He remained silent and sat beside me as apathetically and dull as when he laid on our bed each night. Lost in his head, his dark eyes looked like a dead man's—devoid of emotion. I counted the bunkers on the road as he stayed withdrawn in his thoughts. I wasn't anticipating him talking for long, but I had thought he might utter a word for the eyes of the world. But once more, I was wrong.

I counted fifty-three bunkers in a ten to fifteen-minute ride. Then, we walked through the city to another station and took another fugoni. The fugonis were fast because it was Monday morning, and the drivers wanted to get as many riders as possible during the early turn. As we got off the last fugoni, he bid farewell to the co-riders with good manners. The vehicle sped away, leaving its exhaust behind. He straightened his suit since it had gotten out of shape when he had been sitting in the fugoni. And then, he flicked some dust off it. In that moment, I realized that was all that he had—good manners and a good name.

We soon started up my rugged road, and since it was already the end of August, the road was dry and thirsty. The summer had drained the soil, exposing the jagged rocks underneath, and the weeds, thorns, and shrubs were sharp, deathly spikes. It was clearly torture for him to be walking beside his wife because he let go of my arm and walked on the other side of the path, not caring what people from my village might think or say. He seemed to be focusing only on walking quickly so he could get to my parent's kulla and drop me off. I was walking fast because he was intolerable. His stride was interrupted occasionally by him yelping in pain when thorns stabbed him, and I finally grabbed his arm and pulled him from the edge of the road so he wouldn't get pricked again. He issued his typical "Thank you," a phrase he clearly had decided was enough for a wife like me.

I did not look toward Kol's kulla as we approached it, but I heard someone—probably his wife—sweeping the yard. Then, unfortunately, I heard my name.

"Bora!"

It was Kol calling me.

"Bora," he called again, and I knew I had to stop.

From five feet away from me, my husband asked, "Who is this guy?" He was annoyed and ready to march away.

"A neighbor, I have to say hello," I said, implying he had to wait.

I was more annoyed than he was because Kol and his wife—pregnant for a second time—were the last people on earth I wanted to see at that moment.

He moved toward me as Kol headed closer to us. Kol was holding his wife's shoulders. I inhaled sharply, my heart broken. I wanted Kol to be happy, but seeing him with his wife just hurt. Kol's uneven lips cracked a big smile.

"So nice to see you both," he said, blushing.

My husband put on his fake smile and said "Likewise," shaking Kol's hand.

"Hi," I said to his wife.

"Hi Bora," she said.

She knows my name, I thought, mortified that I did not

remember hers. How on earth had I never registered her name? And because she was quite shy, I had to continue the conversation without naming her.

"Are you almost there?" I asked, seeing that her belly button had pumped up.

"In two weeks," she said.

"Great, congratulations," I said succinctly.

Then, my nameless man and I heard something that neither of us was ready to face.

"It's your turn now Bora," Kol said.

His words plunged into my heart. I looked at my husband, and I saw that he had turned as pale blue as his jacket. Kol was expecting my husband to open up and smile with a manly pride, like another husband would do, and, perhaps, hug his wife, saying something along the lines of: Thank you . . . Soon my mik . . . Hoping for that son. But my nameless man did not do any of it. He could not even spare his typical thank you. I looked at Kol's wife, thinking with slight pity that she and Kol were very kind and sweet to us, but they did not know that we were an unusual couple and that my husband was an atypical man.

"Thank you," I said, finding my voice and squeezing the hand of my man, who was completely disengaged from the conversation.

The merry couple left with a smile, and we separated our hands once we left them.

In distress and fearing that someone else might stop us, he walked even faster than before. I walked fast too, weeping. Because of him, I was left useless and empty like a rifle without bullets. How could he expect me to live like this? My scarred arm twitched, shaking the vegetables, as I thought of the night that I had touched him. Oh . . . I held my guts as my stomach began turning and turning. All it wanted to do was throw up that twisted memory. Crushed and heartbroken, I opened my mouth and doused my throat with mountain air so I could last the few more steps to my kulla without vomiting out his secret.

The whiny wind coming from the mountains was blowing my hair toward the plain and pushing his blue jacket, which caused his jacket to catch on the shrubs and tear the fabric. He did not care about his neat looks now, and I wished he would disappear from my sight so my stomach could ease for a bit. As the road curved, the mountain's body did take him from my sight for a second, but it spit him out immediately, still the futile pit that he was.

Then, on top of our hill, with the pear tree as witness, he stood at our gardh and waited for me. An orange flame color covered the hill's bushes, and Mother's trojë was cracked from thirst. I moved close to him. He opened the wooden gardh door for me, and with that, his good manners were back. Under the shelter of the big mountains, above the sea, among the few trees there, I wanted to tell him: I can't forgive you, I don't care about your polite manners, your good status, or your wealthy kulla, they are all as worthless as you are and I can't forgive you. A long *neigh* came from near the spring, interrupting the rant in my head. It was the white horse, shaking his tail and endorsing my words.

"Bora, don't stand there, come inside," Mother yelled then.

My nameless husband lasted inside for all of five minutes. He couldn't pretend any longer and left without even drinking a glass of water. Mother didn't ask, but I could see by the wrinkle twitching almost imperceptibly between her eyes that she thought I had done something to irritate him. I did not have the courage nor the strength to debate with her, so I focused on the sewn flower that I had made, which was hanging on the wall.

Our kulla looked dark and deteriorated to me after being away for those two months. It must have been surreal for Linda and Llesh to first see what their daughter-in-law was born into. My eyes roved around the interior, taking it all in. I saw the long rug my sister had made and then the sofa Father had made. Despite their rough and meager look, they felt remarkably honest and authentic. They weren't sophisticated and shiny, just truthful.

"I'm leaving," Mother said abruptly as she picked up her bag for work.

"What should I cook?" I asked.

"The food that you brought," she replied in the same way as when I asked a question that I knew the answer to.

"I see," I said.

Then I remembered that there was never much to cook in my kulla. How could I forget? She left looking uneasy as if she were not happy to see me, and I couldn't blame her because I looked awfully low spirited. I cooked, and then I carried the big pot filled with water from the spring, made a fire, and washed the rugs and the other clothing. I did all the work barefoot, trying to feel my old world. In the late afternoon, my younger brother came from school, and I sat on the gravel stairs watching him sliding from the yard down to the spring. His butt was sitting on twigs that he had woven together, and the twigs were ripping his pants. He was hurting himself, but it was humorous. I needed to laugh out my misery for a minute, so I let him do it, very much the best sister, knowing that when Mother came back and saw his ripped pants, I would be the worst daughter. He got up and slid around the pear tree and down the hill to the spring again. As he was swirling around, I noticed that the leaves on the pear tree had changed from flat and green to curly and brown. The tree was sick.

"Hey, how long has the pear tree been like that?" I called to him.

"Since you got married," he said, oblivious.

Mother came home exhausted, reminding me of the old days. I had not worked for over two months. This was after working for four years in a row, six days a week, plus Pascha Sundays. Except for the two weeks before I got married, when I had been required to stay home. I warmed Linda's vegetable soup, and we sat and ate.

"How long has the pear tree been sick?" I asked her.

"Oh, it's struggling," she said, "it's going to take two to three years to come back."

I wanted to ask her how long it would take me to digest a nameless for my husband. Was my timeline two to three years, just like the pear tree?

Once she finished with the food, she took my younger brother to bathe him. She sat on the stairs throwing water on my brother's body beneath the setting sun. He was glowing with innocence and was delighted like a young duck enjoying the dips in a warm lake in the sunset. When Mother went upstairs to put him to sleep, I returned to the kitchen. She came back with some warm water in a plastic tub.

"Put your feet in," she said, "it will calm you."

I didn't want to, but I couldn't say no to her.

"Fine," I said, putting my feet in.

She sat on a tiny stool Father had made while I sat on the stiff sofa, and she began to massage my feet. This is strange, I thought, why is she doing this? That was perhaps the highest level of care I had received from Mother since I had been my brother's age. But she didn't let me be puzzled for long.

"How is Ben?" she asked.

I pulled my feet out. She grabbed them and put them back in the water.

"Perhaps you aren't a daughter here anymore, but I birthed you," she stated.

My stomach began turning again. I put my hand on it.

"Did he beat you?" she asked. "Because men do that."

"No," I said.

"His mother isn't treating you well?" she asked.

"I was told that mothers-in-law aren't supposed to be nice," I replied.

And I can assure you, I wanted to say, you don't want to hear about the nameless.

"Deal with it then," she shot back, thinking that Linda was the problem.

"She is fine," I retorted.

She thought for a moment, then asked, "Did his father yell at you?"

"No," I said again, upset.

178

"Then say it," she pressed, running out of patience.

"You don't want to know," I said.

Her long body stood up, reminding me of the body that I had seen in the mirror on the first night of my wedding. My arm started twitching.

"Say it," she commanded.

"I don't want to," I said.

My guts were boiling, and my chin was quivering. Her forehead frowned, and the wrinkle in between her eyes shrank more.

"You have to tell me," she said soberly in a final, yet effective, push.

Drops splashed into the pan from my eyes.

"He isn't my husband," I said. "He isn't my husband!" I screamed at her face.

She was staring at my lips as I spoke the harsh statement.

"He didn't touch me, I'm still a daughter," I finished.

I heard my teeth knocking in my ear, and my jaw seemed to fly out from my head as she slapped me as hard as she could.

"Don't ever say that again!" she yelled.

She looked around to see if anyone had heard us, then, she grabbed me by the shoulders and stared fiercely into my eyes.

"You listen," she said. "If you want to walk alive from this kulla, don't you ever—ever—say that again."

Then she yanked my feet from the basin. The tub was dripping, and my feet were in a pool of water. My earrings were still shaking from the hit. She went to the door and paused, staring back at me.

"I'd rather kill you than let others do it."

And with those words, she left me.

My body crumpled on the sofa as I realized that I was completely alone. I had wished that Mother would come and take me from their sterile kulla. But once more, Mother had left her daughter alone, not in some hospital room this time, but in a lifeless home instead. Twelve years ago, the dictator had forbidden her to stay with her sick child. This time, her traditions obliged her to cast her daughter away.

On the third day at my kulla, I was alone while Mother was at work. I had been avoiding interacting with Mother, and it would stay this way until I had to leave at the end of the week and live a desolate life elsewhere. After our last conversation, I had realized Mother and Linda were not that different. They were both mothers, both hungry to save their children, and both guilty to the bones.

Below the lawn, I saw the white horse drinking water and decided to go and let his tranquility console me. I grabbed a bucket to fill with water and headed toward the stream. As I was crossing the stream, I felt the icy stones under the water, and my heels woke up, sending goosebumps through my body. I paused for a moment with my feet in the water, trying to revive my barren body. I noticed that the white horse was standing serenely, looking at me with melancholy eyes. I drew closer and saw my face reflected in his large eyes, which were the color of coffee beans. I took his white head and wrapped my arms around it. I was cuddling his head when I heard someone shouting my name from afar.

"Bora! . . . Bora! . . . Bora!"

With the tokë higher than my sight, I couldn't see who was calling to me. I kissed the horse's head, took the bucket, and headed up.

"Bora," I heard again.

This time, I saw it was Maria calling me, and I went to the gardh and opened the door.

"Are you getting deaf now that you got married?" she quipped, reminding me fondly of her snarky attitude.

Her son snuck under the door and went off running. I hugged her and felt a firm belly.

"So nice to see you, dreq," she said. Then, she shouted, "Jan . . . Jan!" at her adorable two-year-old son and told him to be careful and not to get his clothes dirty.

I had missed her. She was always in a booming mood no matter what. We sat on the stairs to keep an eye on her son while we caught up. Maria had not lost her spirit, but she looked tired from motherhood and from being a nuse, as all good nuses were, which I wasn't.

"How are you, how is your family?" I asked, meaning her husband's family.

"You know, I'm good, working in the fields, pregnant, you know how married life is," she said.

"I know," I replied, ashamed to tell her that being pregnant, working in the fields, and being an ordinary nuse did not apply to me.

"How is your doctor husband?" she asked.

"Good," I said, but nothing else, not wanting to lie to her any more than that.

She had once told me that her husband's kulla dripped water when it rained, so she probably thought that I was lucky to have a wealthy husband with a sturdy kulla.

"When are you due?" I asked as I watched her hand lovingly rubbing her belly.

"In four months," she said, standing up, "Is there any name you like?" she asked while she grabbed Jan by his sweater like he was a mop and turned his body toward the kulla, away from the sea.

Knowing that I would not have children, I told her my favorite names as I led her to the kitchen to treat her with coffee.

"Vera, Hena, Gjelina—" I started, but Maria interrupted me.

"Oh Zot, those are all girls' names," she said, hating the idea of having daughters.

"Gent, Gasper, Gezime—" I was naming all our classmates, but she cut me off again.

"Can you find something not starting with G?" she said.

"Dritan, Bes—"

"Wait, wait, wait—I like Dritan," she said, like she was trying to implant the name in her brain so when the pains of the birth shivered her belly, she would remember it.

Sapped by her pregnancy and her son's energy, she sat down heavily on the stiff sofa. Her unborn baby was kicking.

"Bora, you will see how hard it is to be a mother," she said.

I bowed my head, extremely ashamed of being so jealous of her. She had no idea how much I longed to have her life—a drained face, a leaky kulla, a field husband, and being just a simple nuse.

"You look so elegant wearing your new clothes," she said.

She was ready to open the door to questions about the privileges I had as a doctor's wife. But I quickly interjected.

"And you look like a wonderful nuse, bringing a beautiful son into the world like the wife every woman wishes to be," I said as I put her coffee on the old table.

"Alright, because you are a lucky person with a doctor husband." she said. "If my baby is a son, I will name him Dritan."

Oh Zot, I looked up and begged and pleaded with Him for her to have a son so I wouldn't disappoint her.

CHAPTER 23

Three months later, the ground was suffocating from the fallen leaves. I was seated on the stairs of my new kulla mesmerized by the fall colors. I left the three stairs and went inside. Linda was in the kitchen seated on the sheepskin, her hair disheveled. I did not know why her hair was always a mess since she did not do anything besides smile and nap. I walked past the kitchen and went into the odë. Leke and he were at work.

Since August, when I had last seen Mother, the stairs and the bookshelf had been my best companions. That day, I grabbed a book with a green cover out of the book collection. As I was leaving the room, I noticed the locked drawer and wondered if there was something more interesting to read in there, but I had no key. The book in my hand was called *Gjeografia* (Geography), and on the cover, the title was in bold, capital letters. There was an eagle, the symbol of our country, above the title. Between the eagle and the title, it said: *Republika Popullore Socialiste e Shqiperise* (People's Republic Socialist Party). This was also in all capital letters. Next to it, in smaller capital letters, was: *Ministria e Arsimit* (Ministry of Education). Every book that was put into our hands was first translated by the *RPSSH's Ministria e Arsimit* (People's Socialist Republic of Albania's Ministry of Education).

The bold and hard lines on the cover of all the schoolbooks foretold the selective learning that would follow. Seeing the geography book, I recalled the "judicious" teaching method of my school years. The earth is square and made up of stiff borders, and there are only two more countries like ours—I had learned in my school. Every other country was seen as a blank, gray place, and hence, all of them together were called the "gray zone."

Our classes were called: History of Marxism and Leninism, Albanian, Literature, History, Geography, Mathematics, Physics, Chemistry, Biology, Economy, Botany, Calligraphy, Handicraft, Housekeeping, Physical Education, Production Work, and Military Training. The first and last subjects were given extra emphasis.

Standing at the bookshelf, I thought about Uncle Llesh, who was the only one in our family who had learned about the gray zone beyond our borders. I often wondered how he had done it because it was impossible to get knowledge from our classrooms. It wasn't that we weren't curious to learn. But when a student would ask something like "Where does our longest river end?" the educator's face would fume from frustration because the educator wasn't allowed to say the name of the country where the river ended, and someone had dared to ask. One student after another would follow with similar queries, and then another, another, another, another, and so on, asking about the same matters over and over. At some point, most of the teachers would answer in the same way: "The river ends across the border where the enemy is."

After that, a hush would fall over the classroom, leaving us confused about which questions were welcome and which weren't. "Whoever wants to learn about the enemy, is the enemy," the saying went. And there, we understood that if we kept being inquisitive about the enemy, we would be the enemy. We would be traitors. So, we stopped asking and learning. The number of questions we raised varied in accordance with age. The younger the classroom, the more you heard our voices. The older we got, the less we asked.

"Our school is politics, and as such, it requires that even the pupils of the elementary school be clarified. The citizens of the Albanian school, like the Albanian citizens themselves, must be prepared politically, first from the school room . . ." our leader said while eulogizing to our educators the importance of their job and leaving them without a chance for free opinions and views. That's how Leke's job kept us ignorant. He and his colleagues were sold as experts in teaching a fixed and bounded view of our country and the world.

Leke knew, too, that educators were also expected to be informed about the new projects and actions of the Communist Party and to immediately transfer that propaganda to the students. To that end, educators were required to read newspapers every day. However, in a nation where there was no such thing as freedom of the press, the information and viewpoints in those papers only served to convey the warped, limited views of the Party. That there was no freedom of speech goes without saying.

However, Leke and the other teachers in our classrooms, where true education did not exist, knew that their own sons and, perhaps, their daughters would have a different path, one filled with upper-class choices and opportunities. As the popular Communist saying said: "Education for all and higher education for the Communists' sons." Hence, knowledge was provided on a basis of class and favoritism, and no matter how loud our leader's voice rang through the radio's amplifiers declaring that we were all equal, he gave priority to philo-Communist students and parents.

From our desks, we knew that our future was determined by the social and economic class we were born into. Some students, like my husband, could get the answers from their parents because their parents had time and education. Mother, however, in addition to being the impoverished daughter of a traitor, didn't have the energy nor the knowledge to answer my book questions after a long day in the field. In fact, Mother was illiterate. As for Father, he was not a Communist, and he was not home frequently enough to answer anything. Therefore, students with laborers for parents, like me, were left ignorant, and the poorer we were, the more ignorant we were.

Flipping through the pages of the geography book in my new wealthy family's odë, I saw the reason why I had become Leke's son's nuse. It had all begun with the lessons I had been taught in my classroom at school—where truth was strictly forbidden.

The first lesson—suffering. Constant physical discomfort was administered to us inside its decaying, decrepit, inhospitable walls, which forever kept us fraught with trepidation. The school building had been built from rough-hewn stone and covered with stucco cement that crumbled not long after. Those walls never felt safe, hospitable, or warm. The window had bars and cast gloomy, dungeon-like light into the middle of the room. Our desks were worn and felt cold when we put our arms on them. During the winter, the chilly air soaked into the wood of the desks and made our hands even colder.

A tiny stove below the window heated the classroom on winter days. The stove could barely warm our classroom, let alone the desks. On those cold days, we lifted our notebooks up and kept them there so our arms did not have to touch the cold desks. The rows in the middle were the best rows to be seated in because, when the walls dumped in the cold winter air, the side rows felt it the most. I shared a middle desk with Maria in the third and seventh grades, and we felt lucky.

We had a bucket in the middle of our classroom to hold water because the ceiling leaked when it rained. This leads us to the second lesson—obey, which was the cheap role of daughters in our society. In the classroom we—daughters—had to unload the bucket on our breaks. Our parents raised us to be maids before anything else—cleaning, serving, and obeying were our primary duties. In our classroom, we took pride in being the "she" who would unload the bucket first and did not mind never taking turns with the sons. It goes without saying that the only expectation the teachers had of a daughter was that she be a subdued student. Whether she was a studious one didn't matter.

Nonetheless, we didn't mind the ceiling dripping. It had stolen our young hearts because it was the only music we heard the whole time we were at school. Each day, its melody helped us tolerate the cold air that pulsed out from the walls and pierced our bones. That constant sound of the drops falling into the bucket was the only one in the classroom without an agenda. The rest was the noise of terror and war. The rainwater was the sole pleasant sound available to our ears and gave us a bit of tranquility.

In all the classrooms, the teacher's desk sat against a harsh, blank wall in the front of the room, facing the students. On top of it, there was always a book, a pen, a notebook, and at the edge, a radio. The radio was a rectangular wooden box and had an antenna protruding from the top. It had two dials, one on each end. The left dial was the sound dial. The right dial was the tuning dial, which you turned to find the stations—or at least that's what you would have done in another country. In our case, we had only one station: our supreme leader's station.

The third lesson—fear—was drilled into us so we would remember that we were captive of our own country. In the middle of the teaching, a tinny voice would abruptly ring through the radio's amplifier. Roused by the voice, we all felt an audible slap on our faces and were fully awake. The class would pause, and we would have to keep silent until the voice stopped. The speech on the radio would always appear at the same time of the day, close to noon, because that was the time that we felt a bit at ease with our day and were ready to get out on our lunch break. It was a disruptive moment, and it felt as if we had been yanked from the shelter of our desks and reminded that we were someone's hostage.

The teachers, male or female, would be frightened, too. In the off chance that they had loosened up and thought about sharing a point they shouldn't, the voice stopped them short. Afraid of the authorities, the teacher's voice would have a more aggressive tone on the next lesson because fear has a domino effect. That voice blaring from the radio would stay on for about ten to fifteen minutes, talking about nothing, but somehow, it was a nothing that scared us to death.

Final lesson—a muddled brain. The voice, the bunkers, the random training, and so on were just some of the many terrors that our leader used to throw us off balance and brainwash us to keep us under control. From that early—our early grades—he trained us to listen to his awful voice and to understand that we were the property of the state.

Thus, we learned to think about life as a reality full of *suffering*, to *obey* authorities—men—without resistance, to *fear* moments of free will and to be afraid at all times. Our minds were not free to grow and be, they were confused and scared, achieving the final lesson, *a muddled brain*. From a young age, we believed our leader because the fear was greater than us, and it had infiltrated our minds and sucked out our young souls. Later on, many of us still believed him because we were still afraid and thought we were serving our nation.

Once I was married, I was Leke's property, and what he wanted from me wasn't so different from what the state wanted. Leke wanted me to endure my pain. He wanted a docile daughter-in-law who obeyed and served others and was too afraid and confused to seek answers. As a teacher, he knew that these were the lessons that our home, our school, and our leader had taught to a poor daughter like me. That's why Leke and Linda chose me to marry their son, and why my husband married me—because they assumed I was ignorant.

And perhaps I was, because after that week I stayed at Mother's, I went back to their kulla without a fight. I went to their wealthy home silently, dull and obedient once more. That's what my teachers, my leader, my husband, my father-in-law, my mother-in-law, and even Mother wanted from me. And so, that is what I did. I remained dull like a scrap of cloth for them. I had to fight myself and my soul to do so, and sometimes, I fought so much that I could not hear my voice inside my head anymore. But in my heart, I knew that whatever their hands had spared, fate would steer back to them.

CHAPTER 24

After we had been married for two years and winter came, I was stirring water in the pan one day and watching the leeks and onions floating while my beans settled down like heavy stones. At that moment, I decided to ask for a different life.

I left the soup simmering on the stove, opened the mahogany door, and went to grab some wood. It was freezing cold, and I saw Linda's window getting slashed by the wind. Not even our hidden kulla could escape the screams and torrents of the wind. I came back, opening the door with my elbow, and dropped the logs on the floor next to the stove. By then, Linda was in the kitchen laying on the sheepskin.

"You want to sleep?" I asked her.

"The wind is too loud," she said.

I guess Zot didn't want her to forget that He could see her kulla and sent nature for proof. I put the logs in the stove and held my hand over its heat. It was too early for lunch, so Linda got up, her hair disheveled, and went to her room. She napped peacefully everyday unless storms were hitting her consciousness. I kept my hands over the heat and looked at them. I could see that they weren't Bora's tough hands anymore, but those of a weak wife. My callouses had softened; the roughness had become supple; and the cracks had filled with clean, pastel skin. It wasn't until my fingers began to scorch that I finally felt the warmth. It would take a lot more flames, whiny winds, and hard storms whipping my body to make it feel anything.

I had cut some tea branches when I was at Mother's kulla. I hadn't clipped any yellow flowers or other herbs because I had not wanted to reminisce about my old companion and how we had often climbed the mountain to pick flowers. I had brought the tea from my hills to drink for some comfort in Leke's cold, lifeless kulla. I boiled the water for the tea leaves, and when the tea was ready, I sat down in the chair under the window, holding the hot teacup in my burned palm. I was usually alone most of the day, with only the sheepskin cover in the kitchen as a companion. On some days, my friend would be the green curtain in the odë, and on others, it would be a cleaning mania, which made the best companion because it would make me physically tired.

There were also the days when I would walk to the ration supply room with Linda, but the abundance of colorful things on the shelves that the wealthy could buy, while the other people swapped their stamp for a single apple or a potato, would make me ill. As for the books, I had read everything on the bookshelf, so now I would just sweep the dust from them and stare briefly at the locked drawer. Since the books didn't say much to me, sometimes I copied sections from their pages onto a sheet of paper to keep me busy. It was difficult to feel useful and to block my mind from thinking.

I swallowed a sip of tea. It was a strong, pure black tea, but I liked it. I had to let it steep for a shorter time in order to make it weaker for Linda.

If I didn't, she would say, "Please my daughter, can you make it less strong for me?"

"Yes," I would reply to her, having been taken captive by her kindness to me since I had arrived on her doorstep.

I was often mesmerized by Linda, because, on the one hand, she genuinely loved me, and on the other, quite simply, she had targeted my life and destroyed it. But I had stopped analyzing her and her son because it didn't serve any purpose. No decent answer would come out of it.

The wind was forceful that afternoon, and rain was pelting the window glass. I remembered the days when I had to go to the fields while lightening was striking the ground. The days when my soul was so soft that it could feel every breeze. It was almost two years since I had last worked. Two years of dampening all my thoughts so I could remain alive. Two years of sleeping with a lifeless man. Two years witnessing his deadness. Two whole years after being taken to their kulla.

It was water dripping from my neck to my clavicle that brought my thoughts back to the kitchen. I touched the wetness on my shirt—not tears this time. I lifted my head and saw that the force of the rain had opened the window. I grabbed a log and climbed onto the chair. I let some angry wind and rain hit my face, and then I closed the window and blocked it by wedging the log in between the two sides of the window.

Then, I heard Linda's heels marching through the hall. Whatever power she lacked in height, she made up for with her feet. I could hear her from two rooms away. I looked at the soup and saw that it was almost ready. I took the bread from the oven pan and cut it. I had prepared an appetizing meal for Linda because what she was about to hear would fall hard on her.

"It's going to be a big storm," she said, coming inside and quickly closing the mahogany door.

"Here, have some tea," I said, handing her a cup.

"Thank you, my daughter," she replied, pleased.

She laid down again on the sheepskin while I put a cloth over the white table and brought the food.

"Lunch is ready," I said, so she would do me the honor of waking up enough to sit and eat with me.

She was hungry and immediately began eating. I was not hungry, but I had to pretend that I was before I talked.

After I saw that she had eaten enough, I said, "I need to tell you something."

She was smiling blithely, in her own world, and did not hear me, or at least, did not answer.

"Listen," I said.

"Yes," she said, her head still looking down into her soup.

"I need to tell you something," I repeated.

"Oh, yes," she said, "I wanted to tell you too, that if the weather is better tomorrow—"

"Wait," I said, trying to interrupt her, but she continued.

"—and we could go to the ration supply room—"

"Stop, wait for a second," I said louder.

"—and buy some stuff and walk for—"

"Stop talking please!" I commanded.

Her spoon fell from her hand to the table. Her old lip froze above her crooked teeth as she hung on for my next words. It took me a moment to resume.

"What?" she asked, understanding that whatever it was must be important enough for her nuse to yell at her.

"I will start working again," I stated, my voice unwavering so she would hear it clearly.

"What?" she asked. "Where?"

I stared at her without speaking because she knew where.

"No, no, no, not in the fields," she said.

"Where else?" I asked.

"Your father will not allow that."

"He has to," I stated.

"In the fields?" she questioned again, rolling her dark eyes, unable to understand why I would want this.

"Yes, in the fields," I said.

"You are married now, you aren't the field girl anymore," she countered.

I did not speak but instead put the spoon full of soup in my mouth to silence any hasty reaction I might regret later.

"Don't you understand, my daughter?" she said, again asking for my agreement.

I do understand, mom, I do understand many things, I wanted to say to her, but I shut up and waited to see where she was going. I brought another spoon of soup to my lips to buy time.

"Don't you understand?" she asked, irritated now.

"Well apparently I don't," I said after swallowing.

She put her head in her hands as if she didn't want to explain it, but she had to.

"Why don't you tell me," I said again.

"We are different," she said with exasperation.

Hm, interesting.

"How so?" I asked, wanting her to say that we were different because of her son, but no, Linda pointed to something that I had forgotten about.

"We are different, and you are part of us. You are in the upper class now. Don't you see your house—where you live? Did your home have this kind of furniture? Did it have ceilings or even food?" she asked, knowing that my kulla didn't have any of those.

The sound of the spoon falling from my hand stopped her mouth from hurling any more insults. Oh Zot, give me strength to handle her, I said to myself.

"I can't change who I am, Linda," I said, trying to calm my temper.

It was the first time that she heard me call her by her name. In the last two years, I had avoided calling her any name unless I had to, and although she knew that I would never call her mother because she did not merit it, she was expecting to hear at least a "mom."

I stood up ready to leave the table.

"Bora, you are with us now," she persisted, not understanding the impact of the insults she just had thrown at me nor that they were even insults.

But she was right. I had never compared my wealth to theirs. I thought that it was an objective fact that my parents' kulla did not

193

have their furniture.

"It seems that you have forgotten who your son got married to."

"No, it's not that," she countered.

"Yes, Linda, a field girl."

"I didn't mean that," she said, holding her head down.

"But at least you knew who I was," I said, implying that I had not known that her son was a hidden, useless man.

"You don't understand," she repeated.

"Oh please, of course I do. I understand very, very clearly that you wanted to save your son. Why don't you say that out loud? Say it, so you can stop pretending with yourself. Why don't you say that the three of you sacrificed a field girl for yourself, for your name?"

Linda was silent, her head bowed.

"Say it," I ordered. "Say it!" I yelled.

She still didn't move or speak. Her mind seemed to be sinking deep into silence, like when a sinner repents.

"It doesn't hurt me anymore," I said, "so just say it. I live with you and your futile son, and I know how it is, and I don't need your pretense to make it better. But you knew who I was and what you were getting from the beginning. You all did, but I didn't," I finished bitterly, whacked by the forces coming from my insides that had waited for two years to talk.

I stood up and took my plate to the sink. I grabbed the cleaning cloth and squeezed out the water with a vengeance. My heart was beating out loud. Behind my back she was exhaling without uttering a word. At that moment, it was clear that we didn't have to say anything else since it was obvious we understood the same matters differently. I washed my plate and left her in the kitchen.

I went to the back of the kulla, put my spine against the wall, and slid down to the ground. I hugged my knees and took in the sheets of rain to erase my rage. The cold brought me the relief I needed.

Soon my clothes were soaked from the rain, and when a cough began grabbing at my throat, I moved inside. The mahogany door was half open, and I could see Linda standing inside, looking out at the storm, full of sorrow. A trail of water from my clothes followed me up the stairs, to the hall, and into the bedroom, marking my route. I was shivering from the cold until I dropped the clothes on the floor and got under the covers. The red flower sewn on the cover of the blanket leapt up and down until my furiously beating heart slowed with sleep.

CHAPTER 25

I won the battle over me working, and it was because of Linda. Since the first time I saw her from the window of my family's kulla, I knew that she was the head of her family. Linda had conquered her men. But now, she had raised the white flag and was ruled by the field girl.

Leke and my husband did not speak to me during the weeks they were deciding the matter.

Then one day, during our lunch, Linda said, "You can start work."

I didn't thank her. After exploiting me for herself and her son, that was the least she could do. I did not feel that I owed her anything, not even the clothes I was wearing. And, after our last conversation, she understood that their wealth did not seduce me. Caging an underprivileged daughter in a lavish kulla wasn't enough. In fact, there was nothing that she or her son or her husband could do that could make me forgive them.

I pulled the plates from the lunch table and brought a cup of weak tea for her. After washing the dishes, I noticed she was hunched over on the sheepskin.

"Don't begin work right now," she said.

I sat down on the chair, knowing that I had to converse with her and that one of us might say something that would hurt us both.

"Why?" I asked, even though I was not interested in her reasoning.

"Because it's winter," she responded.

"I see," I replied, realizing how used to her comfort she was.

"Wait a little bit," she uttered.

"A bit?" I asked, wondering what a bit was for a woman who did nothing all day and had nowhere to be.

"Wait for spring, it will be warmer," she explained.

I didn't respond because I knew something bitter might come from my tongue.

"Spring would be better," she uttered again.

Better—I turned the word around in my mind and examined it. Perhaps she is hoping I will forget about work by spring, and I will stay with her all day, I thought. That's what better must mean in Linda's mind. It was a Thursday, nearly three weeks after we had first talked about me going to work in the fields.

"Tomorrow you have to come with me to the town offices," I replied.

To be placed on a farm, Linda had to escort me to the town hall. She didn't respond, noisily swallowing her weak tea instead, but I saw the wrinkles on her throat loosening one by one in agreement.

The next morning, Linda was wearing a black shirt, and I was wearing her bright colors. Once Leke and their son left for work, we headed to the party office. As I followed her on the road, I realized that she had bought my upper-class clothes with love and vision and that now she was dissatisfied because they would be turned into shoveling garments. It was the first time I saw her embarrassed about walking with me, and I felt ashamed that I was enjoying it. It was comical and sad to see her downcast and grieving in her black shirt. Only women like Linda had the privilege of being downhearted about their nuse working.

We arrived at the party office in the town hall, and I had to do the talking because Linda was silent.

"Hi," I said to the clerk.

"How can I help you ladies?" she said, looking at the papers on her desk.

Banners posted high on the walls decorated her office in proper Communist style. *Jemi Zeri i Popullit* (We are the Voice of the People), one of them said. Photographs of high-performing miners and model laborers, called *Stakhanovites* (Exceptional Workers), hung next to the banners. Stakhanovites were the ones who produced double their quota, and being designated a Stakhanovite was like being named a hero. In return, you got a good reputation and a portrait of yourself in your local party office. Teachers praised the Stakhanovites in an attempt to install good work ethics in us. It was as if they knew that we were all going to become laborers.

The leader's portrait was on the clerk's desk. He was smiling stingily and tightly, but somehow his smile looked ideal. His orderly suit shouted self-assurance and determination. Every official building from schools to hospitals to government offices had to have a portrait of our leader in case we forgot his face. Next to his portrait on the clerk's desk was his voice—the radio.

"So, I don't have all day for you ladies," the clerk said, hitting her pen on the desk impatiently and waiting for Linda to speak.

"I would like to start to work again," I said, shifting her attention to me.

"Very well. The state always needs its people to work. That's what makes us great, right?" she asked me.

I was startled but did not blink an eye. I was afraid she was provoking me.

"Right," I said.

"And what's your occupation?" she asked.

"I used to work in the fields," I said.

She pulled her legs out from under the desk, stood up, and slowly looked from the top of my head all the way down to my feet.

"You worked in the fields?" she asked skeptically, as if I might be fooling her.

198

"Yes, ma'am," I said, petrified by her.

"When?"

"From age sixteen to twenty."

"How old are you now?"

"Twenty-two."

"Then what about the last two years?"

"I married."

She cast a disparaging look at Linda and looked her up and down, as if trying to assess if it was Linda who was making me go back to work.

"I see," the clerk said and rolled her eyes.

Linda shrunk from the humiliation.

"And now you have to go back to the farms," the clerk said. "I need your identification card."

I didn't have it, but before I could even begin searching my mind as to where it was, Linda handed it to her.

"Alright, workers of the world, unite!" the clerk said, reflexively repeating the Marxist maxim.

Moments later, she handed me a sheet of paper with the field's name written on it.

That night, I put the food down on the white table and said to the three of them, "At the beginning of March, I'll begin work."

I said it not because they weren't aware that I was going back to work. I said it to establish that they didn't have an inanimate object for a nuse. Leke became upset that a poor field girl was asserting herself so strongly in his kulla. Linda smiled from joy because I wouldn't be starting work right away. I had already accepted her request of giving her a couple of months to get used to the idea that she would be alone all day. On the other hand, my husband had lost his appetite and seemed to be debating with himself about what to do with a wife who could not just be dull and quiet. After there was nothing more to be said, I washed the dishes and went to the bedroom and laid down.

My husband came into the room later than me, as he always did, hoping to find me asleep. On evenings when he found me still awake, he would quickly turn off his light and say good night. For two years in our bed, he had never let his body touch me in the dark, even by accident. He was like a ghost, yet his flesh had never shifted to a nebulous form. In the morning, he unfailingly woke up earlier than me and left in order to not encounter me. However, he would always say good morning in the kitchen, and he thanked me when I served his coffee. That was as far as our marriage interactions went. Some days, I was fine with that, but other days, I just wanted to disappear.

CHAPTER 26

Three months later, I woke up early on a Monday morning and left for the fields before Leke and the nameless woke up. I didn't stay to eat breakfast because the three of them would have gotten up by then and would have sat there judging the new addition to the labor workers who was in their kulla. I was wearing the work corset that I had buried in the closet and the skirt that Mother had given me because it was worn and more proper for the fields. I had tools with me that I had found the day before and a big lunch to share with the other women.

It was the beginning of April, and the cold winds were still there, pushing my frame into the bushes and thorns. In March, Linda had asked me to stay home one more month because she was sorrowful about losing her companion, so I had waited until April in order to please her. Despite the chills in the early dawn, I felt satisfied that my body was going to perform something useful after so long.

A few neighbors passed me saying, "*Si ke njeft*" (How did you rise)?

They were my new work people, and from my worn skirt, they knew I was one of them. After we exchanged a good morning, I followed them until we all lined up at the entrance to the farm.

"Bora Zefi," I yelled, when it was my turn, to the man marking the absences.

It had been a very long time since I had said my name out loud. As I left the line and walked toward the farm, the one behind me yelled his name, and then a she yelled her name, and then a he, then a she, a he, a he, a she, and last, a she.

"Zefi, wait!" the foreman shouted.

Upon hearing my name, I halted. Then, I walked back and stood a few steps away from the line. I watched other workers yell their names and rush to go do their jobs, wondering if the foreman had called me back because I was a new worker. Maybe he needed to verify me before I started. When the last worker left, the foreman looked at me and then began flipping through the pages of his notebook.

"Zefi . . . Zefi, Zefi, Zefi, Zefi," he mumbled while he was searching. Within a minute he gave up his search and said, "I don't think you are supposed to be on this farm."

"Isn't this the tobacco field?" I asked.

"Yes, it is," he said and started flipping the pages again.

I held my breath.

"Your name isn't here," he said confidently and closed the notebook.

"I don't know why my name isn't there," I replied. "They told me to come to the tobacco field, I checked last week."

"Here, in Manati?" he asked.

"Yes," I said, "are there any other tobacco fields in Manati?"

"No, this is the only one," he replied.

What now? I wanted to ask. But I stood silent and reserved, waiting for him to tell me what to do, just as a woman was expected to do. Go to work, and we'll figure it out later, I was expecting to hear.

"Look, it's better to go home and revisit the party office tomorrow," he said.

My eyes locked onto his face. I was panicked at the thought of going back to that kulla to be a lifeless nuse for yet another day.

"Look, if you work, I can't give you the points because I have no name to assign them to, and you will not get paid for your work," he said apologetically.

I don't need the points. I just want to work, I wanted to say, exploding inside. But he would never believe me. He stood waiting for me to leave, looking at me like I was crazy, when suddenly I remembered—my name was not Zefi anymore.

"Can you please look for Doda? Bora Doda?" I asked.

"Doda," he said.

He was looking at me skeptically, but he opened his notebook again to check for it. That was the first time I called myself Doda. Bora Doda. I was ashamed, and my eyes sank toward the ground.

"So, you are—Bora Doda?" he asked.

"Yes," I said, looking at the dirt.

"Well, if you are"—he eyed me suspiciously—"I found you."

"Thank you, sir," I said.

"Alright then, you can go and work for 'Bora Doda,'" he said, still doubtful.

"Sure, sure," I replied obediently.

And don't worry, you will see me coming every single day here and calling out her name, I wanted to add, but I left before getting into any deeper trouble.

The tobacco plants looked a couple of weeks old. The crops had grown young leaves on every row.

"Here, grab your container," said a woman, handing me a pump to spray the plant with pesticide. "There is no time to waste. Just spray your row for now and look if there are any dry or rotten brown leaves."

I had not worked with tobacco before, but the only thing I needed to know was that I had to work hard. The container was at least a hundred pounds and broke my back within seconds. The field faced the sea, and the winds were coming directly at us, making it hard to see or even to walk. I sprayed half of my row before lunch, and at 12:00 on the dot, I gladly threw the pump on the ground and went to eat.

When I got in the line to wash my hands, I noticed other workers were peeling dirt from under their nails. I looked at mine and felt proud to see some dirt gathered there too. Finally, my hands didn't look so futile. I still cleaned them well, and after I shook my hands to dry, I looked for a place to find some water to quench my thirst. I noticed a woman on her knees at a stream. She was pulling water from the stream into her palms to drink with her hands. I went and did the same, and when I lifted my head, I saw a frog standing on a wide leaf staring at me and croaking. Mesmerized, I stared at his throat swelling up and at his big, reptile-like eyes, which were inspecting me back. After a short time, the frog got bored and lifted its tiny, green body and jumped away. After that tête-à-tête along the water, I officially re-welcomed myself to the unofficial field workers' association.

The white sheet was on the ground, and once I sat down, I placed my food with the others' and began eating.

"To whom are you?" a woman holding her baby asked me.

"To Doda," I said, remembering this time.

"I didn't know that Doda's had a daughter," another woman replied.

"No, they only have one son," an old woman responded, scanning me thoroughly.

"Yes, I'm their nuse," I said, putting an end to their speculations and hoping for less attention.

"Welcome," the woman with the baby said.

I put some food in my mouth, feeling pleased by the woman's welcome.

"You are a nuse, did you just get married?" a girl my age next to me asked.

I swallowed a piece of cheese and bread. "Two years ago," I responded to her.

"Nice," she retorted, "I'm not married yet."

She was one of the ones that the saying *ka ngel ne der* (was left in the door) was about.

"I see," I uttered.

"But I want to," she assured me.

"Well, then you will," I assured her.

"How old are you?" she asked.

I didn't want to talk more, but I guessed that I had to.

"I'm twenty-two," I responded.

"Me too!" she reacted excitedly. "And did you just get married?" she continued, not remembering that she had asked the same question a second ago.

No, I got married two years ago, I should have responded. Instead, I gave her a plain yes, hoping that the conversation would end.

"Nice, nice," she said and got lost in her own thoughts.

When I got up, I saw the old woman still looking at me. I began thinking that either she had heard me lying about my marriage and was thinking that I was dishonest, or that she knew about the Doda family. Linda didn't talk to her neighbors who were field workers, and the old woman was a field woman. So, the woman most likely didn't know the Dodas. Also, we rarely had miqtë coming to our odë. Besides a few colleagues of Leke's, I hadn't seen any other visitors. Linda had friends but did not like them coming to our kulla, so we usually met them in the ration supply room. As far as I knew, my husband had no friends or colleagues, although how would I have known since he spoke to me so rarely.

The girl introduced herself while we folded our lunch bags.

"I'm Roza," she said.

"Nice talking to you, I'm Bora," I said, and we both got back to work.

I cleaned my skirt and my hands well before I left the field. I had sprayed the other half row of the plants, and my back was hurting. I was still wearing the headscarf from work as I headed to the kulla because it kept my head warm. The whiny wind had never stopped for the day, and part of my hair had slipped out of my headscarf and was dancing in the gusts. In the distance, I could see the grand beauty of the mountains covered in white. The walk from the field to the Doda's trojë was thirty minutes, give or take. Since I was walking by myself and didn't have to hold anyone's arm, I enjoyed it immensely. I realized how much I had missed feeling the physical exhaustion that comes from working the land.

It was almost eight p.m. when I entered the kulla. I wasn't planning to change to be the good-looking, servile, upper-class nuse for them. So, I went straight to the kitchen. The three of them were inside, sitting in their usual arrangement: Linda close to her son and her son close to his father, all on the sheepskin, lost in their family matters.

"Good evening," I said.

"Welcome back," Linda replied warmly, clearly having missed seeing her daughter-in-law.

"Have you eaten?" I asked her.

"No, we were waiting for you," she replied, proud of herself that she had waited for the field nuse.

Leke and his son did not respond, but I was surprised that they had also waited for me. Leke was reading one of his notebooks. I put the tablecloth on top of the white table and brought the plates. Then, we ate in silence.

When we were almost finished, Leke asked, "So, how was your day?" finally addressing me but with a hint of arrogance.

Even his son seemed taken aback by Leke's tone. That was probably the biggest exhibition of emotion that I had seen from him in a long time.

"Good," I responded to Leke, looking at my plate.

"Are you tired?" he continued, not missing a second.

"Yes I am."

"So, you didn't miss the fields then," he remarked.

"I didn't say that," I said, irritated that he had manipulated my words.

"Why would you want to work in the fields? People are desperate to leave, and you go back," he said, revealing that he was annoyed with my decision.

I looked to Linda to speak out against her crass husband, but her tongue was cut, just as her son's was.

"I don't know," I replied and raised my head to his level. "You seem to know better than me what people want."

"I know that you have everything," he thundered back.

Sure, everything that a poor uneducated daughter needs, I thought.

"Everything"—I held myself, calmly peering at him—"and nothing," I said.

"Is this how you talk to your father-in-law?" he bellowed. "Is this what they taught you in your kulla?"

I felt like I was losing my balance like a train on the edge of the rails shaking and grinding on the tracks. He knew very well that his people had taught me, and that's why he had chosen me. He was pushing my temper, and I had no choice but to derail.

"No, actually this is how my teachers, like you, Father, taught me," I said.

And you can take me back to my kulla if you dare, I thought.

Linda's quivers shook my chair, and her son held his head down in disappointment, waiting for the battle to end. I didn't know who he was disappointed with—his wife, his father, or both of us. Leke's forehead was striped with wrinkles and full of rage, partially because there was nothing he could do. He couldn't ask his son to beat me and put me in my place because, despite my husband's futile body, he was not a violent man. Leke couldn't take me back to my parents because he needed me to save his son's reputation and his own. He couldn't reach out his hand and hit me because—how can I say it— because he was an upper-class, educated, and noble man.

Leke's own wealthy manners were burning him up, and he deserved it. Look what a poor ignorant field girl can think and say, I wanted to tell him. I could see every thought running through his mind: it was just unacceptable; how dare she; how dare she be a person and not a poor voiceless daughter. And truly, how dare I? I thought. It wasn't enough that I had to tolerate their life. On top of that, I had to take their offensive implications about who I was. He deserved a rude daughter-in-law because, when you know that your hands are dirty, you don't fool yourself by speaking about the other's dirt. He shouldn't have started this, but he had.

Leke never finished his plate that night. He was left only swallowing his thoughts. Linda looked hurt when he closed the mahogany door. It seemed that she was about to fall into deep sobbing, but she held off until she got to her room. Her son, unable to do or say anything, sank into the sheepskin as if it were a bathtub. The neat collar of his shirt was twisted backwards, and all of a sudden, a whiff of a reminiscent smell came from his body. It was not a cologne. It was the hospital's smell, the scent of chlorine. The same smell that had choked an eight-year-old girl looking for her mother in the halls of the hospital. I realized that the smell in the hospital had been better because it had lasted only seven weeks. As his wife, I had to smell his sterile chlorine scent for life.

How damaged he was made me sick because he was such a handsome and well-composed doctor. How does he cure people when he can't cure himself? I wondered. How does he handle his patient's sickness when he can't handle his own? He was as ill as they were. He diagnosed them, yet he didn't dare to label himself. How could he, a doctor, never have given me a chance? He never gave us a plan, a dream, a prescription for tomorrow. He didn't even pretend that we could make it. He never even said a word to his victim. How many times had I hoped for him to see me as his patient and cure me in his lovely doctor's robe? He didn't have to love me, he just had to treat me. How hard was that for a man who had taken an oath to take care of his people? How could such a man have deserted his calling and fate? As a daughter and his wife, I had no one but him. How could he have abandoned me like that? He unfolded his machine-like, long legs, got up, and grasped the handle of the door. Then, he and his sanitized doctor's hands left.

After the dishes, I went up to the bedroom. It was the first night that he was in bed before me. He had closed his eyes, but the light on his nightstand was on. I changed out of my dirty clothes and quickly put on plain, white undergarments. I got under the covers, feeling scorched from exhaustion. He turned off his light and, soon, was breathing evenly.

In as short time as a flame leaps up, I dreamed of touching his body. Then, deeper in the dream, he moved toward me, as he had longed for this too, and for once, his skin was warm. I smelled his lively flesh for the first time and felt his limbs meshing with mine. He began kissing my neck and loading me up with more warmth. Even though his lips had never kissed me before, they felt familiar. He then moved on top of my body. His head floated from my neck to my chest. My apples suddenly blushed from his touch. He held them softly, just how I had always hoped and wanted. He was mine. I breathed deeply. His chlorine smell had evaporated, and his hands felt new as if they were another man's. He was loving my apples without biting them. He kept his fingers on them and moved his head down, kissing my ribs one by one. He was tasting all of me. How long had I waited for this hedonic state? He kissed me on my sides and went to my stomach. My stomach began turning, but I shushed it.

"I'm now yours," I sighed, feeling his hand on my apples.

He moved back to my neck, and as he traveled inside me, I met his eyes for the first time. They were all green. The one with emerald-green eyes had come back and saved me.

CHAPTER 27

"Bora Doda!" I yelled out.

The foreman lifted his head and took a good look at me. Each day, he seemed to expect to see another woman, but each day, it was me he was looking at. He seemed convinced and quite concerned that I was either an ordinary spy or a high-level rat for the capital, not just a married woman who had forgotten her new husband's last name. I marched away to begin my work.

I hoisted the big pesticide pump and balanced it on my back. An older woman was already spraying in the row to the left of me. I fastened the belt around my belly, grabbed the rubber, and began spraying too. By the fourth plant, we were both fatigued from the weight of the pump. It didn't seem like our bodies were going to get used to the enormous weight, but we persisted. I held on because the old woman was holding on, and she held on because I had to learn to hold on.

After spraying the entire line, I threw the pump on the ground, took the shovel, and moved the stones to loosen the soil around each plant. First, second, third, fourth plant, and so on until I finished the row. Coming back, I weeded the stalks and checked for the bugs that could damage the tobacco. It was midday and time to throw the shovel down to take some rest. The tobacco had grown, and it tickled my kneecaps as I crossed through the rows. In a few weeks, the plants would be ready for harvest, and then we would begin the drying process.

It was a cold day, but the wind was singing mildly because April was almost over. I joined the line for the water bucket so I could rub the dirt from my skirt. I washed my hands, no longer worrying too much about the dirt under my nails—I now could think of a thousand reasons why the upper-classes' clean hands were worse than our dirty fingers. When I was cleaning the brown stains from my skirt, Roza came over and stood over me. We had already said hello that morning, but she seemed to want to talk more. I left the bucket for the next in line and gave her my full attention while I fixed my headscarf.

"*Si je sot Bora?*" she said.

"I'm good, how are you?" I asked her back.

"Good," she said, a bit sad, and we both headed toward the white sheet.

"Let's sit together and have lunch and we can talk," I said.

"Sure," she replied, pleased, and sat down next to me.

We began eating, but Roza was quiet. Perhaps she isn't ready to speak yet, I thought. The other women began to chat, but I wasn't listening because I became captivated by a hawk circling above the field. Even the gray sky seemed wary of its roving eyes. The mountains with the white peaks stood in the background, keeping watch. When the hawk left the ashy sky, a few swallows flew overhead, reminding me that spring was about to arrive down in the low country. Then, before I knew it, I was thinking about the highlanders and their smiles. I had forgotten about them, and I remembered how I once had a mountain smile that was seen only by a green-eyed man.

"Bora," Roza said. "Bora"—she poked me with her elbow—"Bora!"

"What?" I asked.

She pointed to the other women with her head.

211

"Oh Zot, and what?" I said, apathetic.

"Listen," she said, wanting me to eavesdrop on their hushed voices.

"It's just gossip, I don't care," I responded haughtily.

"Listen," she insisted, so I obliged her.

"—it's too long," a woman with narrow eyes was saying.

"It happens. I know it took even longer for my cousin," said another with a long, goose-like neck, her arms full with her restless baby.

"I don't know, I'm just saying she is lucky," the narrow-eyed one responded.

"Lucky!? Why is she lucky?" the goose-necked asked.

"My husband would have left me," the narrow-eyed said.

"Perhaps he loves her," the goose-necked replied. "He is a doctor, he could have any daughter he wants for a nuse. Two years waiting for her to carry his child. No other man would have wai—"

I couldn't listen to it any longer. I lifted my heavy skirt, got up, and left. I walked straight down the first row, knowing that my back was being crossed with their bitter words. Perhaps now Roza would understand that being married could be worse than being a daughter left in your door. My heart was ready to shatter into pieces. Even in the fields where I belonged, my life was not giving me a rest. I passed through the rows of tobacco until I disappeared from their spiteful eyes. When I reached the end of the last plant, I fell to my knees. There, I could sob freely about my fate since everyone was still broken for lunch.

Kneeling on the dirt, I waited. And waited. But no tears flowed. They were all drowning inside my heart, cursing my nameless husband. Why did he have such futile hands that couldn't touch me? Why was I still a daughter and not a woman after two years of marriage? I was so ashamed that even my dreams had chosen to fantasize about Kol. Without any tears to drown out my misery, I closed my eyes and dug my fingers into the loam to sense the earth. The soil was cold, and when I felt it, I finally began to sob. Tears poured down from my jaw, moistening the dirt around my fingers. I felt the cold, wet earth, and with my fingers inside her, I wished for her to take me. I wished to make my life go away.

By the end of the day, I had finished spraying and weeding several rows of plants. I was heading up to the field entrance when I saw the narrow-eyed woman coming from the opposite side of the field. To avoid meeting her path, I crossed the tobacco lines. I couldn't stand the idea of her thinking that I was lucky.

"Bora, wait, I'm done too," Roza shouted when I crossed her row.

It was the end of the day, and still she hadn't had the chance to talk to me about her earlier sadness. She was even quieter now, and perhaps I was the reason for the gloominess on her freckled, red face. If she asks, I thought, I have no explanation to use except for the one that the gossipy lady gave. I am lucky, I was ready to utter while Roza poured water over my dark hands, but an explanation wasn't necessary because she kept mute about her thoughts.

"Bora Doda," the foreman called as I was dusting off my skirt.

"Yes?" I responded.

"You don't take breaks," he said.

"I do," I replied.

"So then why were you not with the others on their break today?" he asked.

"I took a short one . . . I had to get back to work," I said, not caring anymore if he thought that I was a spy or even the enemy. My life was far more pointless than what he could envision. He gave me a glance that informed me that he knew that I was lying. I was, so I said nothing.

"You work a lot," he uttered while opening his notebook.

I couldn't understand what he was recording in his book since he had measured our production earlier. When he was done writing, he ripped the sheet off, walked toward me, and handed me the sheet.

"Here," he said.

I took it without asking what it was about.

213

"You weren't here on your break," he stated again. "Everyone else had to answer these questions. Please do it fast. I don't want to be here all day."

"Sure," I replied.

Four lines of the page had questions about numbers. It took me roughly ten minutes to solve the four mathematical problems.

When I handed it to him, he said, "Have a nice Sunday."

He seemed cheerful that I didn't keep him any longer.

"Same to you," I responded.

I took my bag, and before I left the entrance, a sorrowful woman stopped me to say good night. I understood that she was sincerely sorry about my life and the gossipy ladies. I replied to her without bitterness in my voice, thinking that Linda was right about not wanting me to work. Perhaps she knew that people would talk. Perhaps that's why she stayed hidden. Perhaps that's what I should do too, stay home and look at their nice rooms with ceilings and just lay on the sheepskin.

That night, I wasn't hungry, and I went straight to bed. I was too tired. I just wanted to sleep and not wake up. I wanted to not see Linda, Leke, or him again. I was tired of their faces, and perhaps even more, I was shattered by the fact that I had to live with them forever. I just couldn't handle that anymore. I needed everything to go away. I closed my eyes and wished to sleep before my dead husband laid on the bed. I couldn't live anymore next to a ghost, and I would have given anything to not have to share a bed with him. My chest exhaled while my breast throbbed from waiting so long. I was too tired, and as I lay there, my body began to depart. I was so exhausted that I never felt him lifting the covers and putting the cold air under them as he slid into bed.

I slept deeply and dreamed of the wonderful lives that I couldn't have in my present one. I saw fields filled with lulekuqe and Lule running between their stems. She was as happy as she had been as a puppy. Above Lule, I was flying sedately in an ashy sky like a hawk. Then, I could see the mountains, and when I got closer, I could see the mountain guy waving at me. He was smiling, and this time, I smiled at him too. I swooped down, and we approached each other, so close our palms touched, and then, we let our lips meet. I saw his eyes were green instead of blue. A cloud flew over our heads, quickly traversing across the sky in a strong wind. By the time it traveled down to the country, the green eyes were gone from the mountain.

Then, I heard Lule chewing on something, and I saw the mountain light shining on her belly. The sunlight was so soothing that I sat on a rock watching it for a time, letting it nearly blind my eyes. Then, a few rays crept into my throat and warmed my voice, and suddenly, I was soaring once again. From the skies above, I could hear the spring water roaring, and I looked down and saw Mother working in our yard. I called her, but she couldn't hear me. So, I sat on a rock near her, but she couldn't see me either. Lule was there on our hill, too. She came to my legs, and I rubbed her belly in the hot sunlight. The sunlight became sharper and sharper, burning my chest. The hot rays seared through my throat to my chest and arced into my heart. Then Lule started barking. I turned my head to see her. She was staring at me angrily, baring her teeth, and in a blaze of fire she bit the rock, jolting me awake.

I woke up having just another day to attend to without a husband. The room was freezing and felt lonely. I got out from under the blanket and kneeled down on the cold, cement floor. I dropped my head to the edge of the bed. I wanted to tear up, but this time, I had no earth to put my fingers into for solace. I did not want to live this purposeless life anymore. I looked around to find my weapon like a wounded soldier seeks the respite of the heavens. I saw an electric plug. Tears flooded my eyes as I jammed my fingers through the holes and waited, desperate to depart. It didn't take me. I inhaled some tears and broke the plug to try to find the cables. I saw them and inhaled again as I touched the thin split of the cords. It began to take me, and I held on even more. It shook me, and still, I held on.

The sun came back, and I saw Lule on top of our hill, and Mother was there, bursting with glee. The light was divine, and

Mother and I laid down, soothed by it. Lule ran over and licked my scarred arm and then barked at the sky to show me a rainbow forming. As one color was melting to another, my eyes were locked to its shimmering shades. My heart was delighted as I realized that I was in the heavens, and the rainbow filled the sky, its colors sublime.

"Bora! Bora!" It was Linda calling my name. "Bora!"

I could hear her, but from far away. The rainbow's colors were so bright, so blinding, that I could not see through them to see her, but I could still hear her screaming and begging me not to go. Her voice came close to my ear, and she yelled so hard that she rattled my body, and the rainbow cracked, splitting into shards. Her voice became a moaning whisper, raspy from screaming, as she said that it was her motherly love that was at fault. Lule had bared her teeth when Linda's voice cracked the sky, and she was growling in a low, steady hum. Then tears fell from Lule's eyes, and she came to me and her tears dripped onto my face, and then her tears turned into rain. The rain washed over me, and before it stopped, my eyes opened and I saw Linda, and she was crying.

CHAPTER 28

It was a Monday, and a green vehicle filled with soldiers cut in front of my path when I was on my way to work. I quickly moved next to the bunker that crossed the main road and stood there with my head bowed, waiting for them to pass. Where is the enemy? I wondered. I was twenty-two years old, and beyond the enemies I had in my kulla, I hadn't seen any proof that foreign spies even existed. When the vehicle had disappeared from sight, I lifted my head and scanned the road to make sure there wasn't a rat recording my moves.

Soon, I was calling out my name to the foreman and contemplating whether he was a rat. I had been working in that field for two months by then, and up until a few days before, I had not considered that our foreman might be a rat. But lately, he had seemed anxious and a bit worried, and I wondered why. Also, he had written down our production points for the last two months, even though he was just the administrator for the party office, not our brigadier. And, near the end of the week before, there had been no doubt in his voice when he had called my name. Perhaps he's realized that I'm not a rat, I thought. I had not come to a firm conclusion yet. It was difficult to identify spies, but it was something we were forced to do.

Lightning was lashing the mountains that morning, and in some tokë, it was pouring. It was sunny down in the fields, but we could see the dark storm moving toward us. The thunder and lightning didn't scare me, but some of the workers were asking the foreman for permission to leave early so they would not get caught in the storm. But the foreman said no, leaving them praying for safety.

It was two weeks since Linda had screamed in my ear and forced me out of the heavens. And since then, she had taken the lead in saving me. She had moved me out of my bedroom to hers, and she had become my bed companion. I didn't want to sleep with her, but I had moved into her room without a protest, like a poor daughter. I thought my life would be the same any place in her kulla.

The tobacco plants had yielded flowers, and I began by breaking their heads and separating them from the stalk. All the flowers had to be removed to allow the tobacco to grow well. We topped the plant early on when the flower was still a bud for the plant to have more energy to grow healthier leaves and make good tobacco. I had no clue about the quality of the brown product as I had never smoked, but that's what I was told. The plant was almost three feet tall. I checked each leaf and removed the ones that had discolored spots. In less than a week, we would have to begin collecting the tobacco leaves that were brown and fully ripened.

"*Si ke njeft*" (Good morning), an old lady next to my row said.

"Good morning," I replied even though it was almost afternoon."You are Linda's daughter-in-law?" she asked, despite already knowing the answer.

I lifted my headscarf, telling her that I was, and recognized that she was the old woman who had stared at me on our lunch break when I had first started working in the fields again.

"Linda and I are cousins," she replied.

"That's interesting," I murmured, as we both knew that I had not seen her once in our kulla.

Perhaps she had been at our wedding, but I had not looked at any of the guests. I deduced that maybe they were distant cousins.

The foreman shouted from afar, and we both cut our chat short and turned our heads toward the entrance. Some men in secondhand uniforms were gathered around the foreman.

"The meeting is starting," the old lady said.

She was frightened by the men in uniform, so she immediately headed toward the entrance to the field, walking as quickly as she was able.

"What meeting?" I asked, following her.

I could see that all the other workers had dropped what they were doing and were heading toward the men in uniform, too.

"We're going to have a new brigadier," she said.

"Why, where is the old one?"

"He was a spy, they told us," she said softly, so as not to be heard by others. "He has been taken."

Startled, I didn't respond.

"I knew his family," the old lady said as she stopped for a moment to tighten her headscarf, squeezing her sagging neck. "He had a fine wife and now she will be a widow but that's our world."

When we bowed, dug, sprayed, and shoveled it didn't seem that there were many of us, but now I could see that, together, we were many field workers. As we got closer, I counted four soldiers with an officer—six including the foreman—waiting for us. They had chosen to align their announcement with our break time so that no labor time would be wasted. As if it wasn't enough that we had to work from seven a.m. to seven p.m., now we had to wait for their meeting to end, hoping that we would get some time to sit and eat. Not that field people had much to eat, but at least our guts could loosen up and refresh with a bit of rest.

We waited in silence once we were all gathered. At military gatherings, everyone was afraid of what might happen and tried to be as invisible as possible. I tightened my headscarf, pulling it down a palm lower to hide my face. The five men were wearing army hats with their secondhand uniforms, and they were standing next to each other on a slightly raised patch of ground, looking down on us. Of course, it was already understood that we were below them and that their authority was above us. No one dared argue with that. But standing above us on elevated ground was just rubbing it in. Blood must have forgotten to travel all the way up to their heads because their faces were pale and cold. They looked soulless.

As we waited for the start of the meeting, I looked down and watched a worm emerging from the malleable soil. But the old lady elbowed me to pay attention, so I lifted my eyes and looked at the great, gray-rock mountains instead. I began to wonder who the next brigadier would be. Would they bring a new person? If yes, no one had come with them. Maybe they would send an operative from another farm to be our brigadier. Or perhaps our foreman would be the next brigadier. That would make perfect sense since he knew us and the job already. Maybe that's why he'd been anxious lately. But that raised another question—were we going to have a new foreman and who would it be?

"You all know that we have to proceed," the officer said. "This job is difficult."

My attention fell on the ground to find the worm again. It emerged from the plowed soil then disappeared into another hole.

"Bora Doda to proceed up front."

Just as I realized that the officer had just called my name, the worm reappeared again playing with the earth. I was unable to believe what I had just heard. I looked up at the officer who had just spoken and waited to hear him speak again. He was just standing there, looking at the crowd of workers. I thought I misheard and bowed my head again.

"Bora Doda to come up front at once!"

I felt my spine getting chills. I hid under my headscarf, trying to convince myself that it was an error or that I had not heard him right. That's impossible, I thought, there must be a confusion. Out of the corner of my headscarf, I could see other workers searching the crowd with their eyes.

"Bora Doda, the new brigadier, to report to the front now!" the officer ordered.

My mind struggled to collect the pieces of the statement that the officer had shouted. In disbelief, my ears started ringing.

"We will not continue until the new brigadier comes up front. Bora Doda to report to the front," he said, sinisterly this time.

A steady hum plowed into my head, making my mind dazed. I couldn't hear anything through the roaring in my ears. I was twenty-two years old. How could I be a brigadier? The earth seemed to be spinning, and my knees started to buckle. But a moment before I passed out, a hand pushed my back, making my body lurch forward.

"Bora, you have to move," the old lady said.

One after the other, my legs took me slowly forward, and I moved through the crowd, my head hidden under my headscarf.

"This must be a mistake," I mumbled over and over.

The workers didn't care about my muttering because they just wanted to finish the meeting so they could get time to have lunch. Somehow my legs supported me all the way up front to the five cold military men. My heartbeat became slow once I was standing right in front of them, so slow that I was ready to pass out.

"Bora Doda, you are selected to be the next brigadier," the officer yelled above my head.

Then, he stretched out his hand, demanding a handshake. I couldn't grasp where I was.

"Do you hear me?" his stiff face said while his hand was hanging.

"Yes," I replied and straightened out my arm, looking to the ground in hopes that the earth would open and take me. But it didn't. Why me? I wanted to ask, but I was too scared to say anything whatsoever as he strangled my hand with his.

"Yes, what?!" he yelled.

"Yes, sir, I heard you," I said, awakened by the pain throbbing in my hand from his grip.

The officer then produced a notebook, which he quickly flipped through, showing me the names of the workers.

"This is your brigade," he said and handed me the notebook.

I took it but avoided meeting his hardened face.

"Do you hear me?" he said, ordering me again to show attention.

"Yes, sir!"

"You are a brigadier now, you are responsible for the production of your brigade and your workers," he said definitively. "Do you understand?"

"Yes, sir," I replied.

"Do. You. Understand?!" he bellowed, demanding that I look him in the eye.

"Yes, sir!" I said, frightened but staring at his cold eyes as if I were seeing the dreqi.

Once he was convinced that I understood my new position, he turned his attention to the workers.

"Everyone is released, back to your activities," he ordered.

All the men and women scattered instantly like a swarm of insects sensing a predator. I opened the notebook and saw that each page was filled with tiny squares, the kind used to solve math equations.

"Doda," he yelled.

"Yes, sir!"

"Name, work duty, hours—equals workday pay. We know that you are good at this," he said, then he abruptly turned his back and left. Followed by the fourth army man, the third, the second, and the last. All in a straight line.

The foreman was there and breathed out a sigh of relief once he was sure they were all gone.

"Did you forget your name again, Doda?" he said and chuckled.

I was still stunned and could not utter a word. I knew the foreman had doubts about me before, but now I was sure that he was convinced that I was a spy. What else could he be asking himself besides: Why would they pick a woman for a brigadier? And a woman in her twenties? The answer he'd tell himself was obvious—because she is a spy. My legs were still shaking.

"Congratulations! You did very well on the questions," he said.

"Questions? What, questions?" I asked, shriveling.

"You are good at math," he stated. "They searched your school years, and the questions I gave you."

Astonished and not knowing what to say, I stood fixed like a reed. The foreman began waving at a man who was coming toward us from outside the entrance. The man was not wearing military clothes, yet he was holding papers in his hand.

"Welcome trainer," the foreman said to the man and left us alone. The trainer introduced himself and demanded a handshake too. His hand squeezed my palm hard and held it until I looked at him. They are all the same, I thought. I looked at his big, brown eyes, and they revealed that he couldn't understand why they chose me either.

"You can take your break," he said, "and then you can go back to work."

"Sure," I said quietly.

"You have to talk louder now," he stated.

"Yes, sir," I yelled.

"Good," he said. "Alright then, get ready for tomorrow."

And then, he left. I left after he left and went and sat down on the white sheet. I ate some pieces of bread and looked around me, but all I could see was a blur of arms moving, babies smiling and laughing, and mouths talking. I couldn't hear any of it, and my legs were still numb. I was astonished that I had to be ready to be a brigadier the day after today, while only a fortnight ago, I had been ready to depart these fields forever.

CHAPTER 29

The next day, the sun rose, even though my eyelids had never closed. Linda was sleeping soundly. It was Tuesday morning, and I put on my skirt and headed out, ready to work. I walked briskly, just as Mother did. Now that I was essential, I hoped that Mother's grand walk was mine too so the workers could build some trust in me, but I didn't hope that I had inherited her selfish love.

Outside in the morning light, I saw that my skirt was dirty from the day before. I rubbed the fabric and thought about how a woman, just twenty-two years old, had been made brigadier. I could not process their decision. Once my skirt was clean enough, I jumped from stone to stone on the road all the way to the field because I didn't want to splatter mud on my clothes.

"What are you doing?" the foreman asked, looking at me furiously.

I was waiting in the line to yell my name. Annoyed, he motioned for me to come closer to him. The names of the workers were raining on his ears, and his eyes were nailed to his notebook as he marked the absences. When I approached him, he waved his hand again, motioning me to stand beside him. The line shifted forward, and the workers continued to shout out their names.

"Where is the trainer?" I asked the foreman.

"He doesn't come 'til later," he said, preoccupied.

"I will go and work until he comes," I said.

He turned his head and stared at me with the irritation of a child playing with another who doesn't listen to the rules of the game.

"Are you serious?" he said.

"I am," I responded.

What else is there for me to do until he arrives? I thought.

"I suggest you wait here," he said sardonically.

"For how long?"

"Until he comes!" he shouted.

His shouting startled me, and he softened up, perhaps because I was now of a higher rank than him.

"Look, you are the brigadier now," he said, "I don't know what you want me to say. You can do whatever you think, but I suggest you wait."

"I'm going to work," I said, confident with my decision.

"Well, then be prepared for the message that you are sending to your workers," he bristled.

I went to my row and continued removing the tops of the plants. I avoided looking at the other workers, but that didn't deter them from glancing at their new brigadier. I still could not feel like a brigadier because, for so long, the only thing I had known was how to be a field worker.

By the middle of the row, I heard my trainer talking to some workers. Eventually, he came toward me.

"Hi Bora," he said.

"Hi," I said without stopping what I was doing.

"You don't have to do this anymore," he said.

I was tired of hearing that I didn't have to do work anymore, and for a second, I ignored him and kept topping the head of the plant. He opened his notebook, insisting that I stop what I was doing and pay attention to what he was going to teach me.

He began by describing the method used to record the points of the workers. Then, he took my shovel from my hands and dug the soil out from underneath the plant I had just cleaned, destroying it. He made a square and showed me how to measure the diameter of the roots. After that, we walked to the head of the field and counted the rows by their width and length. Then, we calculated the area of the whole tokë. It did not take too long for the entire field to be turned into a mathematical board of squares, where the lengths, widths, and depths corresponded to the volume of the holes that had been dug for the plants. We also measured how much soil had been shoveled out from the field, a number used to determine whether the worker was planting at a good enough pace, and lastly, we calculated the predicted yield. My head became overwhelmed as the pages in his notebook and the measurements and equations flipped in front of my eyes until the sun set.

It was almost seven o'clock when the trainer and I finally separated. Drained, I dropped my brigadier equipment off and went and stood in the bucket line, waiting to wash my hands and face. It was the first time that I was mentally—not just physically—exhausted from work. It was too early to tell which one I preferred.

Roza was in the bucket line too, but she was intimidated and couldn't say a hello.

"How are you, Roza?" I asked.

"Good," she said merrily, relieved. "How are you?"

How am I? I am exhausted, I wanted to say but settled for "good" instead, to avoid burdening her with my troubles. She already knew one of the worst of them, as she had been sitting with me on the white blanket the day the women had been gossiping about me being childless.

My new role as a brigadier was also heavy. My hands seemed too small to measure the performance of sixty people or dispense loaves of bread or decide who would have enough food for their children. Roza understood, even though I hadn't said it aloud, and she sympathized in silence, patting my shoulder.

She left saying, "Good night."

She said it kindly, and it made my whole heart flood with joy. It had been too long since someone had touched me with genuine kindness, and it felt almost holy, as if Zot was feeling my aches.

"Good night," I said with a smile.

We both headed home, and I went straight to Linda's bedroom and laid down the day.

CHAPTER 30

I had to learn the brigadier's job in a week. On my fifth day of training, I was at a dig site with the trainer, and I was carrying a wooden triangle measure that was as tall as my calf.

"We have to head up to the entrance of the field," the trainer said while I was calculating the amount of soil that had been shoveled out.

The military had arrived for their combat practice and had brought their secondhand uniforms for us to wear. Before I put on mine, the trainer introduced me to the officer.

"*Oficer, kjo është brigadier ë re, Zonja. Doda*" (Officer, Mrs. Doda is the new head of the brigade), he said.

"*Gezohem, Brigadier Doda*" (Nice meeting you, Brigadier Doda), the officer responded and shook my hand.

He did not say: she is very young; she is a woman; why is she in that position?

Once the targets were up, we began shooting. The trainer and I went first.

"Brigadier Doda, shoot again!" the officer commanded when he saw that my bullet had only scratched the enemy's liver.

I put the rifle over my shoulder again, and this time I aimed above the bleeding liver, at the chest. I closed my eye and pulled the trigger. I heard the mountain crying as my bullet punctured the lung. My shoulder started twitching as it absorbed the kickback from the rifle, so I pulled the rifle off.

"Brigadier Doda, kill the opponent now!" the officer ordered, ice cold.

I had a bullet or two left before one of his soldiers would have to refill my rifle. Determined to destroy the other lung, I aimed at the left side of the chest and pulled the trigger. The enemy's heart exploded, and the mountain cried again. I handed the rifle to the worker next in line, without asking the officer's permission. I had performed his order, and the killing had been done.

The trainer nodded his head to me when I returned, acknowledging my good shooting.

"You are going to be a good brigadier," he said and handed the wooden triangle back to me. I had no say in either the shooting or the triangle.

Once the sound of the rifles echoing off the mountains ended, the trainer urged me to get back to work. He was in a rush to keep moving, and we resumed where we had left off before the military training, continuing to go through the rows. He lectured as we worked, expanding his explanations about the restrictions and specifics of the fields and analyzing every point of the soil. Although he seemed pleased with my learning speed, after four and a half days of training, I was struggling to retain all the figures, guidance, instructions, and documentation. But I was trying to absorb as much information as I could.

In the middle of that afternoon, the trainer suddenly and unexpectedly relinquished his duties, saying that I was ready to lead. When he stepped away, I was left to be a brigadier. I was thrown in the ditch all alone to figure out by myself how to conquer the position of a brigadier.

That Saturday evening, I did my first report. I pulled my headscarf further down before I began writing the points for the workers because I was afraid that if they saw how young my face looked, they would kick up some soil in complaint. I walked awkwardly through the rows with my wooden triangle meter and stopped at a young daughter. If she had been more privileged, she would have been in high school instead of in the fields waiting for me to calculate her work.

Once I was done with the young daughter, I crossed the tobacco plants along her row and came to the next worker, a thirty-year-old guy. As my stomach churned, I marked his work too. After that, it was an old woman, and after her, it was a mother, then a bunch of old men, another daughter, a bunch of young men, a girl my age, a man my age, a bunch of young women, old, old, young, young, extremely young, and, finally, the gossipy ladies. The narrow-eyed woman who had called me lucky was expecting fewer points from me, but I gave her the exact amount that she had worked because the last thing I needed was for her mouth to open.

It was already beyond uncomfortable to put the meter next to their plants and record their labor while their worn bodies stood beside me. Labor, after all, translated to food stamps. I would have preferred to remain a simple worker rather than being the twenty-two-year-old woman measuring their production. It was just bitter to think about. But I had to do it, and they had to take it because none of us had any choice in the matter.

CHAPTER 31

The next morning, I boiled eggs and put them on the table, along with fresh onions and flatbreads. I made coffee for each one who came into the kitchen. First, was Leke, who didn't wish me good morning anymore. Second was Linda, her hair combed. Yes, she did comb her hair every Sunday morning because Leke was home that day. And third was he—Ben. I was trying to forgive and forget that he was the nameless one. Ben sat down and began reading the Communist paper. I wasn't sure if he adored or hated our leader, however, he often read the pages with the big headlines.

These papers were given to people who worked in Tirana to remind them that their work was needed to defeat the enemy. My husband and others like him were the noteworthy citizens who the regime had to keep both happy and in check. It was hard to have the enlightened civilians under control, so special perks like free newspapers, portraits, certificates of acknowledgment, vacation days, higher pay, and even apartments in the city were given to them. The laboring class, on the other hand, were handed a portrait of themselves and the title of *Stakhonovite* (Exceptional Worker), if they demonstrated extraordinary hard work and productivity. Our leader knew that the bottom echelon had no choice but to believe in and follow his ruling.

As I sat with them at the white table, I began speaking, addressing all three of them.

"Last week—" I started.

But Linda put her hand on my arm and shook the eggs over the plates, distracting me.

"Last week—" I continued, but she tightened her grip on my arm, trying to make me hold my words. I restarted anyway. "Last—"

"You don't have to talk about that," she interjected, rolling her eyes in annoyance.

"What do you mean?" I asked.

"They know," she said.

"I don't think they do," I reassured her so she would allow me to speak.

Leke lifted his head and stared at us in an attempt to understand why we were arguing. My husband had plugged his ears in fear of what I was about to say.

"They were there," Linda responded quickly.

"Where?"

"Ben found you on the floor," she said.

Her wrinkled lips shrunk, seemingly irritated that I had made her remember the incident. My husband got up, disturbed and not wanting to hear more. For a second, I indulged in thinking about the possibility that he used his medical experience to save me.

"Sure. I wasn't planning to talk about that, but thank you for informing me," I retorted, shooting daggers at Linda to shut up and let me get it out.

"Oh," she exhaled.

Leke was looking at his hard-boiled egg, his ears wide open, and my husband was still standing there.

"Last week," I said, "they made me a brigadier of the field."

Leke lifted his eyes from the egg, scrunching up his forehead in surprise. My husband sat down in relief.

"Ah," Linda uttered, removing her claws from my arm. "And

what does that mean?"

Her question made me understand why the old woman, Linda's cousin, had never visited our kulla, but I refused to tell her because she was looking at me like an ignorant fool. Her privilege to be able to ignore the titles of the people who cultivated her food made me furious.

"The head, the head of the brigade," Leke said, reserved.

Linda was still puzzled by my title, but she seemed glad that I hadn't said anything worse.

"Congratulations," my husband said lukewarmly.

I thanked him without regard to the support in his voice. I ate my egg, then I left the kitchen and let them digest the news. I wasn't concerned about whether they liked the new role or not because becoming a brigadier wasn't my choice and neither was it theirs.

CHAPTER 32

Somehow, the weeks that followed went alright without the trainer. The weather got better so we began to harvest the plants. I kept busy among the workers, pulling out the brown tobacco leaves, and then binding two or three leaves together and hanging them up to air dry. Once the tobacco leaves had dried for six to eight weeks, they would be rolled to make the first cigarettes of the season.

Being a brigadier made me even more reserved than I had been before because I tried to avoid creating any conflict. Somehow, I managed it, and the workers performed their jobs without giving me much trouble. The director from the party office visited us once each month, and when he came this time, he read my report. He seemed satisfied with my work and marked the first month as completed.

Summer was around the corner, and as the weeks passed and we got closer to the June heat, each job got harder. Soon, we were deep into the oppressive summer months, and the stifling heat made the workers get tired and weak more easily. I did not take the physical fatigue into account in my reports, but I did report laziness. It was not pleasant to have to assert myself to the slacker workers, especially men. I was a woman, and our world did not raise women to speak out to men, just as they were not raised to listen to us. Intimidated by the gender, age, and size of the brigade, I laid quiet as if I were prey to hunters. If I were to beat my chest with my title, I knew that I could not win because, to them, I was powerless because I was a woman. I did not confront them, but their wrongdoings did not slip out of my sight for a moment.

On a hot day as the fields were parching, I was hunched over counting the tied tobacco leaves when I saw three men standing around the dry plant stems, holding their shovels and chatting. I squinted in the glaring sun to see their faces. Shortly after, they sat down and continued their conversation. I just watched them from afar and carried on with counting the tied leaves while they kept resting. Their rest lasted until the end of the afternoon.

When the early evening came and it was time to evaluate their work, they actually gathered around me like wolves to see their points. I gave each man two points out of ten because that's how much each one had performed. They threw their hands up and yelled in disbelief, but I didn't utter a word and moved to the next worker. The men scattered away angrily, but I did not change their points because that was fair to everyone.

The next worker in line was the foreman. He was married with children and needed extra stamps for the ration supply store. To earn more, he had begun working some days in the field. The foreman was charming, not physically but verbally, and had been flirting with a woman who also was married. He was fairly smart and had swarmed her head with fast talk, stealing her heart.

That evening, I saw that the foreman had not only ruined his own work by taking time to flirt, he had also ruined the work of the woman. Distracting her with his flirting had reduced the amount she had produced. I gave him two points because that was how many he had earned. I gave the woman the same number of points as her usual production, in the hope that she would prove me right the next day. Who gives second chances to women? I thought while I was writing her points. I guess no one, so then I will because I am one of them. I knew it was a risky practice, but I enjoyed the idea of cutting slack to the woman since society did not. However, everything had a limit, and above all, I wanted to be fair. So, for transparency, I hung the board up on a wall at the end of the day so everyone could see their name and points before the foreman took it to the party office.

I didn't at all mind the measuring and calculating work that a brigadier had to do in order to be precise with the workers' points. I actually enjoyed it. But I hated when workers shirked their responsibilities and expected to get the same points. Sadly, after I had to dock the foreman's points, it did not take long for my nerves to get irritated again.

"Burri im është drejtor" (My husband is a director), one of them said, rubbing her husband's director title in my face while I wrote down her production.

He was a school director, but that didn't matter to me.

"Sure," I said, moving to the next row.

"My points aren't right," she said and followed me.

She wants the full day of work without working, I thought. The dry land was starved for rain, and my headscarf burned from the scorching sun. I had crossed the rows of forty-five workers, and I still had fifteen more to go.

"I think they are," I said assertively.

"You will see," she said, as if threatening to change her production.

I couldn't care less about her and those like her, but she didn't know that. By the end of the day, the board hung on the wall, leaving her even more incensed because her points hadn't changed. The next evening, she had done even less work than the day before. I gave her the same points because that's how much she deserved.

While I was hanging up the board, a man surrounded by other workers said, *"Kësaj zonjes, jepi gjithë ditën"* (Give the whole day to this lady), insisting I give her points for a full day's work.

I lifted my headscarf to look at him. It was her husband—the school director—and she was standing brazenly next to him.

"Happily," I said to him and left the board as it was.

Like a flag flapping in the wind, the woman instantly stared at the director to see how much power he could exhibit.

"Little girl," the director said.

I had just become twenty-three years old, and with Mother's calculations, I was twenty-four.

"Give her the full points," he said angrily, like a dog whose bark is useless.

The wind swept the flag at my side.

"Happily," I said again and took a minute in silence just to hold the suspense of the workers. "I will give her the full points when she works the full day," I said in a very clear–cut voice and left.

He didn't know that I had nothing to lose because I didn't care about being promoted to begin with, let alone being demoted for being fair. Actually, going back to just being a worker didn't seem that bad to me, and it would make my life easier. His wife eventually did get her points, but she earned it with her body, not with her mouth and not because of her director husband.

Shortly after that incident, any complaint or disobedience dropped altogether. And although the three guys were still angry at me, they stopped resting for hours, and each of them did their part of the duty. However, I knew that I had dismissed almost a day of their work, and some of them had young children and needed the stamps to feed them. So, I decided to give them a project that could make up for it. When I showed it to them, they knew it was hard, but they didn't ask questions and went straight to the task. That evening, they surrounded me to see their production, more like coyotes than wolves. I hung the board so they could see the ten out of ten. Thrilled, they jumped and smiled and began playing soccer in the field. I felt delighted, too, because it was a good day for all.

CHAPTER 33

I was sitting on the stairs reminiscing and counting the lives that had gone. As if my fate had taken my existence and left me only watching, I was in disbelief at how many years had crawled through my hands. I was wearing a warm jacket to brace against the cold wind, but my feet were bare, as I wanted to sense the rousing chill. I was leaving that morning to visit my parents and had taken a week off of work.

I heard my husband's light footfalls. His walk was soft, mute even, but time had taught me to register it. The wind stirred my chestnut hair around my face, reminding me how weak and thin it had become. My husband's once black hair had changed, too. It was now rife with ashy gray tones. Yet his face had not changed a bit, and his black eyes still vividly reflected his darkness. His skin had remained clear without any wrinkles, and his long lips parted politely, presenting nice teeth. Even his gray hair looked charming, and for all those years, I was considered the lucky wife of a handsome doctor who kept his wife despite a barren belly.

After nine years of marriage, my face looked tired. Not from births, of course, but from a yearning to look down and see my belly become rounder or a child learning to suckle. Besides Mother, I'm not sure if my family knew why I couldn't have children, yet no one ever asked me, not even Martë.

On my sister's body, there wasn't a piece of fat left under her skin, as it had been consumed by raising her children. She had two daughters, and she got her son. The last time I had seen her, she had said to the sister with no children that she was going to have a fourth baby because it was inferior to leave a man of the kulla with only one son. Mother had been present when Martë spoke of a second son, but she had not spoken against her, disregarding I was suffering from hearing Martë's pain.

Mother had abandoned me the day that I had told her the truth. She showed a lot of care when I visited her, but it was not the caring I wanted her to have. Her love, like Linda's, was only about keeping me alive, and in both cases, it was selfish. Over the years, the guilt about me living in Doda's kulla had filled Mother's pelvis, and she couldn't walk straight anymore. Her grand walk had depreciated in my mind, as life had shown me its real nails.

Father and my brothers thought that I was just the unfortunate one in the family and were very pleased and grateful that my husband and his family weren't turning me back. That's how far their love went. It stopped short of asking if I had any problem or how Ben treated me. They were unable to utter even a typical "how are you," afraid of having to deal with the answer.

As the black sheep of the family, I learned that no one wanted the responsibility of knowing. It was easier for everyone to forgive themselves if they kept out. Your pain is yours to care for, and once shared with the others, it's a guilt for them to bear. That's how we all lose our morals and become murderers, rats, and sinners. A daughter returning to live at her kulla after being married was the most diminishing thing that a man of a kulla could be forced to swallow. Martë and I were a constant liability for our brothers, so they kept us close, yet distant. That was how much the happiness of a daughter, a wife, a mother, and even a woman brigadier mattered.

I had left the foreman to fill my position while I was visiting my parents. He had been very pleased to replace me because, in addition to his foreman points and his labor points, he would get the brigadier points, making him almost a model worker with a portrait. I was twenty-nine years old. I had worked for four years as a regular field worker and seven as a brigadier, and yet, I had never held money in my hands. My brigadier points and worker points were nowhere to be found because, as a wife, the head of the family kept my wages.

Leke, as a noble father, never recognized that his daughter-in-law brought a good wage into his kulla. Ideally, I shouldn't have been working at all. And since his family didn't need the money, he gave Linda the key to our family's finances and the responsibility to figure out the expenses. While I lived in a nice house, my parents' kulla still had no ceilings. A brigadier's earnings would surely help them raise one, but instead, my wage was sitting in a locked drawer on someone else's bookshelf. But a daughter wasn't allowed to be a contributor, only to be the wife of a man. That's what they had chosen for us to be.

After I had spent a week at my kulla, Linda came to pick me up. We got into a fugoni on the main street, and we crossed the river to leave our village. I saw that the river could handle two more storms before it would overflow its banks. A moment after we passed the river, the fugoni stopped at a bunker to pick up a child, a mother, and a nëna. They were on the other side of the road from us, and they had to cross the road and walk around the front of the fugoni to get in. The wind was harsh that day, and as we waited, I was taken by the sheer number of leaves that had fallen onto the top of the bunker, so many it was almost camouflaged. Suddenly, abruptly, and without mercy, nature takes away what it has birthed, I thought. I wished the branches of my miserable life could drop me like leaves, too, but I was too weak to break them.

It was always Linda who escorted me and picked me up from my kulla. Being a daughter and married was the same as being in jail. You were picked up and dropped off like a dog, and at any given moment, you were reminded that you were owned in the eyes of the world. If I had children, it would have been acceptable to ride in a fugoni without a husband or a mother-in-law. But with empty arms, an empty belly, and empty hands, a young female was not allowed to travel alone. However, I had gotten used to seeing Linda owning the coins that I earned and paying the drivers for our rides, and it did not bother me anymore.

The child, his mother, and his nëna crawled into the fugoni, and the child sat next to Linda. His mother and grandmother sat behind us. The boy looked like he was between seven and nine years old, the same age as Kol's sons, who we had seen just a few minutes ago.

Kol's sons had been playing in their yard as Linda and I had been walking down to pick up the fugoni.

"Those boys are beautiful," Linda had said when we passed Kol's gardh.

"Yes, like their parents," I had assured her.

His boys had grown and were running around their trojë, cherishing the day off from school. One of them had Kol's green eyes and his mother's sweet face. I didn't see Kol or his wife outside.

"Who are their parents, do you know them?" Linda asked a second after I saw Kol walking up our rugged road, just as he had when we were seven and nine years old.

"Yes," I said, pointing him out.

I hadn't seen him in a while, and I thought he seemed worried now. He slowed his unpolished body to greet us. His face hadn't changed since he had gotten married, but his hair had changed from a gold color to amber. He still blushed, which he did as his gaze drifted down to my hand that was clutching Linda's arm.

"Bora, it is so nice to see you," he said. "How is Ben?"

"What a handsome man with beautiful children," Linda said when we left him.

I couldn't agree more.

"How is his wife?" she asked, ready for gossip.

"She is very pretty too," I told her because that was the truth.

"Of course, what else could he have married," she remarked.

I didn't reply to Linda because Kol's troubled face was in my mind. A week staying at Mother's and I hadn't heard anything about his kulla. Yet, even if something had happened, Mother would not have mentioned it because his problems shouldn't matter to me.

When Linda and I arrived at our mahogany door, we went inside, and I began preparing dinner. Linda tried to help me, but with the years, she had become sluggish, so I told her to sit. Linda had changed since I had first seen her through the window of my kulla. She had shrunk in height and looked weaker, and one day, just like a snap, Linda's smile had frozen and vanished like lightning from a storm. I never saw her smile again, but I was glad because she finally had relieved herself from pretending.

It had taken nine years for Linda to acknowledge that her son was indifferent to marriage. Her hope and selfish love for her son had cost me my life, but I had accepted it because, every night in our bed before we slept, her hand squeezed mine under the covers, and we shared our burden together.

There were nights when Linda's snoring roared like exhaust from a vehicle, making it hard for me to fall asleep, but she was healthier than her husband, who had still not forgiven me for being a stubborn daughter-in-law. Since last year, Leke's health had deteriorated, and he had problems with his breathing. His doctor had diagnosed him with stress, and then he had deferred to Leke's son.

The first time Leke's lungs had tightened his chest, Ben had said, "It's because it's spring, something in the air is bothering him."

But his condition hadn't improved since last spring. He was a moderate smoker like my husband. Neither of them smoked in our faces, but they always had a pack on them and took a cigarette when the time was right. It seemed like it was a masculine camouflage, a must-do thing when other men were around.

I diagnosed Leke too. His pens weren't as assured about their ink anymore, and his body looked as fatigued as a field worker's. I could see that a man who had once been considered noble had realized that he was plainly a monster. The way he walked reflected that he couldn't deal with his secrets anymore. He had seen his demons, and what you see, well, you can't unsee. The eldest grew older with a heavy conscience or died without one. I was humbled when I discerned that, in his late fifties, Leke might have found his truth.

Once I finished cooking the dinner, I walked down the three stairs to grab some logs for the stove. The wind brought some drizzle on my face, and the clouds were moving fast. The ravine was roaring from the waters coming from the peaks and the rains. I couldn't wait for the cold weather to leave and spring to follow. I wanted to see the gardalinë hopping in the trees and bushes and bees landing on the blossoms.

I brought the logs to the kitchen and fixed the fire. Then, I held my hands above the stove, reminiscing about my childhood when summers were filled with purity and when I could feel the sunsets as if they were passing through my innocent body. The teapot whistled, and I pulled some tea from the bag that Mother had given to us. I added some more water to Linda's cup to make her weak tea and gave the regular cups to the other two. Leke was reading his newspaper, and Ben had some books next to him from the *RPSSH's Ministria e Arsimit* (People's Socialist Republic of Albania's Ministry of Education). My husband was opening and closing the books like he was trying to find something. His black eyes seemed to settle on a verse, and he paused and looked up as if he wanted to read aloud to us. But he closed the book without saying those words.

I moved the cups closer to them and placed the plates on the white table. I brought the soup and pieces of pork, and I served the bread. We all began eating, and Leke began conversing with Ben. As I was dipping the bread into my soup, I looked at Ben. He had combed his gray hair nicely, and it lay tidily on the back of his neck. His clothes were always neat and sharp. His teeth, while they dispatched arguments with his father, were holding bright over the years. If he were different, he could have been the greatest husband, I was thinking—when suddenly, a hand hit the table, jolting it.

For a moment, I thought that maybe my mouth had spoken my mind. But it wasn't me. Linda started yelling, but having been lost in my own thoughts, I couldn't understand what she was arguing about.

"I have to leave mom."

It was Ben. He slammed his hand on the table again.

"No, no, no, no," Linda groaned in great distress.

"I don't have a choice, I have to follow their orders," Ben said harshly.

"Who asked you to do that?" Leke asked, not taking the news well either.

"The director of the hospital," Ben said.

It was sad to admit that if Ben were to leave, my life would not change that much.

"You can say no," Linda stated.

"I can't," he insisted.

"You are not going!" she shouted.

"Mom, it's an order from the state," he remarked.

"You are not going, don't you understand?! That would be the end of this family!" she exclaimed.

I hadn't slept with her son in the last seven years, and he had barely spoken to me—he wouldn't be missed. I found Linda's response overly dramatic and unreasonable. It's the same with or without him, and he will come and visit you, I thought. I could tell her in our bedroom later.

"We don't have a choice," Ben said. "*We* don't have a choice," he repeated, this time screaming the "we."

We, we don't have a choice, we don't have a choice, I thought, trying to understand. For the first time in nine years of living under the same roof and two years of sleeping in the same bed, Ben was finally staring at me.

"Who is 'we'?" I asked.

"You and me," he said, his chlorinated hands pointing from himself to me.

"I don't have a choice?" I asked, looking at Linda for an explanation.

"No," he replied. "You have to come with me."

A moment of silence.

"Don't you understand?" Linda yelled close to my ear. "This would be the end of us."

Another moment of silence.

"Leke, tell him," she implored.

But Leke couldn't utter a word. Ben got up and left the room. Leke had nothing to say because he knew that orders from above were the ones that mattered the most in any kulla.

For the first time, I got up and followed Ben, ready to put an end to this "we." I found him in the odë with his long arms hanging onto the shelf.

"Where are you going?" I asked.

"Where am *I* going?" he shot back. "You didn't hear me?"—he moved closer to me, his face red from fury, his eyes fired up—"*We* are going," he said.

"We? What is this *'we'*? We never were we." I said.

"We have to move," he yelled, "*together.*"

He was staring like he was going to explode. His black eyes had feelings, I saw, and they were indisputably haunted by sadness.

Finally, he said, "We have to move to Tirana"—he took a breath—"They already gave us an apartment"—his voice became ballsy—"I have to work for a hospital there. We have to go."

His words seared my heart.

"These are orders, I don't have a choice," he said as I ran away.

A life married without a husband hurt beyond what words can put together. But that was not enough, now I had to live alone with him and only for him twenty-four hours a day, seven days a week, in a city, just pretending. My throat was choking as I ran, thinking of the suffering that I had gone through and was about to live. I had left our bedroom years ago because I could not bear being unwanted any longer. His "we" reeled in my mind and made my stomach lurch. Oh Zot, how could I endure sharing the same bed with him again? How could I live an already unloved and sterile life, isolated and abandoned in an apartment somewhere? I would be better off dead.

The wind pushed fiercely against my voice and a storm commenced. My legs halted behind our kulla, stopping me from running. I dropped to my knees and sank into the earth. I couldn't hear, I couldn't see, I couldn't think. My heart was throbbing madly. I put my fingers in the soil and rain began to bury them. I couldn't feel the earth. The torrent hit my spine, and my hair fell in the mud as I sobbed.

"Don't worry my daughter," a voice said.

I opened my eyes and saw Leke. The rainwater was falling on his suit. He bent down with his old, crooked knees and pulled my fingers from the earth. The skies were cracking above as he steered me by my scarred arm back inside his kulla.

He left me in the hall, facing Ben. I couldn't see him. I couldn't hear him any longer. I opened the door of Linda's bedroom shoveling his "we" deep into my soul until it drowned. I was soaked, and Linda unfolded her closet to help me change. She stood silent, as if dreqi had arrived in her home and was ready to take me from her. We were both struck down, depleted, and disarmed by destiny's plans.

She covered my skin in warm clothes with feather-like tenderness. Her touch had showered me with care over the years, soothing the state of forlornness that I lived in. Together we forgot our aches, falling into each other's companionship even though we knew that there was no cure for our burden. We had taken our companionship and love for granted, as we had pictured only death dividing us in a far-off future. Yet, throbbing from the fresh, cruel wounds, we both could no longer stay on our feet, and when we laid down, we held our palms tightly together, pressing them with gentle endearment, and turned off the light for the night.

And then, there in the dark, Linda took my face in her hands.

She inhaled for a long moment, gathering her strength, before she uttered, "Bora, I love you."

The words made her lips tremble. Then, she told me her decision.

CHAPTER 34

The day began early in the fuzzy darkness that connects the fading day with the new one. I thought I must have died in my dream and came to light in someone else's life. A sharp slap from Linda woke me up for good.

"Linda—" I said.

"Be quiet," she said.

She took a set of keys and a pair of scissors from the drawer of her nightstand and put the keys in her pocket.

"Sit up," she commanded in a whisper

I did as I was told, and she sat down next to me on the bed.

"Turn your head," she said.

I looked away from her, towards the wall, and heard the snip of scissors as half my hair left my head and dropped to the bed. I touched my neck. It was bare and open. My hair is gone, I thought in disbelief. Linda moved quickly, taking my hair in her hand, and left the room. She was holding her husband's clothes when she came back. A pair of pants, a shirt, a jacket, and a hat.

"Be quick," she said.

She looked at the sky from the window while I put on the clothes.

"It's a good day, it's going to rain a bit, but that will help you," she claimed.

She came close to me and tightened her husband's pants around my waist with his belt and put money in the pockets. Then, she took my identification card from her pocket.

"I hope you will not need this my daughter," she uttered.

Her wrinkled hand was trembling as she put my identification card in mine. My identification paper had remained in the locked drawer of the bookshelf with their wealth for nine years. If that card were to get out of my pocket in the coming hours, it could be worse than death.

I put the card deep inside my pocket, and then Linda forced my head inside the hat, making sure my remaining hair was tucked inside. Then she put my arms into the suit jacket, pulled it up over my shoulders, and checked that the jacket was hiding my breasts.

"Good," she said.

Before I opened the door, she gave me an umbrella saying, "You are going to look down, do you hear me? You are going to look down. You don't dare look up until you get to your kulla."

She kissed me on my forehead, and I left her. I walked through the hall and sensed Ben sleeping. My heart sank saying goodbye to a love that never was. I opened the door, and for the last time, I walked down the three stairs, stepping off them like a fish that was going to swim in an ocean full of sharks.

CHAPTER 35

It was four o'clock a.m., and it had been more than a decade since I had walked without a skirt. The air was damp, and I felt naked. I heard the ravine raging with water coming from the mountains. It was March, the month I liked the least because I felt the cold the most. Each time the leaves along the road moved from the drops of the rain, I could hear my heart beating and thought the worst. My legs were almost numb already, but they had to hold on until I got to the fugoni station on the main road near the bunker. There were two stops I would have to go through, and I would have to wait at each one. A fugoni to Lezhe from Manati and a fugoni to my village from the city. Two stops with my head down or death.

I stepped silently on the stones. My stomach was knotted so tight from the fear that it felt like it had turned into a rock. My hands were clutching the umbrella, and I made sure that my hair stayed behind my ears and under the hat. The first fugoni would arrive at five a.m. I didn't have a watch to check the time, but I knew that I had to undergo a lengthy wait. The fugoni station was along the street and out in the open so the driver could see you. But I couldn't stand in the open, just as I couldn't miss the first fugoni. I had to wait not too close, but not so far that I would be spotted.

I saw the bunker near the road from about one hundred feet away. No one was in sight yet, and it looked like the field grass and shrubs surrounding the bunker had grown high enough to hide me from anyone coming to wait at the fugoni stop. I squatted down behind the bunker and covered my body with the umbrella. If someone walks by, I thought, I can act like I'm fixing my shoe and don't want to get wet doing it. I tuned my ear to the road, hoping to catch the sound of the fugoni's engine in the distance, or maybe its wheels bouncing off the potholes. I needed to hear the fugoni before it got there to give me time to get to the stop. I was a two-minute walk plus a run of a few seconds away.

My heart was pounding, but I couldn't bear to let myself think what I was doing. After I was there about ten minutes, I heard some footsteps on the road some distance away. I lifted my umbrella ever so slightly and saw a couple on the main road, approaching the stop. I ducked back down behind the bunker until the sound of their footsteps stopped. They must be standing there in the open waiting for the fugoni, I thought.

I heard more people, maybe three, walk to the station and stop, as I crouched there in the grass for what seemed like hours. Where was the fugoni? The sunrise had started to emerge already and was shining a dim light on the grass near my feet, the early fog muting its light.

I finally heard the wheels of a fugoni skidding and bumping along the rugged road, so I held my umbrella low, but not too low, got to my feet, and headed toward the station. As I approached, the umbrella was blocking my sight so I could only see the legs of the people waiting. But I could tell which legs belonged to the couple, as they were the only ones standing close together. I moved close to them because men interacted less when they were with their young wives. I had to greet the couple because I was the one arriving, but I waited for the fugoni to pull closer and emit some braking noise first, so the couple would not hear my voice clearly.

"*Si ki njeft*" (Good morning), I said quickly with a manly voice.

"*Mer*" (Good), the man responded absent-mindedly.

Shivers started to rack my body from my feet to my umbrella as the door of the fugoni opened, and I tried to quell them as I watched every leg walking to the fugoni's door. Time ran fast as the driver greeted each rider in a deep, raspy voice: "Si ke njeft." The second that the last passenger left my sight, I dropped my umbrella and got inside.

"Si ke njeft," the driver greeted me as I stepped into his vehicle.

"Si ke njeft," I murmured quietly in a deep voice.

Without the umbrella, the round, black hat hid only half of my face, leaving the other half exposed, and I was terrified. I did not dare to lift my head when I passed the couple and three other men as I walked to the open seat in the far back of the fugoni and sat by myself. I nailed my eyes to the floor, chin to my chest, and set my jaw back to the nuse's position, then, did not dare to move.

The men began conversing, but the driver's raspy voice did not add much, as it was still early, and he had many riders left to listen to that day. This first ride would be short—less than fifteen minutes, but after a couple of minutes, the fugoni pulled over to pick up another rider.

"Si ki njeft, Mark," a man up front said, greeting the new rider.

My blood ran cold when I heard the man's voice. I could tell that the new rider—Mark—was one of my father-in-law's friends. I could hear Mark take his seat and start talking with the other men. It sounded like it was only the other woman and me who were not participating in the conversation. She had a good reason—she was a female. But for me—as a man—it was completely out of the ordinary. Still, I kept mute with my head pointed at my feet, hoping against hope that no one would start chatting with me.

"Here," I heard the friend of my father-in-law say, and the driver stopped the fugoni.

Mark was the only one of six of us dropped off before the city. After a few minutes, the driver entered the city and pressed ahead slowly, knowing full well that there were more rats and uniforms to dodge in the city than in the country. When we arrived at the last stop, one by one the riders paid and got off. I was the last one, and I handed the coins to the driver without expecting any change.

In a fog without rain, I stepped out of the fugoni onto the sidewalk of a wide road. I opened my umbrella and began walking slow, like a turtle in a shell of fear, heading toward the other station. But then, I realized that my speed might draw attention, so I quickened my pace. I tried to walk purposefully, as if I was on my way to work and had done so every single day except Sunday for the last decade. It was still early, and only a few people were on the streets. But those few were enough to do terrible harm. The next station was a ten-minute walk, and a rat or anyone from the military or the police could stop me for interrogation.

My hand got cold from holding the umbrella, but worst of all, it began to vibrate from the heavy footfalls of military troops marching. I couldn't tell where they were at first. It sounded like they were maybe a few streets away, to my right. But the stomping sound suddenly amplified, the pounding on the pavement even louder. I frantically glanced around, still shielding my face, and saw that the first lines of the formation had turned a corner a few blocks behind me, the rest of the lines at their heels. The troops were heading up the same road as me, approaching me from behind.

I did not know whether I should stop or move away or just keep walking. I was afraid that any change would seem suspicious, so I kept on walking, just as I had been, forcing my terrified body to move forward.

As they got closer and closer, the sound of their boots hammering the pavement became louder and louder, thundering with an incessant, torturous rhythm and reverberating from the city buildings. It was a large group, maybe a hundred men. When the troops reached me, I kept my head bowed and my eyes to the ground, but I could see their military boots passing me on my left. They were close to me, maybe two feet away. Line after line marched past me, the sound and the fear driving straight through me.

Then, I spotted a gap between two buildings just up ahead on my right, and I had the idea to try to get away from the soldiers there. One, two, three—I started counting my steps to calm my breath—seven, eight, nine—and focused on the counting, feeling that, if I could just get to that gap, I could escape their bodies and the deafening sound of their boots on the cement. Thirteen, fourteen, fifteen, sixteen—on the seventeenth step, I turned.

There, I dropped into a squat to find my breath, holding my knees and calming my heart while soldier upon soldier upon soldier marched past the gap. Finally, there were no more. They had passed by. I let out the air I was holding in my lungs and felt sobs welling up from my stomach, but I held them down because I knew I had to keep moving to catch the next fugoni. So, I pulled the umbrella down as far as I could and left the alley.

The city's concrete shapes around me loomed out of the fog like a ghost. The few buildings looked stiff and austere as if they couldn't afford color. The city looked severely censored by the men with or without secondhand uniforms who were strolling around them. I made it to the second station as the sky became brighter. It was, maybe, 5:30 a.m. by then, but I wasn't sure. A handful of people were waiting for the fugoni. There was no bunker or safe place to hide there in the city, so I had to wait out in the open with them, shrinking inside my clothes behind my umbrella.

When the fugoni arrived, it was full of people coming into the city, and I heard a stern voice instructing the driver to drop off the riders before it pulled up to the station. Up until that point, I had not seen who was supervising the road. I lifted the umbrella and my head slightly, just enough to spot the legs of a secondhand, blue uniform. A traffic policeman. I forced my head back down, trembling, and didn't lift it again until the fugoni stopped at my feet.

I went all the way to the back of the fugoni again and sat down. I nailed my chin to the nuse's position again, but this time, I kept one eye on the inside of the fugoni. I could only see as far as the floor and as high as the feet, but I needed to keep watch. I knew there would be more riders on this ride and mostly from the city, and who knew who they might be or what they'd do.

So far, we were just three riders in total, four with the driver. That was bad news because it meant that the driver would wait at that station until the fugoni was filled. We had been waiting for what seemed like ten minutes when I heard the traffic policeman outside, greeting some military cars. The driver decided to leave then, even though we were still just three people. I breathed with relief, but it was short-lived because the driver turned the fugoni back into the city to pick up more riders after we had driven for only a few minutes.

"Si ke njeft," the driver said as another passenger got in.

The man sat down in the front row next to one of the other passengers. There was now one open seat left in the first row, two seats in the second row, and two seats in the third row, where I was. Again, the fugoni pulled over and picked up another man.

"Si ke njeft," they said.

The newest passenger sat in the second row. Two single seats in the first and second rows, plus one double seat next to me, were left.

The driver then drove around the city, looking to fill the four free seats. Distress shredded my stomach when he returned to the first station, the one where I had seen the traffic policeman earlier. I pressed my chin down even harder against my chest and waited in agony. Then, I heard the driver greeting someone.

"*Si je zotri*" (How are you, sir)? the driver said with an obedient voice.

"*Polici rrugore*" (Street officers), I heard a rider utter.

My ears were wide open, but I could not see if I was in danger. I couldn't tell whether the street policeman was checking the passengers or the fugoni, nor if he was out for one of us.

"*Shofer, leviz*" (Driver you have to move), the traffic policeman said, ordering the driver to leave the station.

"*Po mor, si te duash*" (As you wish), the driver said.

But just before he closed the doors, I heard two more people step quickly into the fugoni.

"Si ke njeft," the driver said.

"Si ke njeft," a new young rider's voice said, coming straight toward me.

The door closed, and two people squeezed in next to me. They murmured something to each other, and I could tell they were a couple, a young couple it seemed. The driver turned over the fugoni's engine, but its door ripped open again, and two more men got in. The traffic policeman slapped the fugoni.

"*Hik o burrë*" (Leave man), he yelled, ordering the driver to go.

The two men quickly sat down in the empty front seats. That was it. All the seats were filled. It was me, the young man, and his woman in the back row. My entire body breathed out in relief as the door closed and the driver left the station. I pulled down the sleeves of my jacket so the young man next to me would not see my feminine hands, then I figured that it would look unusual to someone sitting so close to me if I nailed my eyes to the floor, so I glued my head toward the window.

This ride was longer than the first by about thirty minutes, depending on the stops that would be needed. There were nine of us, and these passengers were more awake than those in the first fugoni. They began conversing out loud, including the young man sitting next to me. I was the only "man" who had not said a word so far. But their conversation stopped when the fugoni pulled over again.

"We don't have space," a man up front yelled to the driver.

"Of course you have space for one more," the driver replied greedily.

"I'm going to get off soon," the young man next to me said.

I pulled my hat farther down, in case someone looked toward the back after the young man spoke, and I bowed my head into the nuse's position again. I knew that seemed more suspicious, but I had no other choice. The new rider climbed inside while the fugoni idled, and shortly after, the other passengers began chatting again.

Once the young couple got off a few minutes later, the new rider walked to the back and sat down next to me. Then, he greeted me in a slightly raspy voice.

"Si ke njeft," he said.

"Mer, po ti?" (Good, and you)? I responded in as manly a voice as I could.

"Mer," he said genuinely, as if he didn't find me suspicious.

That was good because the other riders probably had heard us talking and now would not find me suspiciously quiet. The man's voice sounded familiar to me. He must be old, I thought, but I couldn't remember where I might know him from. The window glass on my side of the fugoni was cracked and leaking some cold air and drops of rain. I was letting the cold air calm my tension for a moment when I heard a "tsk tsk." It sounded familiar. I turned my eyes and looked toward the man next to me. My hat allowed me to see only his pants. They were black and tidy. I turned my neck ever so slightly and lifted my eyes to his hands. His hands look familiar too. I was right that he was old, and his body was frail.

"Tsk tsk," he whispered again.

And then, I understood. It was the voice of the old man who had spent twenty-five years in jail. The old man from the fields was sitting next to me. And with his "tsk tsk," he had told me that I was a problem, just as he had done with the young guy years earlier before he had let out his story about being tortured in the freezing cold water-tubes.

I stared back down in terror as the wheels of the fugoni thundered over the potholes of our ragged road. Thinking about the odds of meeting him again, I realized that my luck was between terrible and nonexistent.

The old man remained silent without any more tsk tsks, and the passengers talked amongst themselves. The rain began running harder through the window, making it sound like water was coming through. Only a few minutes had passed since I had realized who the old man was, but it felt like thirty decades passing.

The driver pulled over to drop off a rider, and then we were seven, plus the driver, eight. A moment before we crossed the river, we hit another crack, and the wheels veered dangerously across the road. Then, the fugoni stopped again. I felt a sudden breeze. The driver had pulled down his window.

"*Pse hec shpejt*" (Why are you driving fast)? a man yelled from outside to the driver.

I lifted my head, and beyond the windows, I could see the chests of young soldiers and an officer talking to our driver.

"*Na fal,*" the driver said, asking for their forgiveness.

My knees were shaking, and I became covered in a cold sweat. I felt like my mind was falling apart. The driver's window was all the way down, and a wash of cold air and rain was rushing through it.

Then, a rider sneezed.

"What are you saying over in there?" the officer yelled.

"Nothing sir," the one who sneezed replied.

"Don't look up," the old man whispered sideways to my hat.

"Open the doors," the officer commanded the driver.

Suddenly, the old man stood up and stepped out of my row. My blood froze—they would see me, there was no doubt about it. The old man went and sat down up front just as the door opened and the officer stepped inside.

"I just sneezed," the man said, apologizing.

"How many are you here?" the officer asked.

No one responded because no one had counted the riders except me. Seven plus the driver, eight, someone should have told him before he began counting our heads one by one. I heard his one, two, three and was waiting for the last one, the eighth one— me.

When he had counted the last head, he yelled, "Eight! Eight, lift your head up!"

A SPARED FATE

I did not move.

"You! Eight! In the back. Lift your head up!" he yelled.

I lifted my head and discovered that my face was blocked by the old man's head. I couldn't see the officer, and he couldn't see me. That is why the old man had gone up front.

"You!" the officer barked again.

The officer moved his head to try to see me around the old man's head, but he couldn't.

"Eight," he growled underneath his breath and headed toward the back.

He had not taken more than two steps when, suddenly, the old man's throat opened up. He raised his old voice so high and so loud that it slammed against the vehicle's walls like a flood rams the fields.

"HAHAHAHAHAHAHA HAHAHAHAHAHAHA
HAHAHAHAHAHAHA HAHAHAHAHAHAHA!"

His audacious, raucous laughter silenced the officer and froze him in his tracks until the officer could not stand the old voice pounding in his ears anymore. He strode toward the forbidden laughter, grabbed the old man, and dragged him out of the fugoni.

"Leave now," he commanded the driver.

The fugoni sped away forward the flooded river.

That is when I heard a loud, sharp bang. It was a military rifle, with the same bang as when we shot at the fake targets in the fields. But now, the target was real. I spun my body around and looked out the back window and saw the old man lying in a lifeless heap on the ground.

The old man had spared his life for mine.

The driver drove wildly fast after the shot, and the mountains began crying, echoing the fatal news. Tears were streaming down my face in horror, and my hands were shaking. My stomach was crucifying me with grief, the pain turning and turning, over and over. Terrified by the vile attack, everyone kept silent, not moving a muscle. We left the old man behind us, and no other passenger dared look back. Their tongues were all dead.

"Here," I said to the driver when we got to my station.

I held my hat down, put the coins in his hand, and got off. The driver left in a hurry, afraid that he would be stopped again. I stood there, shattered, and watched the fugoni disappear up the road. The sun was coming through the clouds, but I opened my umbrella and rushed to cross the road saying, "Head down Bora, don't look."

I started up the road, but something erupted inside of me right next to a gardh on the road of my kulla. An evil pressure drove up from my stomach to my chest. It tore my throat as it came gushing out. My eyes flooded from the force that had emanated from inside. I saw the dreqi splashed on the rocks, and I wiped my mouth and dried my tears. Then, I pushed myself up using the handle of the umbrella, and for the first time in a long, long time, I felt my stomach free from turning.

I put my head down and proceeded up the road. It was past six a.m., still early for the field workers to be out. But the higher up I got, the more neighbors I saw coming out from under their roofs.

They all walked in a hurry, briskly saying, "Si ke njeft," without waiting for a response.

I heard only women's greetings from under my hat, and I saw more skirts walking down than pants. Perhaps there is a birth occurring, I thought, and moved quicker.

I arrived at my hill, opened the wooden door of my gardh, and saw our pear tree, its leaves fresh and green. It was welcoming me. I closed the umbrella, taking in what I had done. Bora Doda would never exist again—there was no going back.

But I did not know if the Zefi's would accept their daughter back on her trojë.

I walked into the kitchen and found Father seated on his stiff, handmade sofa. I felt relieved, yet terrified, that he was the first person I encountered. He saw his daughter wearing a jacket, a man's pants, and a hat, all soaked by the rains and the storms that she had lived through to arrive back at his trojë.

I heard Mother walk in, but I didn't turn to look at her. It was Father who I had to come up against first. Mother came next to my shoulder and stood alongside me, facing her husband. Father looked at us unmoved, as if he was too befuddled to be either pleased or outraged with his daughter. He did not speak a word, not even a good morning. He left the kitchen without saying or doing anything, just as he had all those years. At least he didn't throw me out.

I breathed a sigh of relief and sat down on his sofa. Mother was silent, too. She reached out her hands and pulled off my hat. My hair fell onto my face again. Mother took me by my hands and gently pulled me up from the sofa and helped me take off the jacket.

Then, somber, she said, "Get ready, Bora, we have to leave."

My heart sank so deeply that it went through to the bloody basement. I looked at her amber eyes surrounded by fine folds of wrinkles. I was ready to erupt in screams.

"Nine years of torture, endangering my life to escape and sparing others, all just to go back!" I cried.

I was devastated. She put her hand gently against my cheek.

Puzzled and in wonder, like it was a mystery that she didn't know how to explain, she said, "No. Get ready Bora. We have a funeral to attend. Kol's wife died this morning."

The End

Made in United States
North Haven, CT
25 October 2021

10564088R00152